Simrita Dhir grew u[...] distinguished academic [...] actor in school and college, she is a Duke of Edinburgh Gold Standard Awardee. A recipient of the Chancellor's Medal for Academic Excellence in Post Graduate Studies, she received her PhD on Toni Morrison from the Department of English and Cultural Studies, Panjab University, Chandigarh.

An avid reader, some of her favourites are Prem Chand, Sarat Chandra Chattopadhyay, RK Narayan, Ismat Chughtai and Nirmal Verma alongside other literary stalwarts of Indian and World Literature.

Simrita has contributed to leading national newspapers including *The Times of India, The Indian Express* and *The Tribune*.

She now lives with her husband and their son in San Diego, California where she studied Advanced Rhetoric at the Department of Rhetoric and Writing Studies, San Diego State University. She lectures on Writing, Diversity and Imagination at the University of California, Art Institute of California, among others.

The Rainbow Acres is her debut novel.

Readers may connect with her on:
Facebook @TheRainbowAcres
Twitter @simritadhir

THE RAINBOW ACRES

SIMRITA DHIR

Om Books International

First published in 2018 by

Om Books International

Corporate & Editorial Office
A-12, Sector 64, Noida 201 301
Uttar Pradesh, India
Phone: +91 120 477 4100
Email: editorial@ombooks.com
Website: www.ombooksinternational.com

Sales Office
107, Ansari Road, Darya Ganj,
New Delhi 110 002, India
Phone: +91 11 4000 9000
Fax: +91 11 2327 8091
Email: sales@ombooks.com
Website: www.ombooks.com

ISBN: 978-93-5276-668-0

Printed in India

10 9 8 7 6 5 4 3 2 1

For Nik, Lalit, my parents and Ajaiveer

"And once the storm is over, you won't remember how you made it through, how you managed to survive. You won't even be sure, whether the storm is really over. But one thing is certain. When you come out of the storm, you won't be the same person who walked in. That's what this storm's all about."

Haruki Murakami

A carpenter building a sawmill by the American River in Sutter Creek, California first spotted the glimmering yellow in the water in 1848. Scooping it up and gazing at it closely, he could hardly deny that it was the coveted metal. He, however, bit it just so he could be sure, really sure, before yelling out, "Gold!"

His cry reverberated far and wide reaching many reckless and restless men and women all over the world who responded with a fervour so crazed that even though the journey threatened to annihilate them, perilous as it was, it couldn't deter them from taking off for the land of gold. Many perished on the way, but those who made it, took on the great quest along the mystifying Pacific in the enchanted land called California. At first, the pursuit was for the shimmering amber, but soon it became the glorious chase after all things marvellous, all objects elusive, all wishes big and small, emerging as an insurmountable urge impelling people to reach the golden port and pursue fame and success, opportunity and fortune, day after day, until their aspirations came alive, changing their lives forever. In the process, California changed as well. No more a frontier in the far distance, it became the ultimate destination for dreamers across the world, the melting pot of diverse cultures and fantastic ambitions, as eclectic as the multi-ethnic people who had come to inhabit it.

In 1916, a heartbroken Kishan Singh heard the call thousands of miles away in a dusty old village, Noor Mahal, in Punjab, British India. A loud vigorous cry, it shook his being, enticing his mind with audacious hope to where all the colours of the rainbow came down to blaze his path.

In 1925, the shout reached Sophia in the faraway Mexican fishing village of Bahía de Kino, propelling her to follow glitzy butterflies to yellow afternoons and violet sunsets, to reignite a submersed passion, to start anew and dream afresh.

There was no telling if the journey would be worth the struggle, worth breaking hearts and bones, worth burying the throbbing past in a subterranean pit, worth starting again with the uncanny belief in second chances.

There was really no way for Kishan Singh and Sophia to know except to live out their stories and flow with their cryptic twists and turns as they unfurled along the coast of dreams.

KISHAN SINGH

Kishan Singh walked briskly along the swaying wheat fields in his village Noor Mahal in Punjab, British India. Twirling the large melon that he was carrying, he grinned. At seventeen, a grin invariably split his face. It happened when a girl walked by on the streets, or when he slid in the mud, or when he recalled a Bulle Shah verse in the midst of milking the cow. And sometimes, even when a dog barked at night. Kishan didn't know he could blame it on adolescence. Shrugging his shoulders, he just grinned. That spring afternoon of 1916, it was the melon. It had him chuckling from first sight. Luminescent, perfect, round like the moon, it was a melon like no other and it knew his name.

He slumped under a tall banyan that stood by a canal, carrying the burbling waters of the River Satluj and ran his long fingers over the bright green lines that spread across the pale yellow of the melon in a stunning symmetry. At once reluctant and eager, lifting the bewitching fruit, he hit it hard on the ground, smashing it open. The heady aroma of the fruit spread in the air. Grabbing a piece, he gulped it, his mouth flooding with delight, the thrill spreading all the way down his throat and chest before settling into a pool of gladness in his stomach.

Kishan lived with his maternal uncle and aunt, Baldev and Nihalo. His mother had died giving birth to him and his father's people had declared him ill-starred and given him away. As his father moved on, got himself a new wife and in time, three children — two boys and a girl — Kishan slipped through childhood into adolescence in Baldev Mama's two-room earthen house.

Bordering the tiny house were the courtyard, the kitchen, the bath and the barn. Everything about the place comforted Kishan — the bare-walled back room with an old wooden cupboard that stood in a corner, the little front room, which served as both living area and sleeping space for him and his cousins Lakhwant and Khushwant, and the stout mulberry that grew in the courtyard bearing sweet-sour berries that attracted birds, bugs and the village boys. He had come to befriend the cow too, leaping at the first chance to take her for a dip in the pond. His favourite thing, however, was reading in the barn on hot afternoons about places far and near and the intriguing people who lived in them. As a child, he devoured school readers but now into his teens, he relished the gripping books that his teacher, Master Imtiaz Ali lent him. Thanks to Master Imtiaz Ali, he had read numerous books in Punjabi and Hindi and a few in English too. Being well versed in English could open many doors, Master Imtiaz Ali had told him. He had also given Kishan some English novels to keep so Kishan could familiarise himself with English words and phrases. The Dickensian novel was no different from the novels of the Bengali writer, Sarat Chandra Chattopadhyay, Master Imtiaz Ali had said. Kishan cherished Sarat Chandra Chattopadhyay's *Bordidi* and *Biraj Bou* for their tender, nostalgic take on love. Equally fascinating, he thought were Dickens' *Great Expectations* and *Oliver Twist*, which he had read with extensive help from Master Imtiaz Ali. By letting him into the lives of two intense boys who grow up to become perceptive, intelligent men, those Dickensian novels urged Kishan to dream.

Living in the quiet of Noor Mahal where people went about working the fields, eating and sleeping and doing not much else besides, books were his only windows to the astonishing world, taking him to unseen, unimagined lands, transforming ordinary days into remarkable ones.

Kishan knew countless stories, some true and some make-believe. He was always sharing his stories, at school and at home, with villagers and visitors. Every afternoon, he would tell a story even to the mooing cow who sat across from him in the far corner of the barn. It was a story that he didn't tell anyone else, a story that was forever running through his mind — about the most beautiful girl in the village, Roop. He had gone from building mud castles with her by the canals in childhood to discovering a fathomless friendship in the teen years, his infatuation budding into profound love. And she enjoyed his stories, especially the ones about kings and queens, old forts and ecstatic lovers. So, he rehearsed those tales in his mind over and again before presenting them to her, just so he could see her open her mouth in amazement before smiling a smile that stretched far beyond the farthest stretches of the River Satluj. Around Roop, he forgot that he was gawky, large-eyed and awkwardly tall, that he was motherless and abandoned. Around her, feeling inspired, he walked with a victorious swagger despite being destitute. Around her, a song echoed. He called it Roop's Song. Happy, spellbinding, mesmeric, it calmed his storm, stirred his soul.

Kishan would tattle on about Roop to the cow slapping flies with her swishing tail as afternoons turned into evenings and the aroma of Nihalo Mami's cooking began hollering him out. Though Baldev Mama and his boys often complained about Nihalo Mami's cooking — about how the daal was not salted enough and about how the rotis were burnt — at such times, Kishan would be quick to declare that Nihalo Mami had dished up the most delectable daal and that the rotis were crisp and not burnt. Each time he did that, Nihalo Mami would hand him a treat after the meal such as a lump of brown sugar and on lucky days, a melon.

Nihalo Mami's brothers were melon growers in nearby Sherawala, a sunny and marshy village by a bend in the River Satluj. Melons not only grew there but abounded. Her brothers would ask Nihalo Mami over many a time, especially when babies were to be delivered, or a wedding feast had to be prepared and she would set off to help them for a few days. On those days, Kishan helped Baldev Mama with the cooking even though he disliked it, not because he saw it as women's work, but because he found it slow and monotonous. There were other things that Kishan would rather do like read new quirky stories or roam the streets with the village boys, talk about girls or better still, tell tall tales that made the boys buckle up with laughter. But unlike his cousins, Kishan couldn't blatantly refuse to cook. As the forsaken nephew who had been taken in, he felt obliged to his uncle even though Baldev Mama had never so much as shown the slightest preference for his sons over Kishan.

Rolling rotis in the kitchen with Baldev Mama, Kishan liked to tell him about the wondrous planets that adorned the universe, one of which was the blue and green Earth embedded in the splendid Milky Way. "The Milky Way is a strip of luminous stars that looks like milk spattered across the dark sky," he would tell Baldev Mama.

Baldev Mama would have none of it. "Kishan, haven't you had your fill of telling far-fetched tales to the village boys that now you have started throwing your fantastic stories at me?" Baldev Mama would ask, frowning.

Kishan would hang down his head in silence for a bit. What a pity that Baldev Mama couldn't read and that the astonishing world of books was unknown to him. Then, adding salt and chillies to the daal, Kishan would turn his thoughts to the melons that Nihalo Mami would bring back. And the day that Nihalo Mami returned home with a bag of full of melons, Kishan and his cousins would buzz around the bag like bees. Before his cousins could raid the bag, Baldev Mama would hand Kishan the largest melon as a reward perhaps for his help in the kitchen.

Gulping down the melon under the banyan that day, Kishan thanked Nihalo Mami loudly even though he knew she was nowhere around, for bringing the most delicious melon there could be. Then he figured a way to trap the wonder of that melon forever. Quickly, he scooped the pearl-like slimy seeds off its middle and slipped them in his pyjama pocket. Just then Roop's face shone before him. His grin returned. He shook his head at the nerve of that melon. It had made him forget for a wink the love of his life, or his *beloved*, as the village boys called Roop. Even though he pushed those sneering boys away when they joked to him about her, the truth was that the mere thought of Roop set his heart racing.

Picking up what was left of the fruit, he sprinted towards Roop's house. He just had to share that melon with her. He hoped that her mother would not be around. Of late, Roop's mother had begun to scowl at him, grumbling that because he and Roop were no longer children but well into their teens, she didn't want him around her daughter. Kishan understood all too well that it was his destitution that she didn't want around her coveted daughter. He couldn't care less for what Roop's mother wanted. Staying away from Roop was not humanly possible for him. He lived on her smiles. On his way back from school, he was always devising ways to see Roop.

Roop didn't go to school. Embroidering, cooking and cleaning with her mother, she, too, waited every afternoon to meet him.

"Kishan, how I love your stories," she had said once, coiling her braid. "They give me reason to wonder, to smile."

"Is it only my stories that you love?" Kishan had probed with bated breath, hoping that she'd say if only just once, that it was he that she loved, far more than any of his stories.

But withholding a chuckle, Roop had replied, "Yes, it's only your stories that I love."

It didn't matter what Roop said, he knew. He knew that she turned crimson when she saw him watching her. He knew also that she saved her special smile only for him. And that smile, a stupefying amalgam of desires and dreams, made him want more than ever to clench her wrists, kiss her on the mouth, sense her breath upon his skin. If only he could throw propriety to the dogs.

Barely had he started for Roop's house when three British horsemen galloped by, blowing giant dust clouds in his face. Their red coats had him musing about his grand plan.

"Kishan, you must aim for good scores in school and win a scholarship to college. A college education would ensure you a job with the British government," Master Imtiaz Ali had told him.

Kishan intended on doing exactly that, knowing well that once he had a government job, Roop's mother would rush to marry her daughter to a college-educated government employee. He couldn't even begin to count the number of times that he had envisioned Roop as his radiant bride, clad in an exquisitely embroidered phulkari, her kohl-lined eyes smiling, her translucent skin rosy, her straight-set teeth sparkling, her hennaed hands and feet fragrant with happiness. Only a job with the British government could turn that vision to reality. Recently, however, the Indian Independence Movement had begun sweeping across the nation like a storm, leading Master Imtiaz Ali to comment in class one day that the storm would blow the British out. Kishan looked up to Master Imtiaz Ali. If Master Imtiaz Ali thought the British would be ousted, they surely would be. In any case, he had nothing to worry about. If the British left, he would work for the newly formed Indian government. His goal was to land a job with the government. It didn't matter which government — British or Indian. A government job was his means to the end — Roop.

Feeling satisfied again that afternoon with his plan of securing a government job, Kishan frisked into Roop's courtyard. He found Roop sitting on a manji, embroidering yellow flowers on a red bedspread. Seeing no one else around, he called out to her. She looked up, both alarmed and amused. Setting the bedspread aside, she tiptoed to him. When he handed her the melon pieces, she smiled. Kishan thought she was irresistible in her old pink salwar-kurta to where he wanted to grab her and kiss her red lips. He also wanted to tell her that he woke up, walked around, breathed, lived and lusted only for her but transfixed at her sight, he was unable to utter a word let alone braid a sentence.

Watching melon juice trickle down his pyjama pocket, Roop giggled. Seeing her gushing, he smiled. She poked the dimple on his right cheek and whispered, "Kishan, go now," before running inside with the melon pieces.

Kishan's mouth fell open. Roop had poked him. That was reason enough to keep grinning for a whole week. He turned around and headed towards Baldev Mama's fields. Pulling out the dripping melon seeds from his pocket, he sowed them along the edges of the fields. He was growing wonder, he thought, to one day, reap elation.

But even as Kishan waited day after day for the seeds to sprout, for the saplings to dash and colour the space with glorious saffron flowers that would give way to alluring melons, the melon seeds never took root in Noor Mahal.

The soil was not marshy enough for melons, Baldev Mama said.

It was not fertile enough, his cousins opined.

The soil in Noor Mahal indeed was unrelenting, Kishan thought. If only it had welcomed hopes and melons, if only it had let the rainbow shimmer it with the colours of his dreams.

At the peak of spring, Basant Panchmi announced itself with a bang. Roop sneaked out of home on the pretext of embroidering with the village girls, joined Kishan, and the two took off for the celebrations being held in the adjoining village. Kishan couldn't believe his luck. Roop was walking by his side. He had to turn and look at her every few seconds to reassure himself. Roop was too tickled about the festivities to bother with where he looked. Exuberant like a bird out of the cage, she walked uninhibited, her eyes sparking defiance. Even in the terror of being caught together, there was joy. Revelling in that, she was basking in her audacity to rebel, to break free. Kishan's heart skipped a few beats. It happened every time his fingers or arm rubbed against hers. He thought his chest would rip open from the excitement. They came by Serai Noor Mahal, the rest house that had been constructed in their village back in the seventeenth century upon the whim of none other than the legendary Mughal empress, Noor Jahan who had spent her childhood in their village and after whom their village Noor Mahal was named. Looking up at the serai, Roop stopped in her tracks. "To think, I have never strolled inside the serai. Bibi wouldn't let me tread close to it. She says it's haunted," she said.

Kishan smirked. Only Roop's mother could call that serai haunted. He cherished the ethereal serai, having spent many mornings, noons and evenings inside it, applauding Empress Noor Jahan's amazing architectural feat. "There isn't an adventure more exciting than touring the serai," he said.

"Let's forget the celebrations and do that instead," a thrilled Roop suggested. It was her day to revolt, to tread the forbidden.

Kishan could have jumped and touched the sky. His fascination for the building had found a match in Roop's delight in it. "Roop, the double-storeyed arched gateway to the serai is made from sandstone brought from faraway Fatehpur Sikri!" he said, hastily leading Roop towards the serai.

Roop stepped up to caress the eclectic art embossed upon the red gateway — lotuses sprouting out of ponds, nightingales and peacocks, royal riders and effortless archers. They walked through the magnificent entrance, past a desolate courtyard into a thick grove dazzling with trees. The pungent odour of a neem had Roop wrinkling her nose, making her all the more tempting to where Kishan wanted to forget the empress and her serai and kiss Roop hard.

"Kishan, why would the empress plant a neem here," Roop asked.

"The empress knew that the neem dispels mosquitos and other bugs," he replied, his desperate fantasy lingering.

"You sure are smitten with the empress? You know every bit about her and her serai," Roop laughed.

"I like talking about the empress, but it's you I am smitten with," he replied.

Roop turned red. He had said similar things to her a few times before, always leaving her wondering if he were serious or jesting. She peered into his face. He knew she was reading it, trying to gauge if he'd really meant what he had said. His heart jiggled. Unsure if she were angry or elated, he let out an awkward laugh. Seeing her break into a smile, he heaved a sigh of relief. They wandered along the serai's high quadrangular walls lined with mysterious arched rooms, 140 in all. A mosque with a quaint tomb stood by a well and four octagonal minarets glowed in each corner of the serai. Awed by the details, Roop sat down on the steps by the well and looked around. Kishan wished that moment could last forever so he could continue watching her, but the afternoon was fleeting. Above them, birds were flying home across skies reddened by the receding sun, their twittering reverberating through the serai like a timeless melody.

Roop got up with a start. She had better rush home, she said. To hold her back a little longer, Kishan tempted her with a story saying that he knew exactly how the mighty empress came up with the idea of building the momentous serai in Noor Mahal.

Curiosity got the better of Roop. Tugging at his arm, she demanded to hear the story right away. So, looking into her luminous eyes, Kishan began, "Legend goes that sitting in the royal court at Agra, unnerved by the rising advances of her callous stepsons, Empress Noor Jahan often worried for her throne. All four stepsons abhorred her but the third, the most arrogant, Khurram had robbed her of her sleep. First, he had shattered her pride by rejecting her gorgeous daughter, Ladli, in marriage and then had wedded instead her listless niece, Arjumand, going on thereafter to call his new wife, Mumtaz Mahal — the Chosen One of the Palace. Worse still, Khurram's lust for the throne was growing stronger than the strongest walls of the kingdom. Nothing however, bothered Noor Jahan's husband, Emperor Jahangir, who let alcohol and opium waste him away, leaving Noor Jahan to single-handedly avert the insurgencies that threatened to topple their reign.

On most days, Noor Jahan thought she held the reins tight but on others, the anxiety baffled her. One evening, hoping to drown the angst that was gnawing away at her, she dabbed on a perfume brought on a ship from France, especially for her. Not liking it, she dismissed it scornfully. It was no match, she declared, to the fragrances that she made from the radiant roses growing in her court's summer retreat, Kashmir, and began to scour the room for something else to engage her and rid her of her pervasive anguish. Not finding anything interesting and feeling irked, the empress looked down at her dainty little hand. And what do you think Noor Jahan saw?"

Raising and dropping her shoulders, Roop shook her head. She had no inkling.

"It was a coin," Kishan said, "that the empress had dug out from the ruins outside of her childhood village so long ago when she had gone to play hide-and-seek there with the little girls. Yes, there it was shining bright on Noor Jahan's palm. At the sight of the coin, Noor Jahan's face lit up and she pulled out a smile from that distant time. Alien to the ornate palace, that smile belonged only to her childhood village, where, when out looking for adventure, she had found a little fortune instead. The great empress gazed at that glinting coin, staring at it so long and hard only to find it gone. All Empress Noor Jahan could see then was her bare palm and it appeared very empty indeed. The smile disappeared too. Her rapturous face now mirrored her perpetual worries. It was empowering to be the empress, but her tranquil childhood in the old village would remain her most cherished memory. Recalling her life there made her long for the little girl who chased bugs through blooming flowers on cool, orange evenings.

It was to soothe that persistent longing that the empress ordered the building of a signature monument in her childhood village and in the subsequent years came about this famous serai, a relic as fascinating as its royal builder. Thereafter, every summer, the mighty empress came to Noor Mahal to rest at this serai. Here she would again become that carefree girl in search of adventure and each time, she would find her treasure too, not in a piece of shiny silver but in the much-needed peace of mind and her empty palm would be full again." Kishan smiled as he finished the story.

Roop clapped, her cheer spilling over. "I feel so lucky to have heard the story here inside the serai. I loved it," she said.

"What about it?" Kishan asked, arching his brows.

"The empress's pluck and that it was our Noor Mahal that she loved and chose to build a serai in!"

"The empress had some pluck and what about the smarts of the storyteller who told you the story?" Kishan asked, annoyed.

Roop let out a laugh. "Ah, so, that's what you are waiting for — to be complimented. Kishan Singh, how must I thank you for that story?" she joked.

"Perhaps you could let me hold your hand?" Kishan asked abruptly.

"In your dreams!" she chortled, starting off for home. The brave adventure was over.

"But you haven't heard the best part yet. It's about the serai's secret mesmerising spot!" He couldn't bear to see her go.

"Another day," she replied, walking past him.

"I can walk you back," he said.

"I'll manage," she replied.

"Don't miss me too much," he shouted.

"Miss you? Not even after every other creature in the world is dead!" she exclaimed.

"That's a fat lie, and I know it," he said.

Laughing, she kept going.

"You'd better watch out. There are foxes and scorpions and God knows what creeping out in the evening," he called out again.

Turning around, she smirked. "It is you that I have to watch out for," she said and began walking faster.

Kishan guffawed. He wondered when he would see her next, his anxious eyes following her as she walked the trail by the now sleepy fields.

That night, turning and tossing in his sleep, he did indeed see her in a dream. She was swinging on a rainbow in an unknown village, more captivating than ever, her perky eyes dancing, her long brown hair grazing her slender waist. Despite stretching this way and that, he couldn't reach her. The rainbow was much too high up in the clouds. His heart hammered hard against his chest, an unbearable pain rising in his throat and choking him. He woke up, wheezing and sweaty.

SOPHIA

Sophia Morales had one childhood memory that would never fade.

It was from a November morning when she was twelve years old. Playing along the beach, she had wandered through the palms into the wilderness by the lagoon in her coastal Mexican town of Acapulco. She was very proud to have found a spellbinding new space all on her own. Lilies, lupines, primroses and phacelia were in full bloom, kicking up a riot, tickling her senses, immersing her in wonder. Tall old rosewoods stood bunched together. Wild geese cackled in the distance. A hummingbird twittered somewhere. Or was it a cuckoo? She didn't care. All that mattered was that she had found herself a riveting nook. Gathering some flowers in the folds of her dress, she sat down on a grassy patch and began to arrange them in a careless bouquet. She knew it was unlikely that her family would notice her absence, busy as everyone was in the mornings. She could leisurely enjoy her new hideout. She looked up. The sky above was an incredible blue-green with runaway streaks of white. The bewildering mosaic of colour and sound evoked happiness and an obscure nostalgia, leaving her longing for her hometown, Acapulco. How strange it was to miss a place that one hadn't even left? A spark of sunlight caught her eye. Squinting, she got up, pushed back her dark brown hair and walked over to nestle in the shade of a rosewood. She was all but ready to kneel against one when she saw them.

There were hordes of them clustered on the tree. And many more on the neighbouring trees. Wide eyed, she stared harder. Sure enough, it was them. Yes, throngs of butterflies lay resting on the trees, the black and gold of their wings glinting in the morning sun. Never had she imagined that Acapulco was home to so many butterflies. She had always been enamoured of butterflies, drawing the most remarkable ones with big dark eyes and large symmetrical wings on the beach, on banana leaves and on the streets. In drawing life-like butterflies, she revealed an extraordinary understanding of the bugs as though she had studied them for hours, months or even years, when in truth, she relied only on her imagination. Watching swarms of butterflies was a fantasy come alive. She tiptoed to see the butterflies up close. An enchanted smile spread across Sophia's face. The butterflies embodied grace and mystery, colour and beauty, hope and dreams.

That evening, when she shared her new discovery with her father, Antonio, after dinner, he smiled. "Butterflies start their journeys in early autumn from way up in the north. They latch onto warm air currents and float thousands of miles to reach Acapulco to roost down here for the winter. The rosewoods and the wildflowers in the lagoon offer the most perfect habitat for them. They like to rest by the water, you know," he said.

A blaze caught Sophia's eyes. It was astonishing. Butterflies were not just beautiful, they were also gritty. Undertaking hazardous journeys, they learned to adapt to unfamiliar new environs.

The sight of the roosting butterflies would be forever caught and held in Sophia's mind. Little did she know then how much she would come to embody their courage and resilience. Or that her life would echo the journey of the butterflies and that she, too, would one day travel long and far in pursuit of sunnier spots.

Acapulco formed Sophia's world. She grew up frolicking along its deep blue bay, golden beaches, mango groves, lush lagoons and undulating hills, living in a three-room wood house with her parents and grandparents. On the tiny front patio, four tall banana trees swayed in the ocean breeze. A street shaded by avocado trees connected the house to the beach and she would run back and forth between the two all day, swimming, laughing and watching the red sun sink into the ocean in the evenings. Not only was she the centre of her family, she managed somehow to charm neighbours and friends alike, which was surprising because she wasn't particularly compliant. If anything, she was a rebel, always choosing to walk new trails instead of towing the line. Gutsy to the point of being risky, she insisted on swimming in the wild ocean instead of the safe bay since she learned to swim at age three, spending each day dangerously chasing after adventure, welcoming challenges and cherishing trials, even accepting a dare once to jump into the ocean for a swim on a stormy day. And while her gutsy choices made her appealing to others, her family often worried themselves sick about her well-being.

One rainy afternoon when she walked into her house, cold and shivering from being out on the beach for hours, her grandfather, Jacin was aghast. "Sophia, you should know better than to roam the beach on a rainy day," he chided.

"Abuelo, I was collecting sea-shells. So many of them get swept ashore on a rainy day, especially after a storm," Sophia said smiling and showing him her basket full of shells.

Her grandfather didn't smile back. Nor did he look at the sea-shells. "Sophia, the storm could have swept YOU away!" he said sternly. "Only fools go about risking lives without rhyme or reason. Life is a gift. Savour it and be grateful for it. Many never get a chance to live it through."

Sophia bit her lip and nodded. "Don't you worry, Abuelo," she whispered. "I'll try to be careful in the future."

Changing into dry clothes, she told herself that for her family's sake, she must try to keep herself out of harm's way. If only routine could be as exciting as adventure. Her grandfather's words rang in her mind. There was pain at the heart of his chidings. After dinner, she climbed into bed next to her grandmother, Paula, and leaned against her. "Abuela, you know that Abuelo was upset with me today. I guess, he doesn't like my ways," Sophia whispered to her grandmother.

"Your grandfather knows the thrill of adventure, but he values life more. He and I have seen young life snuffed out. It is the worst tragedy," Paula said wistfully.

Sophia knew her grandparents had sailed all the way from Spain to Mexico, overcoming many a storm. She had heard bits and pieces of that story from here and there. That day, her grandparents' words left her wildly curious for details. "Abuela, tell me your story, the whole story, from the very beginning," she said.

Paula smiled and embraced her granddaughter, glad to have her huddled close and evincing an interest in the family story. Most days, Paula would be calling after Sophia to help her with the house work as Sophia flitted in and out of the house, too preoccupied with herself to pay heed, let alone help. Looking deeply into her grandmother's face, Sophia squeezed her hand, imploring her to start right away.

She and Jacin were born and raised in a vibrant village called Pals along the Mediterranean in Spain, Paula said, looking far out of the window as Sophia sat and listened without blinking or stirring. "Back there, your grandfather ran a confectionary serving cakes, bread, fritters and also the most delicious chocolate. He was somewhat of a musician, too, who entertained clients with thrilling bouts of the banjo," Paula said.

Sophia let out a laugh. On rare days, her grandfather still played old Spanish songs on his banjo, the melodies resounding across the house and the patio, spilling onto the street and the beach, enrapturing neighbours and passers-by.

Paula said she had chosen Jacin over many a local bachelor all for his music. "It wasn't so much the man, but the banjo that I'd had fallen for," she said blushing deeply.

Sophia smiled. It was the first time that she had seen her grandmother thrumming with happiness.

In 1840, besotted with the New World's promise of prosperity and happiness, Jacin and Paula along with their three teenaged sons sailed to Mexico on a crowded ship called *Liberty*. Co-passengers said that the west coast of Mexico was geographically similar to coastal Spain. It was warm, thinly populated and held out opportunity. "We decided that Mexico's west coast would be just the place for us to live out our dream for a fuller, wealthier life. Your grandfather decided to set up a bakery to earn a living, panaderías being the heart of every Mexican neighbourhood, where people flocked to buy bread each morning," Paula said.

They settled in the coastal town of Acapulco because it was deeply reminiscent of Pals.

"Like Pals, Acapulco sat by the coast, snuggled by mountains. Acapulco's old fort reminded us of the Tower of Hours back in Pals," Paula said.

"Tower of the Hours?" Sophia asked. "Is it a fort?

"No, it is a captivating clock tower on a hill," Paula said. "They say an elf lives inside the tower."

"Really?" Sophia asked bewildered. She had grown up on stories about elves and gnomes.

"Yes," Paula said, swelling with joy. "Legend has it that the elf leaves sweets for children at the bottom of the hill and runs back to hide in the tower. Sneaking from behind a window, he laughs watching the children eat the sweets."

Sophia was happy to see her grandmother's eyes dancing on recalling her hometown. It took the years off her, ironed out the lines on her face.

Paula and Jacin tried as best as they could to assimilate in Acapulco and for the most part, succeeded. The ambience of Acapulco was familiar, making them feel as though they had never left home. The ocean was warm, offering a bounty of fish all year long and the mercado was always overflowing with fresh produce from nearby farms. The days were long and sunny, the nights pristine and cool. The people, however, weren't nearly as welcoming or friendly as the town. There were many Mestizos, the mixed race born of the mingling between the Spanish and Natives. They looked suspiciously at the new immigrants from Spain who were fewer in numbers. Then there was the language. The Spanish spoken in Mexico was not the Castilian spoken in Spain, but a softer version heavily influenced by the indigenous languages of the land. Jacin couldn't understand many of the words. For starters, everyone got his name wrong. After correcting the locals to no avail, he gave in, resigning to being called Yay-son. Paula had a harder time with the language.

"I couldn't even guess the meaning of several words," Paula said.

But the bakery that Jacin set up in Acapulco hit big, attracting a stream of customers all year long. The expert confectioner in Jacin effortlessly took to baking Mexican delicacies. People swore by his scrumptious churros, pestinos and fresh-baked bread.

"Why did Abuelo not sell chocolate here?" Sophia asked.

"He would have loved to, but the locals had different tastes in chocolate. Selling bread and churros was foolproof and reliable."

Though Jacin and Paula were grateful for the steady income that the bakery brought them, making them economically sounder than they had been back in Spain, Paula said the political turbulence that rocked the newly independent Mexico made them wonder from time to time about how lucrative the move to Mexico had really been. What delighted them, nonetheless, was that their three sons had taken to Mexico like fish to water. Befriending the Mestizos, they loved everything Mexican from the food and drinks to the language and locale.

In 1846, calling it their honourable duty to Mexico, Jacin and Paula's two older boys, Claudio and Jose, joined the ranks of the Mexican Army and died fighting in the Mexican-American War of 1848. Paula and Jacin were crushed.

"I couldn't pull out of bed for months. It was as though I had died too," Paula said gravely. "Your grandfather never played the banjo with the same passion again. Something in him just stopped singing. The melody slipped away."

That part didn't need to be told. Sophia knew. Even though her grandparents always had a smile ready for her, some days, if she looked beyond the curves of their smiling mouths and the twinkle of their delighted eyes, she could see the pain peering back at her from behind her grandmother's white dress with big red flowers, and from underneath her grandfather's old straw hat, making her want to hold them tight and comfort them.

"We swore by the cross never to let our third, your father Antonio, out of sight," Paula said. "He took over the bakery from your grandfather, pouring his heart and soul into his work. And what a fabulous job he does. He is the son all parents aspire to have."

Sophia knew that all too well. Not only were her grandparents proud of her father, they were fixated with their only surviving child. He worked late into the evening and they waited for him to return home, anxiously walking to the bakery to fetch him if he were ever running too late.

"Tell me about the time Pa and Ma got married," Sophia asked her grandmother, trying to steer the story in a happy direction. The meeting of her parents was where her own story began, and she wanted so much to regale in the joy of that instant.

"Your mother as you know, is astonishingly beautiful. Your father saw her selling flowers in the zócalo one spring morning. He bought all the flowers from her only to present them back to her," Paula laughed.

Sophia laughed too. It was an awfully romantic story, the kind they sang about in the songs. Her mother indeed was beautiful. Sophia loved it that she had been named after her mother and she wished on many a day that she would grow up and look like her mother too. Her mother's Spanish heritage shone in her sharply chiselled face and in her tall frame. Her dark long hair ran down in a cascade, her eyes were neither black nor brown but a chirpy mix of the two and her teeth were glossy and tightly set. As of then, Sophia looked nothing like her mother. Her teeth were uneven, her hair flew wild and she had freckles on her face from being out in the sun all day long. She thought herself far from beautiful. Her grandmother thought otherwise.

"Sophia, you are a gift from Virgin Mary, presented to us after fifteen years of your parents' marriage," Paula said, cupping Sophia's face in her hands. "We were beyond ourselves with happiness to have you. You were the loveliest baby with bright eyes and the most perfect little smiling face. Oh, how we prayed tirelessly for you to come. You are precious beyond measure. Now, do you know why your grandfather worries for your safety?"

Sophia nodded. It felt nice to be so awaited and so loved. It was burdensome as well to be an only child, to be constantly reminding herself to be sensible when all she wanted at times was to break loose, give in to impulse and do the impossible. Being the only child was like trying to reach for the stars with one foot on the ground. She sighed. As much as she loved her family, she couldn't let that love hold her from flying high, from running after the changing horizon, from jumping at the next exciting venture.

She would never stop chasing clouds.

KISHAN SINGH

Spring made way for a promising summer. To Kishan's good luck, the Teej Carnival was announced on the faraway meadows along the River Satluj. Hearing of the summer festivities, Roop, too, was thrilled. Excitedly, she shared with Kishan how much she looked forward to singing, dancing, eating sweets and looking at trinkets. On the day of the carnival, dodging prying eyes, the two took a secluded route to the fair, walking through kachnaars laden with purple and white flowers. Joking and talking, when Kishan's shoulder brushed against Roop's, far from moving away, she knocked hers against his, again and yet again. Kishan's eyes blobbed out as though he'd been sparked by thunderbolts. His heart thumped. There were goosebumps on his arms, fire in his chest. He felt a sweet sting, an insistent urge to hold and kiss her. He was wondering if she would let him when banging her shoulder against his again, Roop rippled with laughter. Kishan smiled. If only Roop knew how his heart beat for her; how thoughts of her sent him zipping to the moon one moment and panting for air in the darkest dungeon the very next; how the uncertainties of his life made her so bewildering to him — within reach and yet unattainable.

Throngs of people — men, women and children in bright, new clothes from all the nearby villages had made it to the carnival. They circled the many food joints, eating sumptuous chhole-puri, delicious reohri-gachak and refreshing kulfi. Roop, however, made a dash to where the gypsies were selling colourful clothes and flashing jewellery, Kishan following close behind her. Enamoured of the many ornaments, Roop strung a necklace around her long neck, slid a bangle down her pretty wrist. Then bending over a pair of gleaming silver anklets, she tried them on, entwining the delicate hooks on each end. Kishan thought she looked like a princess, her silver-clad ankles blazing, her smile glistening. On an impulse, he decided that he would buy her those anklets. But just as soon he knew that he hadn't a paisa in his pocket, let alone the three rupees that the gypsy was asking for the anklets. As he stood there thinking, Roop unhooked the silver anklets, put them back and walked up to look at the hair trinkets that another gypsy was selling. Kishan continued staring at the silver anklets. Roop had outdone the fabulous summer day when she had worn them. One way or the other, he had to get them for her. He was considering begging and stealing when his mind murmured that there was a way he could buy them. But it would mean leaving Roop behind at the fair for a bit. He wanted to spend every second of every minute at the fair with her, but he knew he must go so she could have those anklets. He walked up to the gypsy. "Can you hold those for me?" he asked, pointing to the anklets. "I'll be back before you know."

When the gypsy nodded, he started running through wind-ruffled trees, past the wheat fields turned orange by the afternoon, towards Noor Mahal, his pulse racing. He imagined the look on Roop's face when he would present the anklets to her, when he'd tell her that they were hers to keep. Reaching Baldev Mama's house, he rushed into the front room. Under the bedstead lay an old sack in which he stored his books, a few maps and his precious silver medal that he had won a few years ago for finishing first in the district in the middle school board examinations. Kneeling by the bedstead, Kishan reached for his sack and emptied it. Clenching the medal, he recalled the day when the Education Officer in Jalandhar had awarded it to him at a ceremony attended by students, teachers and dignitaries from across the district. Never had he imagined that he was the best middle schooler in the district. He remembered how proud Master Imtiaz Ali had been of him that day, how Baldev Mama and Nihalo Mami had looked at the medal in wonder, unable to even grasp what that thick circular piece of silver was all about, how he and his cousins had taken turns to hold it and look at it, how after showing it to an enthralled Roop one afternoon, he had wrapped it in white muslin and tucked it at the bottom of his sack for safekeeping. He was fortunate to have that medal, he thought. Trading it, he could get the silver anklets for Roop, making her gorgeous smile last till eternity. Shoving the medal down his pocket, he began running back to the fair. He saw the sun was ebbing and ran faster still on the muddy trail, fearful of missing the chance of buying the anklets.

Back at the carnival, he scurried through the crowds to reach the gypsy's shack. Pulling the gypsy aside, Kishan told her that he wanted to trade his silver medal for the anklets. The gypsy held the medal, scratched it with a coin and then rubbed it against a boulder that lay on the ground. "It is silver all right and good, clean silver for that, but it is of lesser value than the anklets," she said, puckering her lips and handing the medal back to Kishan.

Kishan's heart stumbled but thinking fast, he told her, he could give her a few pumpkins along with the medal. Three or four pumpkins?

"Make it five pumpkins, large ones," the gypsy said.

Tucking the medal in his pocket again, Kishan began running towards Baldev Mama's fields, a horde of robins flying overhead. He thought of how Roop might be looking for him and how much of their precious time together he had missed with all the running back and forth. He mustn't let the entire evening slip away; he must run faster.

Baldev Mama had grown pumpkins so they could eat something other than lentils all summer long. As he tore off five large pumpkins, Kishan knew a beating lay in store for him but fired by love, he was ready to get not only beaten up but also killed just so Roop could have those anklets. With three pumpkins in one hand, and two in the other, he began walking back to the fair, it being impossible to run while holding five pumpkins. He worried that on not finding him, Roop would have headed home with the village girls. If Roop had left, he would have to come up with a way to meet her and hand her those anklets. Then, he took to thinking about the gypsy. "Gypsies are devious," Nihalo Mami had said once. "Their words are as shifty as their whereabouts. Stay away from them."

What if the gypsy decided to sell the anklets to another, Kishan wondered. Gripping the pumpkins tighter, he began walking faster. The only way to know what was happening at the carnival was to make it back there as soon as possible.

Reaching the carnival, he carefully waded through the crowds and placed the pumpkins and the silver medal in front of the gypsy. The gypsy stared at the pumpkins and the silver medal. "Boy, who are you buying the anklets for? The young thing who stopped to try them on?" she asked, smiling impishly.

Kishan nodded.

The gypsy laughed. "The girl sure is beautiful. Just like these anklets. And you are mad!" she said, handing him the anklets.

Kishan could hardly believe that he was holding the anklets. It didn't matter that the chortling gypsy had called him mad. He was convinced that he was mad in love. Tossing aside Nihalo Mami's warning about gypsies, he stepped up and gave the gypsy a squeeze. "Boy, you are not just mad but raving mad," the surprised gypsy cried, gurgling with laughter.

Kishan shoved the anklets in his pocket, his eyes searching frantically for Roop. Then he saw her. She was walking towards him with a kulfi. "Kishan, where did you take off? I've been looking for you everywhere and for so long. You missed seeing how much I danced and how loudly I sang with the village girls," Roop said, shaking her head.

Kishan smiled. She was even more beautiful when annoyed.

"I wonder what you are so thrilled about," she said, frowning.

He was still fumbling for an answer when she handed him her half-eaten kulfi, saying, "I got this for us to share just in time before the kulfi man wrapped up."

Kishan began lapping up the half-eaten kulfi. They had shared treats since they were little, bonding over sweet gulgullas, churri and gur. But that day, after all the toing and froing, slurping the kulfi was like biting into paradise. Cooler than the chill waters of the River Satluj, the kulfi had him swaying to a song from another age. Licking the stick clean and swinging it in the air, he said, "Let's go home."

They took the trail along the river where rows of gulmohar and amaltas grew, their red and gold blooms, lighting up the evening. Roop was in a dream world, singing.

The trees are tall and lofty
Oh, so tall and lofty, my friend
The river rolling below them...

Kishan sneaked close to her. "Close your eyes and hold out your hand," he whispered. Just as she did that, he swiftly placed the anklets on her palm and asked her to open her eyes. Seeing the anklets, she gasped, slumping down on the sandy riverbank with a thump. "How did you get these?" she asked.

"I bought them," he said.

"Bought them?"

He nodded.

"Let's go back and return them. The last thing I want is you in debt." Getting up, she clutched Kishan's arm to lead him back.

"Roop, I am not in debt. The anklets are paid for and yours to keep," Kishan said.

"Paid for?" Roop was stunned.

Though he knew that she would fume, Kishan told her.

Sighing, Roop lapsed again on the riverbank, one hand on her forehead and the other holding the anklets. "I fell hard for the anklets, but God knows, I never wanted for you to give up your medal to buy them for me," she said.

"Roop, buying the anklets made me happy like I've never been," Kishan said, kneeling by her side.

Roop smiled. It was her special smile, lucent and unrestrained. Kishan remembered how long and how fast he had sped that afternoon to earn that moment. He thought that if he tried to kiss her then, perhaps she would let him, but he didn't. The air was already charged with exhilaration. He could barely handle it — the twinkling anklets, Roop's riveting smile, her ravishing eyes. A kiss on top of that would delude him. So, he smiled and asked her to try on the anklets instead. She poked the dimple on his right cheek before fastening the anklets around her ankles one after the other. Then standing up, she lifted her salwar so Kishan could see her glittering feet. Even as he smiled, Kishan Singh was burning with ecstasy. It felt as though buying the anklets for Roop was the only good thing that he had done in his life, as though Empress Noor Jahan's love for Noor Mahal had melded with his for Roop, setting him ablaze.

Lying on his manji that night, all Kishan could think about was how achingly beautiful Roop looked with the silver anklets on her feet, and how close he and Roop had come to kissing. Soon, he would kiss her. Loving her as much as he did, it seemed the most perfect thing to do.

The next morning in the schoolhouse, sitting cross-legged on the hard and dusty floor, in the middle of the arithmetic lesson, he wondered again what it would be like to have his nose rub against Roop's, to have their lips twined in a kiss. He was lucky that Roop didn't attend school else he would have failed in every subject. In the afternoon, he went to help Baldev Mama on the fields but couldn't. His mind kept sketching scenes of him and Roop holding each other, of them staring into each other's eyes. But most of all, he imagined them kissing each other again and again in the thick cornfields by the bustling river under the clear green sky. Perhaps a geography book could help, take him for a spin across the world, finally wean his mind off her. He set out for Master Imitiaz Ali's house down the alley to borrow one. Reaching there, he just had to ask. Master Imtiaz Ali pulled out his thick book of continents and oceans and handed it to him. Grasping it, Kishan thanked him and was about to step out when Master Imtiaz Ali said, "Kishan, the Maharaja of Patiala has announced scholarships for smart boys who are needy. If your scores are high, you could win a scholarship to the Maharaja's College in Patiala."

Kishan's heart soared. It was an amazing prospect. "I sure could, Masterji!" he said.

Going home, the scent of Roop satiating his brain, Kishan resolved to work harder at school and win a scholarship. That would ease his way to his dream. With no expenses to worry about, he could breeze through college, get a job and marry Roop real soon. Then she would be his, to adore and to cherish forever.

Kishan would have spent the entire summer like he had the seasons before, planning, dreaming, fantasising about being with Roop but then one day, he ran into Jaspal, the wrestling hero of not just Noor Mahal, but of all the villages along the River Satluj. Training under the legendary wrestling instructor, Ustaad Gulbahar Khan, Jaspal had beaten many veteran wrestlers of the land at mere seventeen. Kishan was proud of Noor Mahal's champion but he had never got around to rubbing elbows with the iconic wrestler. With his ongoing training and matches, Jaspal rarely attended school. On days that he did, his many admirers would surround him, applauding his famous wrestling feats. Kishan had a mind to one day wade past Jaspal's followers and let Jaspal know how much he admired his strength. But the day when Kishan finally came face-to-face with Jaspal, their meeting was nowhere close to how Kishan had imagined it would be.

It happened abruptly. One day, roaming the meadows with the boys after school, when Kishan spoke of the incredible strength of the human mind to accomplish far beyond the physical limitations of the body, his friends, Gurjas and Pyara dared him. "Kishan, surely you are not suggesting that a weakling with a strong mind can scale a mountain?" Pyara asked.

"Certainly, you don't mean that sickly Rama of our village can win a running race with the strength of his mind?" Ramjas asked.

"Why yes, even a frail man with a strong mind can climb a mountain and yes, Rama, even though he is sickly, can win the village race if he makes up his mind to do so," Kishan replied. He recounted how he had once taken tests while reeling under a high fever, describing how his body had hurt, how his eyes had watered, how the village hakim's medicine had made him drowsy but he had held on tenaciously in the midst of shivers and stupor, finishing first in his class.

Pyara and Ramjas laughed him off. Soon, other boys joined them, all refuting Kishan's contention about the strength of the human spirit. "Kishan, going by what you say, with the strength of your mind, you should be able to swim the length of the River Satluj from the town of Phillaur to the far end of the next town?" Sukha asked.

"I sure could," Kishan replied, "if I picked up the resolve to do so."

"In that case, you could wrestle the greatest wrestler too and with the STRENGTH of your mind, knock him to the ground?" Sukha sneered.

"Of course, if I am determined enough, I could," Kishan said, his voice rising.

"Let's take him up on that challenge," the boys cried in unison. One of them ran to fetch Jaspal.

Kishan was still reasoning and explaining in a high-pitched voice when Jaspal came along. Listening in on the discussion, he rubbed his chin and smiled.

"Let's see the match," Sukha said, pointing towards Jaspal. "Strength of mind against the muscle."

Kishan looked at the well-built Jaspal. Arguing with the boys, he hadn't had a notion that he would have to prove his point by fighting the famous six-foot tall wrestler. Not only was Jaspal winsome and energetic, he was a disciplined sportsman who exercised for hours each day to maintain his position as the undisputed greatest wrestler of the land.

"Come on, Kishan. Certainly, you won't back out now? Will you?" Sukha shouted.

"You can't go back on what you said," Ramjas cried.

"You are not a chicken, are you?" Pyara jeered.

Though completely taken aback, much to everyone's surprise, Kishan turned towards Jaspal and said, "Let's head to the wrestling ground."

Cheering and shouting, the boys followed the two to the wrestling ground.

Throwing off their shirts, Kishan and Jaspal walked to the centre of the ground and faced each other. Kishan blinked. Clearly, he was out of his mind. His whole life he hadn't wrestled anyone but his cousins and that too in jest. How would he hold his own even for a few minutes against the supreme wrestler? The best that he could do now was to keep his head and deal one blow at a time.

Jaspal stepped closer to him. "Kishan Singh, I hear you are somewhat of a wonder when it comes to writing and math," he said. "Now, wrestling is a different game. I'll quite understand if you want me to back away. I could even say that I don't feel up to wrestling today or something like that. You know what I mean?"

Kishan knew exactly what the famous wrestler meant. "Thank you, but I wouldn't want the great wrestler of Noor Mahal to turn his back to the wrestling ground for me. Let the match begin," Kishan replied.

Reluctantly, Jaspal walked towards Kishan and grabbed his arms. They grappled and Kishan slid away. Then Jaspal aimed for his waist but again Kishan wriggled, not letting Jaspal clench it, reaching instead for Jaspal's right leg. Surprised at that move, Jaspal pushed Kishan off only to have him reach for his left arm next. The match continued. What everyone had imagined would be a leisurely win for Jaspal stretched beyond a few minutes. When Kishan reached a second time for Jaspal's right leg, pulling free, Jaspal tried to tackle Kishan hoping to knock him down with a jerk. Kishan, however, wouldn't let him. Jaspal then resorted to the more extreme measure, his famous lock. He clasped Kishan's arms, trapped his shoulders and slammed him to the ground. Kishan felt his body shudder. Never had he experienced a jolt of that magnitude. Would he ever be able to get up again, he wondered?

The boys who had been cheering and clapping all along, shouted, "Bravo, Jaspal — the hero."

As Kishan slowly rose to his feet, Jaspal gestured to the boys to shush. "I may have outdone Kishan Singh but there is some truth in what he says — strength of mind can carry a person far. Why, another man would have run away just at the thought of tackling a wrestler, but Kishan Singh persisted despite never having stepped on the wrestling ground before. I'd rather you cheer for him," Jaspal said, touching Kishan's shoulder and walking away.

Kishan was sore all over. He could barely stand but limping home, instead of groaning, he smiled. At night, when his body stiffened, and his cousins rubbed ghee on his bruises and Baldev Mama called him a fool for shouting out to trouble, down on the manji, kindled by an unaccustomed joy, Kishan smiled again. It didn't matter that he had been knocked around bad, he had made a friend.

In the days after the wrestling match, he began spending time with Jaspal, helping him on his fields after school, even going to the nearby villages with him to get seeds and manure. Tickled by the new friendship, Kishan was on a high — talking and laughing with Jaspal outside the sweetmaker Ramdeen's shop in the afternoons, even jumping and swimming in the canals with Jaspal in the evenings. He realised that the most famous wrestler was also the one who stepped up after harvest to hand a bag of produce to the farmer who had reaped the poorest yield. Kishan also noticed that Jaspal could barely sit around during the day. Moving and shaking, he was forever anxious to bend over and start working — sowing, weeding, tending the fields. After the day's work, however, calming down, Jaspal would share with Kishan his wrestling adventures as also his many failures at school, confiding that he would soon be dropping out of school to take to his fields full time. Anticipating a rich cotton harvest at the end of summer, Jaspal hoped to pay off the debt on his land and rid his father of the deceitful moneylenders.

In Jaspal's company, Kishan discovered a nonchalance. Where he had previously begrudged his absentee father, he now told Jaspal that his mother was dead and for all practical purposes, his father too and that he had made peace with it. He also began unleashing his swarm of tall tales for Jaspal, one after the other. Jaspal liked Kishan's stories, his favourite being the one about the boy and girl, who blown away by a hurricane, landed and romanced on the moon. Befriended by

someone as strong and resolute as Jaspal, Kishan forgot that he
was alone with no father or mother, brother or sister. Instead,
he felt important and cared for. It was as though he had found a
brother to walk with, to trust and to patch the hole in his life. In
a sea of ambiguity, Kishan thought that he had found something
of which he could be certain — Jaspal's friendship, even as the
many uncertainties in his life continued.

He slogged through his final year of school battling the
doubts — would he make it to college, would he land a job,
would he be able to marry Roop?

SOPHIA

"Paula and I wish to go to Mexico City to pay homage to the Virgin of Guadalupe," Jacin said one Sunday morning.

It was October 1890 and the family sat on the patio after breakfast, talking and sipping coffee.

"Yes, there is nothing more that we want than to go to the Basilica of Our Lady of Guadalupe in Mexico City," Paula entreated.

Antonio was taken aback. "What? It is over 200 miles away!" he said. "And unsafe too. Not a day goes by without a riot breaking out in Mexico City."

Jacin shook his head. "We won't let turmoil hold us anymore from offering our respects to the Virgin," he said.

Antonio wouldn't have any of it. "I would be a callous fool to put my parents' life in danger. Rebels are relentlessly protesting economic inequality," he said.

"We have been hearing about the upheaval for years now. Conflicts fail to resolve. We are old and hunched and getting weaker by the day. It is now or never. We must go," Jacin said.

"If the Virgin so wills, we will return safely," Paula said, leaning over to touch her son's face.

Antonio looked around and sighed.

Sophia who was sitting in a corner, drawing butterflies on the mud floor with her finger and listening to the conversation, looked up at her father. "Pa, if Abuelo and Abuela want so much to visit the basilica in Mexico City, please let them. The town traders go to Mexico City all the time to bring back goods. No harm has ever come their way. Abuelo and Abuela will be fine too," she said.

Sophia's mother was cooking pork stew in the kitchen. Setting her ladle down, she walked over to her husband. "The

Virgin looks out for her flock. She will keep your parents safe. You mustn't hold them from taking the trip," she said intently.

Antonio looked at his wife. She was a generally quiet woman, not one to butt in with opinions or advice. He knew she had stepped up only because she was an impassioned believer herself, having hung a large picture of the Virgin of Guadalupe in the front room. "Give me a few days to plan things out," he said, stepping out of the house.

In the days that followed, Antonio arranged for his parents to travel to the basilica with one of the town traders in a horse-drawn wagon. "The trader will take the safer roads to Mexico City. He even knows of taverns that offer food and lodging along the way and has assumed complete responsibility for your well-being on the trip," he told his parents.

Paula and Jacin embraced their son, grateful to have finally come by the chance to pay respect to the country's beloved saint. In the days leading up to the trip, they spoke and walked briskly, lingering smiles lighting up their faces. Sophia was excited for them too, filling the neighbourhood in about her grandparents' upcoming trip, loudly sharing with everyone how visiting the basilica in Mexico City was a dream come to life for her grandparents.

The night before the trip, she helped her grandparents pack their things — clothes, soap, oil and hairbrush in a large jute bag. More anxious as she was than Jacin and Paula, Sophia was hardly able to sleep that night, and was out of bed at the crack of dawn. She insisted on helping her grandparents get dressed. Only the nicest clothes would do for a visit to the basilica, she said. She pulled out her grandfather's new black trousers, felt hat and grey shirt from his box. Then she polished his shoes till they shone. Putting on his new clothes and sparkling shoes, Jacin kissed his granddaughter's forehead, blessing her profusely. For her grandmother, Sophia chose a blue velvet dress, slipping into which, Paula appeared to have magically reverted in time to a decade ago when she was not nearly as bent over or wrinkled, when she walked taller and smiled crisper. Watching her grandparents all dressed up, Sophia flushed with joy. When they left in the trader's horse-drawn wagon, she waved enthusiastically, even ran behind the wagon for a bit before it sped out of sight.

In the days that they were gone, Sophia missed her grandparents sorely. Everything felt unusual about the house. Breakfast was not the same without her grandmother's sweet bread rolls, the afternoons were long and boring without her grandfather's chidings. Most of all, she hated sleeping by herself in the front room every night. Some mornings, on waking up, she would reach over absent-mindedly to nuzzle her grandmother only to find her bed vacant. A vendor at the mercado who had visited Mexico City told Sophia that there was no place quite like it. "It is a huge city with royal buildings and majestic splendour," he said. "The basilica sits atop a hill and is always bustling with people from across the world. One has to watch out for violence and theft though. The city is infamous for unrest."

Sophia imagined her grandparents having a good time in Mexico City, riding past tall buildings and big shops. She could even see them staring in awe at the Madonna's statue inside the basilica.

One evening, as she was walking home with her mother after picking mangoes, the excitement gave way to anguish. The vendor at the mercado had also echoed what her father had said. As exciting as Mexico City was, it was also unsafe. Sophia took to suddenly worrying about her grandparents. They hadn't been away from Acapulco in years. They were very old too. Her grandmother complained often about her aching knees and joints. Her grandfather's eyes were bleary, and his walk unsteady. Some nights, he coughed incessantly. Her face creased. "Ma, would Abuela and Abuelo be able to climb the hill on which the basilica stands," she wondered aloud to her mother, her mind sketching scenes of shouting protesters in front of the basilica, trampling and shoving pilgrims.

"Sophia, don't you worry," Sophia's mother reassured her. "The Virgin called for them; she will stretch out her hand and lead them to the top. If you so like, you could pray to our Lady of Guadalupe for your grandparents' well-being."

Sophia immediately closed her eyes and muttered a prayer to the Virgin to keep her grandparents safe.

When the horse-drawn carriage finally pulled back into the street one afternoon, a fortnight after her grandparents' departure, Sophia was out on the patio, trying to pull down a banana bunch off a tree. She shrieked, ran and threw her arms around her grandparents who showered her with kisses.

As the family huddled together in the front room after dinner that evening, Sophia sat between her grandparents, clutching their hands, wanting to hear every detail of their trip.

"The basilica is unforgettable," Paula said. "Story has it that on a radiant winter morning back in 1531, the Virgin appeared and blessed an honest farmer named Juan Diego as he hiked a hill on the outskirts of Mexico City. So, to honour the Virgin's love for the pure of heart, the basilica was built on that very hilltop."

Sophia smiled. "And what did you think of the city," she asked.

"Mexico City is the oldest city in the Americas," Jacin said. "People from places far and near work and live there. The roads are wide and always busy. The wealthy ride in large carriages."

"The rich must be very well dressed," Sophia asked, wondering if her grandparents' clothes made the cut.

"Yes, people were luxuriously dressed in fine silk gowns, neatly tailored coats and leather shoes," Jacin said. "Not everyone is rich though," he added wistfully. "The City of Palaces is also the abode of numerous poor and homeless people."

"Your grandfather is right," Paula said. "We saw many destitute and hungry people roaming the city streets."

"It is this rising economic inequality that is causing the unrest," Antonio said. "The poor are starving to death while the rich roll in wealth. No wonder riots break out every day."

Sophia imagined a poor man in tattered old clothes and worn-out shoes throwing a stone at an ornate horse-drawn carriage. Suddenly the political upheaval did not seem so distant in her mind.

"I take it that you were able to safely hike up and down the hilltop to see Our Lady of Guadalupe," Sophia's mother said. "Why, Sophia worried a lot for your health, even praying that you would make it up to the top and back safely."

"Of course, we did. We forgot all our aches and pains at the basilica. The Virgin led us to the top, healed our wounds, touched our souls. We feel so at peace," Paula said smiling.

Sophia and her mother smiled too. Sophia thought her grandparents looked happier and healthier. And surprisingly enough, they seemed to have gotten younger, walking faster, joking more and laughing much.

For Sophia's fifteenth birthday, a few weeks later, Paula and Jacin declared that they would oversee every detail of the big quinceañera party to celebrate her coming of age, making Sophia leap up with joy. She could hardly wait to be quinceañera, God's own princess.

The morning of her birthday, her grandparents presented her a necklace with a picture of the Virgin of Guadalupe on the locket.

"People have overcome ordeals because of their belief in the Virgin. Such is her power. Sophia, your necklace has been personally blessed by the high priest at the basilica in Mexico City," Paula said, kissing Sophia on both cheeks. "Life is not fair, but it is beautiful and worth every struggle."

Sophia kissed the locket and slipping the necklace around her neck, she thanked her grandparents.

"May the Virgin watch over you always," Jacin said, touching Sophia's forehead. "Always hold the Virgin in your heart; she will pull you out of all predicaments. Live bravely and smile often."

Smile, Sophia did for the rest of her special day. She wore a flowy pink gown with fuchsias embroidered all over. It had taken her mother several months to hand stitch and embroider her princess dress. For Sophia's hair, her mother had woven a tiara of fuchsias to match Sophia's outfit. When she saw her reflection in the mirror, Sophia smiled in amazement. For the first time, she looked somewhat like her mother, her teeth didn't seem nearly as uneven, her hair not really as wayward as before and her freckles, too, seemed to have faded somewhat in the bright happiness of the day. She left for church, carrying a bouquet of pink primroses, her rosary and Bible, her dark hair glistening in the red sunshine. Her family, friends and neighbours followed behind her, their song and laughter echoing in the streets. At church, Sophia offered flowers to the Virgin Mary and thanked her for her love, promising to honour her faith and her family till eternity.

"Sophia, remember that you are a quinceañera, Daughter of God, the King. In all circumstances, happy as well as sad, you must honour your promise to the Virgin and stay true to your faith," the priest said, sprinkling holy water on Sophia and blessing her rosary and Bible.

To carry out the last doll tradition, her father handed the last doll to Sophia. "Today, you will leave behind your toys and take on the role of an adult. Here is your last doll; she will be your bridge to adulthood — independence and responsibility," he said, his misty eyes smiling.

Sophia gazed at the endearing fabric doll. Dressed in a pink gown with primroses in her hands, she was Sophia's exact replica. What's more, she had Sophia's freckles too. Sophia kissed the doll and held her father in a long embrace. Walking out of the church, she tossed her last doll to a group of little girls huddled in a corner. The little girls screamed with joy. Sophia didn't look back. She was happy to leave behind the world of toys and savour the indulgences of adulthood. It seemed a heady place and she couldn't wait to dive right into it.

Returning home, she gasped.

On the celebration table lay fluffy bunuelos de viento, almond cakes, cookies, pestinos and flao. And a huge clay pot piñata, the largest that she had seen at a quinceañera party, hung on a banana tree on the patio.

"Sophia, your Abuelo has been hard at work in the bakery. He insisted on personally baking all the goodies for your birthday," Antonio said. "And your Abuela stuffed the piñata with all your favourite treats before hanging it on the tallest of the banana trees. She had to climb on a ladder to do that!"

Tears of joy ran down Sophia cheeks as she flung her arms around her grandparents. They were a prayer and a blessing, a source of unconditional love and joy. Her life was richer and fuller because of them.

The crowd took to eating, raving all along about Jacin's baking as Sophia's father handed out large tumblers of tepache, which he had made by adding spices to fresh pineapple juice. Soon everyone was taking turns to break open the piñata with a stick. Slowly and gradually, the clay pot piñata began to crack as Sophia's grandmother sang the piñata song.

Hit it, hit it, hit it,
Don't lose your aim,
Because if you lose it, you get lost on the road.

The piñata requires much skill, but it only contains oranges and sugarcane...

It was Fidel, the tallest boy in the neighbourhood who finally broke the piñata open; bananas, oranges, sugarcane and candy spilled out of it. Children flocked to grab a treat and Sophia's father asked her to waltz. Everyone clapped and sang, joining them in dance as her grandfather played old tunes on the banjo, conjuring images of faraway coastal Spain through his melodies.

Sophia went to bed very jubilant that evening, her grandfather's tunes playing softly in her head. She was still smiling in her sleep the next morning, when her mother shook her awake. "Sophia, your Abuelo died in his sleep last night," Sophia's mother said, stricken with anguish.

Sophia's heart sank. Leaping out of bed, she looked out of the window. She saw her grandmother crying on the patio. She rushed out. Her grandfather lay still on a cot. Reaching for his hand, she stared at his old bony fingers that had enthusiastically played the banjo the evening before. They were also the fingers that had kneaded the dough and baked goodies for her quinceañera party. The truth came to jolt her. Life could be happy one moment and horrific in the next. It was uncertainty and not heady happiness that epitomised adulthood.

In the days after her grandfather's death, Sophia noticed her grandmother slipping into seclusion. Insisting on staying to herself, Paula stopped talking altogether and a month after they had buried her grandfather, Sophia walked home one evening after collecting firewood only to find her grandmother lying lifeless underneath a banana tree on the patio. It was the same tree on which Paula had hung the piñata for Sophia's quinceañera party. Sophia thought back on the day of the party. It had marked her transition into adulthood with a bang, ruthlessly snatching away her beloved grandparents. In truth, it was their death and not the quinceañera celebration that catapulted her into adulthood. Bereft of her adoring Abuelo and Abuela, who were the centre of her tranquil childhood, Sophia grew up overnight and began helping her father at the bakery.

KISHAN SINGH

Summer lingered on. Hot winds blew all day, dust circling around and landing in Kishan and Jaspal's eyes and hair as they worked the fields. Waving off bothersome flies, they'd wait for the sun to sink, for the moon to come up, for the earth to cool a little. Kishan looked forward to watering the fields on full moon nights when a cool breeze blew along the canals. Walking the trails, he would relish how rapidly the crickets chirped, how brightly the fireflies burned and how loudly the jackals howled in the far distance on nights like those. It was as though all creatures were maddened by the moon, the fullness of it too beautiful for creation to behold.

The days got hotter. One afternoon, the heat was sweltering. Despite downing large tumblers of lassi, Kishan and Jaspal had parched throats. Beads of sweat reappeared on their foreheads seconds after they had wiped them clear. Jaspal said that the river was the only respite and they ran and jumped into a large quavering canal. Relieved somewhat after the dip, they sat under an old teak and looked up at the cloudless sky.

"The rain will be later than usual this year," Kishan said. "Even the mynahs have not flown in yet. They bring rain with them."

"The birds will come and the rain too. You tell me about your mynah," Jaspal laughed.

Kishan's heart fluttered. Excitedly, he shared with Jaspal his grand plan of making it to college on scholarship, landing a government job and marrying the love of his life, Roop. Jaspal listened closely and offered to request his wrestling instructor, Ustaad Gulbahar Khan to put in a word for Kishan to someone at the Maharaja's College.

Kishan thanked Jaspal. His dream seemed a little more within reach. After the carnival, he had seen Roop just once by the trees behind her house. She was embroidering purple flowers and blue birds on a shawl, she had told him. And he had told her about the novel, *Parineeta* that he had just finished reading. It was about a boy and a girl who loved each other as children, but on growing up, were separated by the boy's unscrupulous father. The novel was quite the rage all over, he'd told her, but she didn't want to hear any more of the story. It was morose, she had complained. The end was memorable he had pressed, but she had shaken her head. Giving up, he'd promised to recite love poetry to her at their next meeting.

Sitting with Jaspal by the canal, Kishan visualised the next meeting with Roop. She was leaning against a tree and listening as he sang to her a verse from Waris Shah's legendary love poem, *Heer*. Kishan was still smiling at that vision when Jaspal said, "Kishan, even after you have a government job, I see a hurdle in your way of getting Roop."

"What hurdle?" Kishan asked. "Her mother?"

"Nah, not her mother. It's yet a bigger hurdle," Jaspal said in dismay.

"Really?" Kishan was muddled. "What hurdle would that be?"

"You see," Jaspal, replied with a straight face, "the hurdle unfortunately is your own nose."

"My nose? What's my nose got to do with anything?" Kishan asked.

"Well," replied Jaspal letting out a chuckle, "your nose is so blunt. A pretty girl wouldn't look good with a blunt-nosed man!"

Fuming, Kishan chased Jaspal through the cotton fields all the way to the village.

That night, lying next to his cousins, Kishan asked the older one, Lakhwant what he thought of his nose.

"There are other things I'd rather think about at night than your silly nose," Lakhwant grumbled, turning the other away. Before long, he was snoring.

Kishan couldn't stop wondering about his nose. He felt it again and again. It was flawless, flawless indeed. Besides, he had killer dimples that cracked his cheeks every time he smiled. Why, all the village girls swore by his dimples. And even though she wouldn't say it, Roop loved his dimples too. Why else would she poke the right one every time he smiled? Relieved somewhat by that conviction, Kishan tried sleeping but couldn't. Strange thoughts started chugging through his mind like a train. What if Roop's family objected to his landlessness? What if a government job failed to win over Roop's mother? What if Charan Singh, the respectable farmer from the neighbouring village, stepped up and asked to marry Roop? Kishan had caught him staring at Roop once when she was walking back home from the gurudwara. Charan Singh was well-to-do and handsome. What if Roop's father accepted his proposal?

Kishan twisted and twirled. The thoughts now completely unreasonable began pounding harder. What if Roop's mother objected to his nose even though it was perfect? What if Roop's father thought him gawky? What if Roop's people married her off when he was away at college? What if? What if? What if?

Kishan sat up with a jolt. Darkness hemmed him in from all directions. Clenching his fists, he blamed it on the heat. It was turning him into a maniac. If only the rain would come. He collapsed back on the manji. Waving off a fly, he tried again to strangle his wayward thoughts and sleep.

SOPHIA

"Pa, the future belongs to chocolate. Why, the town traders tell me that chocolate is a rage all over the world. We must start selling it, just like Abuelo did back in Spain," Sophia said one warm winter morning as she and Antonio were baking bread rolls at their bakery.

"The locals will never take to Spanish chocolate, never having known the old country and its tastes," Antonio said. "They will refuse to even try it."

"Pa, we don't have to replicate old recipes. Inspired by them, we can create our own. People are bound to love chocolate. Chocolate forms the Mexican consciousness! The natives from the Mayans to the Aztecs treasured chocolate! While the Mayans had it hot, the Aztecs liked it cold, even calling it a gift from the God of Wisdom, Quetzalcoatl."

Though Antonio wasn't nearly as well versed about the local cultures and traditions as his Mexican-born daughter, he was not unaware of the Mexican fascination for *chocolatl*. "If you are so hopeful, we can try," he said hesitantly. "God knows that baking bread, cakes, churros and cookies are our mainstay, I can't risk losing my loyal customers as well as my living all for a chocolate experiment."

"You wouldn't have to," Sophia said. "We can start by lacing cakes in chocolate and thereafter, when we have tested the waters, maybe we can begin making chocolate confectionery. Pa, people are tired of the same old churros and pestinos. They crave change and we could give them that. Who knows we might hit it big. One has to take a chance."

Antonio recalled his father's old recipe for chocolate sauce. Together, father and daughter got to work. First, they cooked sweetened milk on low heat, condensing it to just the right consistency to where it was gooey without being runny, gradually adding ground chocolate beans and stirring the mix till everything blended smoothly.

Antonio dipped a spoon into the sauce and tasted the blend. His eyes brimmed up and his throat tightened. "Your Abuelo would've been proud," was all he could manage.

Sophia tasted it too, and clapped. Abuelo would indeed have been proud. Then recalling how her grandfather had urged her to live bravely and smile often, she added cinnamon to it. "Pa, the spice will lend a unique flavour to the sauce, winning over the hearts of the locals," she said.

Her father tasted the blend again. "Hmm," he said. "Cinnamon does give the sauce a local, intense pull."

Inspired by her grandfather's legacy and driven by the thrill of a new adventure, Sophia started icing cakes with her special chocolate sauce and began taking orders for birthdays. The neighbourhood responded with excitement, raving about the fluffy cakes but most of all it was the chocolate icing. They couldn't quite fathom its enigma.

"The chocolate icing is sweet, dreamy and smooth like silk. And it has an aroma, too, which is befuddling. I have never had anything like it," the cloth merchant Luis Garcia said, walking into the bakery one evening on his way back home from work.

He had had a slice of one of Sophia's chocolate-laced cakes at a birthday party, he said. "I would like to order a large seven-layered chocolate-laced cake for my niece's wedding next month. It will be a big wedding at the church. Would you be able to deliver the order?" he asked.

Sophia took to thinking. A big wedding at the church was rare in the neighbourhood. Everything must be perfect at such grand a wedding. Would she be able to meet the expectation, she wondered? Her father was in the back, baking bread. She knew she must consult him before consenting. She knew also that he would be reluctant to take on such a big order. They had never done a wedding cake before, not even for a friend or a neighbour. The chance, however, was too tempting to resist. She decided to jump off the cliff, hoping to grow wings along the way. "Senor Garcia, we would be so delighted to!" she exclaimed hurriedly, fearful all along of her father stepping in to erode her plan. She made note of the details and the date. It was unbelievable how a well-known merchant was willing to place a stake in their bakery.

"Seven layers?" Antonio was stunned when she told him. "Sophia, you haven't done even a simple wedding cake before. How in the world will you manage a fancy seven-layered one? Surely, you know what you're getting into, don't you?" he asked. "You can't go ruining people's wedding celebrations."

"Pa, don't you go worrying. I may never have done wedding cakes, but I have done birthday cakes. A cake is a cake. It takes flour, eggs, milk, sugar and chocolate. One layer or seven, it is the same recipe. I will have it done," Sophia said.

On the day of the wedding, stacking the seven large cakes one on top of another, drenching each one in decadent chocolate sauce, Sophia asked her father to help with the decorations on top. Her father slowly made a groom and a bride in white icing and Sophia added two kissing butterflies in orange. Delivering the cake, they crossed their fingers hoping for the best.

Never could they have imagined the vistas that cake would open up for them, leading to new, enigmatic spaces. Not only did the town merchant pay them heftily for the cake, he recommended their bakery to all his friends and clients. Word about the bakery spread beyond their little neighbourhood to the other end of town. People began swarming the bakery. Soon Sophia was taking numerous orders for multi-layered chocolate-laced cakes. People wanted them for fiestas and picnics, celebrations and birthdays. Sophia and Antonio hired three neighbourhood boys to help them about the bakery, the work load having multiplied manifold in six months. Sophia also set up tables and chairs on the bakery patio and began serving coffee and cake to neighbours who stopped by for a snack. Soon the bakery was frequented by young men and old, travelling traders and locals, bored wives who needed a break from chores and restless young women who wanted to get away from home to show off their good looks and new dresses, flirt with young men, or just dance to a tune of youth.

Sophia was delighted with the bustle around the bakery. She woke with a renewed vigour each morning, smiling, singing and sprinting to the bakery as though the wonders of the world awaited her there. In her waking hours, she imagined herself making inspired variations of all the rich chocolate delights that her grandfather sold back in Spain — chocolate bars, chocolate truffles, chocolate bonbons, chocolate fudge, chocolate toffee, chocolate caramels and more. If only her father would throw caution to the wind and chance their luck at chocolate confectionery. That would open yet bigger, more elusive doors for them, catapulting them from being small-time bakers to becoming celebrated confectioners.

KISHAN SINGH

When the heat became torturous, when farmers began to worry that the sun would crack open the dry earth, when the cattle started huddling around searching for shade and water, when mothers took to forbidding children from stepping outdoors even for a bit lest the hot winds scorch them, the mynahs flew in and soon thereafter, the monsoons. Bathing in the showers, the fields began to dance, the leaping frogs croaked, and the wet soil, bursting with fragrance, invited farmers and children to frisk and frolic. Hopeful of a bountiful cotton harvest, Noor Mahal swam in monsoon euphoria. Bidding bye to the hot summer, the village welcomed the downpour as it rose and ebbed, going away for a day or so only to return with verve.

Children bathed in the rain, floated paper boats in puddles, munched on gulgullas that grandmothers fried in large woks. The air was resplendent with song, dance, the beating of drums and the aroma of malpuras and kheer. Everyone was basking in monsoon fervour, everyone but Kishan.

His nose was in his books. Monsoons had brought along not only rains and celebration but also high school tests. Aiming for good scores, Kishan shut himself in the house with his books. Turning a deaf ear to the cooing of the mynahs, he trudged like a donkey. Good scores could change his life. He strove his hardest, practising his math facts over and again and reading his books till he fell asleep, only to start practising his math facts and reading his books again as soon as he woke up. On the days of the tests, he was excited, eager to take them and get them out of the way.

After the tests, he dashed to the jamun tree in the schoolyard, ecstatic to have caught the tail end of the rains before they slinked away with the last of the jamuns. Gulping jamuns, his mouth smeared with purple juice, he waited for Roop by the trees behind her house. The sprightly wind was beating to the rhythm of the season. Swinging to it, Kishan hummed a verse that he had memorised for Roop from the love poem *Heer*.

As wine-addicts cannot give up wine,
As opium-eaters cannot live without opium,
So, I cannot breathe without my lover.
As the stain of mango juice cannot be washed away from clothes,
So, the stain of love cannot be wiped off a lovestruck heart.

He waited and waited, his patience running out. First, he hadn't seen Roop in thirty days. Then, it was the monsoon, heavier than ever that year. Caught between the two, he was lovesick. How would he be able to keep his hands off her?

Roop came in. She had gone cucumber picking, she said, and had got delayed. She was distracted and jittery. "Sing me the verse that you had promised to sing. Make it fast before the rain comes again," she said hurriedly.

"Wah! Someone's in the mood for romantic poetry! But wait a minute. That's how you greet me? After a month? Let the rain come. Won't you ask how I did on the tests?" Kishan said.

"Oh yes! The tests? How did you do?" she asked.

"I will soon be packing my things," he winked.

Random drops of rain began falling from the skies.

"But you will return for the holidays? Won't you?" she asked.

"Someone's missing me even before I've left," he teased.

"Who said anything about missing?" she pouted. "How long will you be in college?"

"A few years. Then I will be a government officer and all the girls from here, there and everywhere would want to be my wife," he smirked, raindrops hitting his head, trickling down his face.

"Oh really! In that case, you'll have a hard time picking a girl," she said, looking away.

"I won't have to bother with picking. You know that," he laughed.

"I know nothing. Now stop laughing as if the Princess of Paradise is dying to marry you," she frowned.

"Why, yes. She is a princess indeed. And there is nothing that she wants more than to marry me even though she wouldn't EVER say it," he smiled.

Blood rushed to her face. She looked down. He felt her breath on his kurta. His heart pounded against his ribs. Bending, he drank in the smell of her hair. It was a delicious, layered-with-promise scent of wet fields and wild flowers, of playful breeze and fresh corn. He imagined her wedding dress. What colour would she choose? Red? Orange? Magenta?

"Yes! Magenta," his mind whispered.

Just then she looked up, her face glowing, her hair dripping raindrops.

"What colour?" he asked.

"Magenta," she replied, turning pink.

Blown away by that meeting of minds, he gazed at her in wonder. She was flushing irrepressibly. Their eyes met. He leaned. She moved closer. Greedily, they kissed and kissed, his hands feeling her curves, fondling her hair. In the bushes, the mynahs cooed. The unsung verse from the love poem played in his head.

In the days that followed, Kishan remembered the kiss with frenzy, adrenalin rushing through him like a flash of lightning. Most of all, he remembered how the kiss tasted. Sweet. Sweeter than the looping bright orange jalebis in Ramdeen's sweet shop, sweeter still than the sugarcane flaming in the faraway fields.

Noor Mahal was bouncing with monsoon fever and Kishan with love. Hardly able to wait for the results and his dream to unfold, he walked to Jalandhar every week in the pouring rain to enquire after the results and ask around about the Maharaja's College in Patiala. One evening, after dinner as he and his cousins sat around joking and slurping on mangoes, Baldev Mama came along. "Stop blabbing! The rains are refusing to halt. The canals are going to spill over and flood the fields. Here I have been sick with worry that the cotton crop may be ruined, and now Nihalo has come down with high fever. I want no yapping here!" he shouted.

Khushwant and Lakhwant ducked under the sheets. Kishan too slouched on his manji. Dismissing floods and swamped fields, he pictured himself walking the exalted hallways of the Maharaja's College. His bright dream sat beckoning around the corner. He could hardly wait to live it.

The next morning, however, was far removed from Kishan's dream. He was sleeping restfully when cries of Nihalo Mami woke him up. Rushing to her bedside, Kishan held her hand as Baldev Mama went to fetch the village hakim.

Heavy rains had triggered influenza and it had caught Nihalo Mami's brain, the hakim said. He gave Nihalo Mami medicine and left. Hours passed but the medicine brought Nihalo Mami no relief. Moaning on the manji, she shivered and shook like a fish out of water, blubbering deliriously. Kishan and his cousins began running to the hakim and back with one medicine or another but to no avail. When night came, Kishan trembled. Even though Nihalo Mami never quite loved him as she did her sons, glowing with pride at the very sight of them, Kishan remembered how she carefully sewed the seams on his shirts when they came undone and how she cooked kheer every time he finished first in the annual examinations. Seeing her bellowing with pain, he was afraid of losing that maternal figure in his life. He fed her medicines himself, massaged her hands, rubbed oil on the soles of her feet, but Nihalo Mami died before the crack of dawn and they cremated her at noon.

Soon the entire village fell under the deadly spell of influenza. Almost every family was hit. As horrid as it was, funerals became a frequent sight in Noor Mahal. To make matters worse, the cotton stood damaged by the heavy showers. Farmers had been excited when monsoons had arrived. The water would help the crop, they had hoped. But too much of it had brought along influenza, flooded the canals and turned the fields into swamps, destroying the cotton. Far from reaping a rich harvest, farmers were now bogged by disease and debt. As they mourned their dead family members and failed crops, the moneylenders rejoiced. A poor harvest meant farmers in debt wouldn't be able to pay off their loans, thereby losing their land to the moneylenders. The monsoons had flown in with promise but departing, they had left behind death, disease and landlessness.

Kishan was still coming to terms with Nihalo Mami's death and the wrecked crop when the cow died one night. He was convinced that misfortune had narrowed in on their house, slamming it over and again. But soon thereafter, he heard that adversity had struck Jaspal as well. The moneylenders grabbed Jaspal's land because with the harvest ruined, Jaspal's father could not pay back the debt on his land. Becoming landless was horrific but the worst followed right behind. Within days of losing the land, Jaspal's father, mother and sister succumbed to influenza, dying one after the other. Everyone in the village twitched their tongue and called it Jaspal's bad luck. Jaspal's strong shoulders drooped. Helplessly, the village watched the farmer boy make his way around even as everyone wondered if Jaspal could still call himself a farmer? Whoever heard of a farmer without a piece of land?

Jaspal felt the same. He told Kishan that it wasn't influenza but the loss of a sense of self that had killed his bapu. How could his father have retained a sense of self without a piece of land?

Or for that matter, how could Jaspal? A farmer's sense of self and his land merged to where there couldn't be one without the other. Kishan was sorry for Jaspal. Soon however, tragedy of the worst magnitude came to jolt Kishan. Like the heavy torrents that had ruined a beautiful harvest, destiny washed away Kishan's elusive dream, ran him down, stole his boyhood, his careless talks, his heady dips in the canals. He stopped grinning altogether. In time to come, those who remembered his laughs scanned his face, and ended up studying the brooding looks and curtailed smiles that had come to replace his toothy grins. Somewhat sad, somewhat reflective, his grim glances told them Kishan Singh's story of crushed dreams.

In the midst of death and disease, Roop's mother announced that her wildest fantasy for her daughter had come true. In what she called her daughter's good fortune lay Kishan's doom. Over and again, Kishan reviewed the situation. If only Roop hadn't accompanied her friend Mina to Mina's cousin's wedding in a village far away. If only the wealthy landowner's son hadn't seen Roop at the wedding. If only that importunate lad had not declared on an impulse that Roop was the one for him. If only the landowner had not pressed for his son's immediate wedding with Roop.

Kishan hit his head against the wall. He shouted a curse to the sky. Throwing himself on the ground, he yelled that "If" was a devil who was a friend to none. Not even to the fools who bet on him. He braced himself for the worst — Roop's family had not only accepted the landowner's proposal but also begun preparing for the wedding. A magenta wedding dress flashed before Kishan's eyes. He pulled himself up and went to Roop's mother to sell his tattered dream to her. He couldn't live without Roop, he told her. There was nothing more that he wanted in his life than to marry Roop.

Roop's mother dropped the blanket she was folding. "You, worthless swine! How could you even think?" she mumbled. "Just because I let you play with Roop when you were little, you went so far as to think of…"

She couldn't bring herself to say the word, "marriage."

"Now Kishan, we knew your mother," Roop's mother whispered, knitting her brows. "She was noble, but she has gone. Your father has remarried and got new sons. We feel sad for you. You and Roop grew up together, but how could you think of…"

Again, she could not say the word, "marriage" as though saying it would demean her daughter's beauty.

He stood there listless. Stripped of his precious dream, he felt languid as if life had been sucked out of him. "Ask Roop what she has to say," he said, his eyes pleading.

"Ask Roop? Ask Roop what?" Roop's mother thundered impatiently. "What does a girl like Roop have to do with a waif like you? If someone so much as gets a wind of this, you could lose your life! Go now! I don't want you around here. To think that you thought of…"

Again, she could not say the word "marriage."

Kishan's eyes blinded and stumbling home, he saw that Baldev Mama had returned from the fields. Staggering, he found a manji in the courtyard and sat down. He felt faint, barely able to sit straight.

Scuttling around, spicing the daal, Baldev Mama said, "Kishan, did you hear that your friend Jaspal is going across the waters to a new world? They call it America. It is farther than China and is nicer than England. It has thousands of acres of flat farmland. The right place for a hard-working boy like Jaspal. Why, Beant Singh from Phillaur went to Canada and from there to America. The fare alone is a hefty three hundred rupees. It's not like anyone can hop on a ship."

Roop's mother's scoffs iterated in Kishan's ears. He couldn't even nod. Seeing him droopy, Baldev Mama shook him once and then again. When Kishan fell, Baldev Mama was shocked. "Shame on you, Kishan! How could you get drunk with the village goons when people are dying of influenza and the cotton crop has failed! Shame indeed!" he cried before walking back to the kitchen.

After Nihalo Mami's death, her brothers had given Baldev Mama a young cow, out of pity perhaps for the poor widower who had to fend for two motherless sons and one abandoned nephew all by himself. Whatever their reason, Baldev Mama, his boys and Kishan were grateful for milk to drink, for ghee to cook their meals with. Every morning, Baldev Mama would boil a pot of daal on the earthen stove. Come evening, he would add ghee, salt and chillies to it and either Kishan or one of his cousins would knead the dough, roll it out and flip rotis on the fire. Then the four of them would eat rotis and daal.

Flat on the manji that evening, Kishan saw that Baldev Mama had begun rolling out rotis, his cousins not having returned from the fields yet. He knew he must get up and flip the rotis on the fire for his uncle. But courtesy was miles from his mind. He was miserable, in a way glad to be thought of as drunk and left alone. Perhaps it would be best to actually get drunk and declare to the village that he loved Roop and wanted to marry her and that she loved him back. But he knew that no one would approve of it. As of that day, he had no standing to propose to Roop. He had no house, no land, no college education and no job. Certainly, Roop's family was not going to wait for him to start college and finish it, to apply for a government job and get it.

Then he thought about how he was an outsider to Noor Mahal. In a way, not just Baldev Mama, but the entire village had obliged him by taking him in, nurturing him, giving him a chance at life. By stepping in the way of a village girl's marriage to a prosperous man, instead of offering gratitude, he would be letting the village down and maligning Roop's name. No one would stand up for him. Not even Jaspal would approve of compromising a girl's honour by disclosing her involvement in a romance. Baldev Mama would be shamed beyond redemption, compelled to hang his head forever because of a waif of a nephew that he took in.

Kishan considered eloping with Roop. They could go somewhere, anywhere, so long as it was away from Noor Mahal. The very next minute, however, he remembered the disastrous result of such a reckless deed. Fleeing with a girl provoked the worst consequence. Death. The village men would hunt them down and kill them. Like hapless deer. The farmers of the village had little land, but an abundance of honour. And they held on to it staunchly. It wasn't himself that he was worried about. They could kill him, cut him to bits. It was for Roop's life that he feared, a life full of hope, of yet-to-be-savoured dreams, of sunny tomorrows. He had no right to deprive her of a bright, beautiful life when he had nothing to offer her except uncertainty.

Roop's mother's taunts cut into his being. Perhaps she was right. How could he even have chalked out such a plan? Because the fact of the matter was that even though Roop's family was in debt, Roop was no ordinary sixteen-year-old. There wasn't another girl like her, so beautiful and so kind, not in Noor Mahal, nor in any of the surrounding villages. No wonder the landowner had thought her worthy of marrying his son.

He recalled how he had been madly fixated on Roop since childhood. He never stood a chance of marrying her except in his imagination. An attractive girl even if born to a farmer in debt had her beauty to change her luck. But a luckless boy like him, remained forever that. Neither his imagination nor his grit could get him the girl. He rebuked his smarts. What good were they anyway? In his most trying time, they had failed him. He saw himself going crazy, walking around in torn clothes with ruffled hair and confused eyes, rambling nonsense. He closed his eyes in despair. The River Satluj bolted through the darkness. It struck him how the river had taken in many a hopeless soul, relieved them of anguish, put an end to their misery. Now that there was nothing left to live for, the river could drown his suffering. Jumping into the river would save him from watching Roop marry another. He imagined that his cousins and Baldev Mama would pull out his body from the river when it washed upstream, cry a little and cremate it. And life would go on like the moon entering a new phase. The blue of the river was flickering in his eyes when Baldev Mama's words from a long time ago came to pound him. "Suicide is a sin," Baldev Mama had said. "It is the resort of a coward. By choosing that path, a Sikh would defame none other than the epitome of courage, Guru Gobind Singh."

Remembering that, Kishan opened his eyes and sat up. Invoking strength from the brave Guru Gobind Singh, who with his unwavering spirit had continued to march on even after losing his father and all four sons to the cause of righteousness, Kishan told himself he wasn't a coward. From a sunken labyrinth in his mind, his grit resurfaced. He began to find an escape in something other than death. He must escape from Noor Mahal and bury all memories of his life there, a life tinged with Roop's smiles and giggles, a life that sang her song. But where could he go? At best, he could go to the college in Patiala. That was hardly far enough. Chaos engulfed him. Bogged down by scenes, memories, pain, his breathing was heavy, leaden, interrupted. He needed to go far away, very far away.

Breaking through the mounting turmoil, Baldev Mama's words came to jolt him — Jaspal was going to America. AMERICA. The name itself was revitalising, like the first perky monsoon showers that made the fields dance.

Kishan had read about America. It was a new country in a new continent, sitting across from Europe on the other side of the Atlantic Ocean. It was a captivating land with mountains, rivers, and lakes, promising justice, liberty and good life to everyone who landed on its shore. Though the early settlers were Europeans, now gutsy people from all over the world were heading there. There was a lot one could do in the new country — build railroads, work in lumber mills and factories and best of all, farm. He could go there with Jaspal and plunge into farming. His clan, the Jats had been farming for generations, growing wheat, sugarcane and cotton on the vast plains along the banks of Punjab's five glorious rivers — Satluj, Beas, Ravi, Chenab and Jhelum. He would continue his farming tradition in America. He had read that there was so much land in America that some of it still sat untouched by man. In as vast a nation, he was bound to find a strip to call his own. He had also read that America was the country of workers. He would put his nose to the grindstone and slog in the new land, ending his misery forever.

Getting up from the manji, he saw that his cousins had come home and along with Baldev Mama were gulping down rotis and daal in the kitchen. He set out for Jaspal's house. Baldev Mama and his cousins called after him. Kishan didn't look back. He had decided on his destination — America.

SOPHIA

One bright May morning in 1894, two ladies, one young and the other middle-aged came by Sophia's bakery in a horse-drawn carriage. Their immaculately tailored flowery dresses and glossy leather shoes spoke of a lavish, extravagant lifestyle, their lily-scented perfumes filling the space with vitality.

Sophia was by herself at the bakery that morning, baking cakes since her father and the three helpers had gone to the mercado to buy groceries. Having turned nineteen several months ago, with every passing day she was assuming more responsibility for the bakery and café. A visit from the wealthy was occasional and far between in the area. She gazed in wonder at the women and their finery. The women smiled slightly and introducing themselves as Esmeralda and Elsa Guzman, said that they were the wife and daughter of a wine trader from the other side of town.

"How may I help you?" Sophia asked, somewhat taken in by the women and their aura.

"I had a slice of your chocolate-laced cake at a picnic. I must say I really liked it. It reminded me of my visits to Mexico City. The cafés there serve similar cakes and pastries — soft, moist and delicious. Did you ever live there?" the trader's wife asked resting her sequined purse on the table.

"No, Senora Guzman," Sophia replied. "I have always lived in Acapulco, my parents too. My grandparents came from Spain though. My grandfather sold confectionery there. I do spin-offs of some of the age-old Spanish recipes that have been handed down from him by embedding Mexican flavours in them."

"I would like to order a large seven-layered cake with double the chocolate icing than you would normally do," the lady said. "It was for a soirée which will be attended by distinguished people from town, including the mayor." Then with a quizzical look, she asked, "Would you by any chance be able to deliver chocolate as well? About fifty slabs? I so want to serve some with coffee."

Sophia was at a loss for words. She swallowed an imaginary lump. It was as though her dream itself had come knocking at her door. As titillating as that was, a volley of counter thoughts began scurrying through her mind. The soirée would be a big event, attended by eminent guests and the mayor. She mustn't disappoint anyone with her experiment. She hadn't ever sold chocolate slabs before. She must only promise what she could deliver. She mustn't let her father down. Just as she was going to whisper, "No," a voice from within held her back. It was imprudent adventure again. She mustn't give up the chance, it told her. This was her one opportunity to take the leap and start making and selling chocolate. So even though she hadn't a clue about how she would put together the chocolate slabs, giving in to the domineering voice, she said, "Senora Guzman, I sure could!"

The lady nodded.

"Let me take down all the details, the date and such," Sophia said, pulling out her father's notepad hurriedly.

The soirée was only ten days away. She thanked the ladies for giving their little bakery some business. "It's awfully nice of you to come so far out to order from us," Sophia said, both excited and nervous.

"Oh! I couldn't forget your chocolate-laced cake. That chocolate icing was unforgettable — zesty and gripping! I know you will do an equally commendable job with the chocolate slabs," the lady said, leaving some money on the table.

"Thank you," Sophia said.

"I will pay the rest after you make the delivery," the lady said, walking back with her daughter to the carriage.

Sophia began thinking. She recalled helping her grandfather make chocolate slabs years ago for relatives who were visiting from out of town. That was when her grandfather's eyes were still good and his hands firm. She could do a twist on the old recipe and churn out fifty slabs, she told herself.

Her father's return broke her reverie. He was furious on hearing of the new order. "This is ridiculous," he said. "Just because we somehow pulled off the multi-layered chocolate-laced cake, now you are jumping on to chocolate slabs. And that too for the wealthy and famous. I have no inkling as to how your grandfather made chocolate slabs back in Spain. Besides, we wouldn't even be able to lay our hands on many of the same ingredients. And God knows that distinguished guests will not be easy to please. Sophia, I may run a small bakery, but I have an honest name. How you have compromised my reputation!"

"Pa, I have not! I helped Abuelo make chocolate slabs once. Even though I remember the ingredients, I don't intend to follow his recipe. I could make the slabs in a style of my own, something distinctly Mexican. The guests will love the local flavour."

"A style of your own! Sophia, this is no time to experiment. What do you know of chocolate making anyway?" he said. "It takes practice and patience to perfect something as fine as chocolate." He shook his head.

"Pa, I stand firm on what I promised," Sophia said. "I will try making a tiny batch tonight."

Listing all the ingredients, she left for the mercado. Upon returning, she took to work.

Heating butter and sugar syrup in a saucepan, she gradually added ground cocoa, stirring and whisking all along until the paste was thick. Then she placed a sheet of wax paper on a tray and spread the mix on it.

"I will leave it in the cool of the window to harden during the night," she said covering the tray with another sheet of wax paper.

"Sophia, I wish you luck. But if it doesn't work out, I will have no choice but to walk over to the other end of town to cancel the order for chocolate slabs. It is terrible to mislead people, you know," Antonio said as they closed down the bakery for the day.

Sophia was quiet. Though she could hardly deny that her heart was beating fiercely, her face was unusually radiant. Life meant drifting away from convention, owning your ideas, owning yourself. If one had belief in one's self, there was no need to convince others. In time, her father would believe in her too. Her venture could be small but if it took off, it could pierce through the night sky and sparkle like a million blazing stars.

KISHAN SINGH

Slumping his way through the deserted dusk, Kishan reached Jaspal's house. As he stepped into the courtyard, he sensed the quiet sadness of a house in mourning. Jaspal was sitting on a manji by a lantern on the far end of the courtyard. His paternal aunt Basanto was clearing the dinner dishes. Basanto Bhua lived in the nearby town of Nakodar, but after the death of Jaspal's parents and sister, she had moved in with Jaspal for a while to help him get on.

"Kishan, is that you?" Jaspal asked, getting up from the manji and lifting the lantern.

Kishan saw that Jaspal was still reeling under the shock of his father, mother and sister's sudden death. Unable, however, to exchange niceties or ask after him, Kishan got to the point just as soon as they sat down on the manji. "Pali, are you sailing to America?" he asked.

Jaspal nodded. With his family and his piece of land gone, it was clear to him that his destiny lay elsewhere. "Kishan, I was going to come by and tell you myself first thing tomorrow morning. Fate is leading me to California. It's the prosperous port of America. I will farm there. An agent, who I met in Jalandhar a few days ago, has helped me to plan the trip. He says California is a chunk of heaven. Everything not just grows there but thrives," Jaspal said, smiling at the prospect of what lay ahead.

"What is the name of the port, again?" Kishan asked.

"California!" Jaspal exclaimed. His eyes shone like gold.

"California!" Kishan echoed. The flash caught his eyes too. "Pali, I will go with you," he said hastily.

Jaspal's mouth fell open. "Why would you? You are smart. My story is different. I dropped out of school to work the fields but now I'm landless and orphaned. I have no choice but to board the ship. Things aren't dire for you. Why would you break your back in foreign fields?" Jaspal asked.

Kishan fumbled that his mind was made.

"Kishan, going to America is not like going to nearby Amritsar or Lahore. You may know more from reading your books. America is far away, on the other side of the great water. Many who go never come back. They are gone forever, somewhat like the dead. I know why you are upset. I heard about Roop's upcoming wedding. It is most unfortunate. But you must go to college and beyond," Jaspal said insistently.

Kishan sighed and shook his head. "Pali, I am coming with you. I have no plans anymore of attending college, of becoming an officer or anything else. Noor Mahal is unflinching, resistant not just to my melon seeds but also to my romance. I'll have the fare by next week. My destiny lies far away too," he said.

Jaspal told Kishan that the fare was outrageous and that he had to sell his house and his dead mother's jewellery to a moneylender and on top of it, borrow from Basanto Bhua to put together three hundred rupees. Reluctantly, he also reminded Kishan how difficult it would be to raise the fare with nothing in his name.

Kishan mumbled that he would manage. Then as if to reassure himself, he said again, this time louder, that he would surely manage the fare in a day or two.

"Kishan, I will take off on Tuesday morning for Jalandhar to catch the Hooghly Express that leaves for Calcutta at noon. If you can arrange the fare, great, else I will send word on reaching America. Go now!" Jaspal said.

"I'll have the fare by Tuesday morning. I'll see you then," Kishan said, getting up from the manji and leaving quickly.

Walking back home, Kishan had no clue how he would lay his hands on three hundred rupees. Tuesday was only five days away. There was never any money around the house and he had hardly ever known the need for it. Baldev Mama's little plot of land gave them grains and lentils for their meals and in the spring, they pulled some vegetables off it too. Every few months, Baldev Mama would bring home earthen dishes from the porter by bartering bowls of grain. Other knick-knacks like an occasional cake of soap or a new hairbrush were luxuries that they indulged in at harvest by bartering grain at the village bania's shop. For clothes, too, Baldev Mama gave a sack of grain to the cloth seller and another to the tailor and the whole family had clothes to last until next harvest. Their needs being few, Kishan's only brush with opulence was through Bengali novels, which let him into the world of wealthy landowners with coffers full of gold and silver.

Reaching home, Kishan saw that Baldev Mama and his boys were sound asleep in the courtyard. He fell on a manji that lay to a side. Baldev Mama's loud rhythmical snoring resonated in the dark, drowning the occasional snorting of the cow. His sons lay knocked down on either side of him like two tired dogs. Kishan looked at the sky. His sleepless eyes spotted many flashing stars, but the moon was nowhere in sight. Masaya — that's what they called a night like that when the moon went into hiding and the stars took over. Staring at the blinking stars, Kishan was at his wit's end. Three hundred rupees was a huge sum. Baldev Mama had no money and because of the bad harvest, he even had a debt to pay. Nobody else in Noor Mahal had money to lend either. After influenza and the failed cotton crop, people were barely getting by. Amassing three hundred rupees in five days was like trying to bathe the cow in a puddle that the rain had left behind.

His only other relation was his father who lived in the nearby village, Jandiala. Having given him away after his mother died, never once had Kishan's father tried to contact him. Baldev Mama hadn't asked Kishan to visit his father either. Encouraging Kishan's knack for learning instead, he had insisted that Kishan would be better off keeping some chapters closed. So Kishan had begun to rely on books and school to bail him out of the denial that life had thrown his way. If anyone so much as mentioned Jandiala in passing, Kishan would manoeuvre the talk in another direction. Of late, he had come to associate that village with his paternal grandmother, Dadi. She had begged Baldev Mama to see Kishan and Baldev Mama had taken him to meet her once at the gurudwara in the neighbouring village and then another time, on the outskirts of Noor Mahal.

Kishan remembered the last meeting under an old banyan well. Like most grandmothers, Dadi was old and wrinkled, humped and always weepy. She had held his hands and cried at the death of his young mother, at having to give him away and at her helplessness in the face of it. Kishan so wanted to tell her that he was okay and that she needn't cry, but instead overwhelmed by all that crying, he had got up to leave. Hungry for a few more moments with him, Dadi had grabbed his arm to pull him back and asked if he went to school. Baldev Mama had butted in to tell her that Kishan was the best student Noor Mahal ever had.

Dadi was thrilled to hear that. "Oh really! Do you read English?" she'd asked.

When Kishan nodded, she had said, "So like your grandfather. He could speak and write in English too!"

In his seventeen years, Kishan had heard many people talk of his paternal grandfather. A soldier in the British Indian Army, he had served for years at the British cantonment in Burma. Since Kishan's hurt heart so wanted to sever ties with his father's people, he never let himself be roused by stories of his grandfather's sojourn in Burma or elsewhere. So, when Dadi mentioned his grandfather, Kishan had looked away. But Baldev Mama, priding in Kishan's cleverness, had begun boasting of Kishan's plans. "If he fares well in school," he had told Dadi. "Kishan will go to college on a scholarship."

At that, Dadi had put her arms around Kishan. "Kishan, don't go without saying bye to your old Dadi. I have a good luck charm from your grandfather saved for you," she had said before starting to cry again. Not being able to bear another minute of that crying, clutching Baldev Mama by the elbow, Kishan had slid away.

Slouching on the manji under the starry sky that night in Noor Mahal, suddenly recalling Dadi's words, Kishan sat up. Dadi had mentioned a good luck charm. Surely that good luck charm would amount to something. It would give him a little of, if not the entire fare. Perhaps that Dadi of his was worth more than her tears. She could forge his passage to the new world. Impatiently, he began waiting for the sun to break through and dim the sparkling stars.

The next morning, he was out of bed and dressed up, ready to go even before the first rooster clucked. When Baldev Mama woke up, Kishan told him that he was going to meet a friend in a nearby village. Upset about Kishan's presumed drinking, Baldev Mama started off about how he had hopes for Kishan. It was only when Kishan swore by his dead mother that he had never so much as brought any spirit to his lips and that he had just been tired the night before that Baldev Mama let the matter go. Promising to be back in time, Kishan took off for Jandiala.

Walking for an hour, he rested under a pipal hoping to reach Jandiala mid-morning. His father would be out working the fields by then. The last thing he wanted was to run into his father. Seeing a bullock cart loaded with sugarcane pass by, Kishan hopped on, letting the farmer riding on the cart know that he would jump off at Jandiala. The farmer nodded and said he was headed to Jandiala as well to drop off the sugarcane at his sister's. He asked Kishan if he was visiting family. "No, I am visiting a friend there," Kishan replied. Then not wanting to divulge more details, he lay down, closed his eyes and pretended to nap.

As the cart moved on, many questions popped in Kishan's head. What would he do if his grandmother wasn't home? What if his father was at home instead and recognised him? What if his stepmother lashed out at him? As he took to imagining probable scenarios and the ways to deal with them, the farmer began humming an old song.

O pretty damsel!
Besotted with you,
Your lover has turned ascetic
Fly o bumblebee, fly along,
Hum here and there and soak up the colours of youth.

Kishan smiled and shook his head. It was unbelievable. The farmer was singing Kishan's story. When the cart made it to Jandiala, thanking the mirthful farmer, Kishan leapt off. Realising that he had arrived a tad early, he sat under a large sheesham and looked around before scribbling Roop's name on the hard earth with a twig. It was a subconscious act done out of habit. Quickly he wiped it off and wrote "America" instead before starting for his father's house.

Kishan had imagined his father's house many times. Though he never liked to admit it even to himself, his boundless thoughts had flown to Jandiala often and he had pictured himself growing up there, basking in the love and care of both a father and a mother. That day, however, facing the large wooden gate, his feet were shaky. Reluctantly unhinging the gate, he walked into a large courtyard that led to a brick house. The house was much bigger than Baldev Mama's two-room earthen one. Kishan saw a few cows in a corner by the barn. Then he saw a little girl playing with a rag doll. He didn't know what to say or do. Then thankfully, he saw Dadi coming out of the barn.

Seeing Kishan, Dadi was startled. "Kishan, is that you?" she asked.

Kishan nodded. She led him to a manji that lay in a corner under a small tree. She was in as much of a rush to know why Kishan had taken the trip as he was to spill the story. "Dadi, I need money. An opportunity has swung my way to make a life for myself. You said you have a good luck charm for me from my grandfather. I need it now," he said.

"Are you going to college?" Dadi asked.

"I am pursuing my destiny in a faraway land. I can only go if you help me. Dadi, it is now or never," Kishan said.

"Come with me to the outhouse by the fields," Dadi murmured.

With no other place to store things safely, many villagers buried their belongings underground. Kishan imagined Dadi had done the same at the outhouse. They got up and started for the door. The little girl followed them. Dadi said they would have to take her along, there being no one at home to watch her. Just then, a young, happy faced woman of medium height carrying an earthen pot of water on her head and another in her hand walked in. The little girl ran to her and called her Ma.

Kishan knew then that the young woman was his stepmother. Quickly, he folded his hands and greeted the young woman. Suddenly, Dadi was flustered. "This is my cousin's grandson. He has come from the neighbouring village to ask after my health. I will walk him out and be back," she said.

A smile spread across the young woman's face. She placed the pots on the ground and lifted the little girl in her arms. "Boy, what village do you come from?" she asked.

"Shankar," Kishan replied. Shankar was a famous village in the area. Kishan was glad he had come up with a name.

"Why, that's a long way to walk. You can't go without having lassi!" the young woman exclaimed.

Despite Dadi and Kishan asking her not to, putting the little girl down, the young woman rushed to the kitchen and was back soon with a small pack and a glass of lassi. Handing Kishan the glass, she dragged a manji and gestured for Dadi and Kishan to sit as she slumped on the floor. The little girl went and sat on her mother's lap. "I hear there is a temple in your village. I so want to visit it. Can you tell me about it?" the young woman asked Kishan.

Her face evinced an inquisitiveness that Kishan had known only himself to have. Thankfully, he had been to that temple in Shankar, not just once but many times. "The village is named Shankar after Lord Shiva and houses his temple. Since the first God cares not for plush offerings, you can walk in with some fruit and be assured that all your prayers would be answered," Kishan said, taking in a gulp of lassi.

"Now, I can hardly wait to go," the young woman said eagerly.

Downing the lassi to the very last drop, Kishan got up and said goodbye to the young woman. Dadi got up too. They were already walking out when the young woman handed Kishan the small pack. "Maroondas for you to munch on the way," she said.

Thanking her, Kishan reached to take the pack from her hand when suddenly she pulled her hand back a little. "Boy, what did you say your name is?" she asked.

Before Kishan could say anything, Dadi stepped up. "Ram Ditta, that's his name! Now girl, why don't you let anyone be? You ask question upon question. You have unusual interest in far-flung temples and an unnecessary curiosity about visitors' names! Go and tend the house!" Dadi snapped.

Quickly, handing Kishan the pack, the young woman rushed inside the house. Placing the snack in his pocket, Kishan thought of how in bringing him lassi and a snack, the young woman who happened to be his stepmother had in a sense made up for all the meals that she didn't provide him in all those years that he was growing up in distant Noor Mahal. He was still reminiscing when Dadi hit him hard on the arm. "Boy, now move along. First, instead of responding to questions with answers, you start to spin yarns and now it seems you have taken to dreaming," she said sharply.

Kishan followed Dadi out of the house. Dadi kept looking back as she walked him to the outhouse a few hundred feet away. Once there, she opened the jaded wooden gate. Leading Kishan through a small courtyard, she unlocked a dilapidated little room that stood by a stack of cow dung cakes. Stray strands of sunlight were peering into the room through the frame of the tightly shut window in the back. Logs of firewood, stacks of dried branches and a pile of quilts filled up the space. Knocking down the quilts, Dadi found an old and dented chest. She dragged it out and opened it. Pulling out a pouch from the bottom of the chest, she handed it to Kishan, who quickly pushed it down the inner pocket of his pyjamas, glad that no digging was involved in the hunting of the treasure. Dadi slammed the battered chest shut and covered it again with the heap of quilts. Stepping out and rushing out through the wooden gate, they began walking towards the outskirts of the village as fast as Dadi's worn knees would let them.

Pausing under an old teak, Kishan pulled out the pouch and groping inside it, found a watch. It felt heavy on his palm. Dadi swam her fingers down to the bottom of the pouch and pulled out a glittering red stone. "This watch is your grandfather's. It is precious as is the stone. Now that I am handing these to you, you must know the story," she said.

"Story! What story, Dadi?" Kishan asked, dazed. The watch and the gem were the stuff of books, far from the realm of their everyday lives. And now Dadi had a story as well.

"Son, your grandfather was not like the peasants here," Dadi began. "His bearing and demeanour were different. So, when the British came to recruit men into the army, a British officer chose him right away for his orderly and took him all the way to Burma. In time, because of his sincerity, your grandfather became a favourite of the British officer, who began to trust him with everything, even his life. And Son, your grandfather never let the British officer down, going as far as to jump in front of him on a hunting trip when a tiger leapt upon the British officer. The tiger grabbed a chunk of flesh from your grandfather's leg before another officer shot the tiger down.

The British officer, overcome with gratitude for the great sacrifice that your grandfather made, gifted him money, his own watch and this peerless stone. With the money, your grandfather bought land in the village and he treasured the stone and the watch his entire life, even though his weak leg meant being prematurely discharged from the army and having to limp his way for the rest of his days."

Kishan looked at Dadi's face and then at the watch and the stone. It was a story like no other.

"I had saved the two items for you. I know you will put them both to good use," Dadi said, touching his shoulder.

Kishan clenched the stone and the watch. He would put them to the best possible use, to transform his life, to forge his way into the new world. Never would he forget that his Dadi had saved two relics for him, paving his passage to the land of promise. He slid the watch and the stone back into the pouch and snuck the pouch once more into the inner pocket of his pyjamas. Then he got up, bent down, touched Dadi's feet and said goodbye.

Dadi got up too and said, "Son, forgive us. Giving you away was not what I wanted. Your father was so in love with your mother that when she died giving birth to you, he was devastated. He walked around like a lost lamb for four years and then was on medication for another two. To keep my only son sane, I kept you away and got him remarried. I've wronged you."

Kishan recalled how heartbreaking it had been all those years to live with the fact that he had been disowned at birth, that he had been held responsible for his mother's death and declared unlucky. Now he wanted to forget it all. "Dadi, there is something you must know," he said. "All my growing up years, people marvelled at my storytelling and some days, I would wonder myself but now I know. I get it from you. Today you handed me my heritage wrapped in a remarkable story."

Dadi held him in a tight embrace for a long time and when she let go, tears ran down the eyes of both. Abruptly, Kishan walked away.

When he looked back on reaching a bend in the path, Dadi was still sitting under the teak, following him with her tired old eyes.

The next morning, draping a turban and slipping on a clean kurta, Kishan discarded the dusty pouch and slipped the watch and the gem in a clean one that he had hurriedly sewed the night before after ripping his grey pyjamas. Sneaking the pouch into his pocket, he took off for the largest jewellery shop in Jalandhar, which boasted of many elite clients including the Maharaja of Kapurthala.

The owner, a grey-haired, bespectacled, well-dressed man sat on a chaise behind a broad table. Kishan remembered from his books that confident folk walked straight, sat upright and looked others in the eye. Intending on doing all of that, he greeted the owner, who nodded and asked him to sit.

"Lalaji, I hope to sell you invaluable heirlooms," Kishan said. Reaching for the pouch, he pulled out first the watch and then the gem and placed them in front of the Lala.

The Lala picked up the watch and looked at it closely. Putting the watch down, he picked up the gem. Resting the stone in the middle of his palm, he moved his hand around to assess the stone from different angles. Placing the gem next to the watch, he put his glasses back on. "Sardarji, how, if I may know, did you come by these items?" he asked.

Having anticipated the question, Kishan presented his well-rehearsed answer, "Lalaji, my grandfather served the British Indian Army in Burma. He was presented this watch and stone by a British officer for extraordinary service. I would've never parted with them, but foreign shores beckon me, and I need the money. I came here because you are the only jeweller in Jalandhar who can value the pieces for their rarity and hand me what they are worth."

The Lala blinked his eyes. "Sardarji, what village do you come from?" he asked.

Again, Kishan had known that question would come. "Shankar," he replied.

Kishan had the answer to the next question too. "What may your grandfather's name be?"

"Sepoy Maheshwar Singh," Kishan said.

The Lala was quiet. He examined both items again. "Sardarji, I need time. Please come next week, I will surely strike a deal then," he said.

Kishan had thought of that possibility as well. He didn't want the Lala inquiring after him at Shankar and other places. Besides, he did not have time until next week. "Lalaji, time is of essence. Today is all I have. Either you make a transaction now, or I will take the train to Amritsar and meet a jeweller there," Kishan said, trying to stay calm.

The Lala was taken aback.

Sticking to his guns, Kishan said, "Lalaji, this is an IWC watch. The British officer who presented it to my grandfather had purchased it in Switzerland. The stone is the finest Burmese ruby. If one looks at it too hard or long, it scorches the eyes." Since he had nothing besides those items to bank on, Kishan had created the stories about the watch and the stone from what he knew of history and geography.

The Lala sighed. "Sardarji, how much are you hoping to get for the two items?" he asked.

From the little economics that he had read, Kishan knew not to quote first. "How much do you estimate them for?" he asked back.

"Two hundred and fifty rupees," the Lala said.

"Three hundred rupees is what I am hoping to get, not a paisa less," Kishan replied, his heart wobbling.

"Sardarji, that's not possible," the Lala said.

Kishan's heartbeat was completely out of sync now. A part of him wanted to leap at what was being offered but he knew that that recourse would be open for later. "I won't settle for two hundred and fifty rupees," he said, wrapping up the items. As soon as he returned the watch and the gem to the pouch, the Lala said, "Sardarji, how about closing the deal at two hundred and seventy-five rupees?"

Desperation told Kishan to relent. "Three hundred rupees are what the two are worth, but I'll take two hundred and seventy-five rupees," he said.

The Lala walked to the back of the store. "My son will get the money soon," he said upon returning.

Kishan nodded.

"Headed to England, are you, Sardarji?" the Lala asked.

"Yes," Kishan replied, not feeling the need to explain how different and far and away America was from England. An unannounced pang of anxiety overcame him. "Lalaji, now that we have agreed on two hundred and seventy-five rupees, I have a request to make," he asked leaning forward.

The Lala raised his brows.

"Loan me twenty-five rupees so that I'll have the entire fare for the trip. I will mail it back to you with interest on reaching abroad," Kishan said.

The Lala reclined on his chaise. Before he could ask for a surety, Kishan said, "I have nothing to leave behind as security. All I have is my word that I will mail back the money with interest."

The Lala thought for a while and said, "Twenty-five rupees is no small change. My business is facing a low now. There is a daughter to be married off by the end of the year. I don't know you Sardarji nor do I know of your family, but something makes me want to believe you. I will lend you twenty-five rupees, hoping that on reaching England, you'll keep your word."

Kishan reassured him that he would indeed return the money to him with interest.

The Lala scribbled his mailing address on a piece of paper and handed it to Kishan, who folded the paper in four and put it in his pocket. Unlocking a drawer, the Lala quickly counted and handed Kishan twenty-five rupees and hastily, Kishan put the money in his pocket. The Lala said that he would keep that bit from his son.

Soon the son walked in. Sitting down beside his father, he counted two hundred and seventy-five rupees before placing them in a pouch and handing them to Kishan. Clutching the pouch, Kishan got up. The Lala and his son got up too. Kishan smiled, his eyes reassuring the Lala that he wouldn't let him down. The son, not privy to that moment, laughed. "Thank you, Sardarji. We hope to see you again," he said in a rehearsed manner.

Kishan walked out of the jewellery store with more than just the fare for the trip. He knew the meeting with the Lala would stay with him far beyond their brief nervous interaction. By believing him that edgy afternoon, the Lala had given Kishan a lesson in trusting another, setting him on the path of reaching out to strangers at forlorn, forsaken moments. By loaning him the money, Kishan knew the Lala had handed him a legacy that he would never forget.

SOPHIA

Sophia was out of bed and ready to leave for the bakery much before sunrise. The chocolate weighed on her mind. She had to go and see how it had come out. Not a man, woman or child was in sight when she set off from home early that May morning, walking briskly over dry fallen leaves. No sound could be heard either except the beating of her quaking heart and the clucking of hens digging out insects from tree trunks.

Opening the bakery doors, she reached for the chocolate tray in the window, removed the wax-paper covering, dug a spoon into the chocolate and took a bite. The chocolate was surreal, melting in her mouth, jostling her mind, singing to her soul. The consistency, however, got her thinking. The chocolate hadn't hardened all the way. She must strive for a thicker consistency. Butter was the answer, her mind whispered.

Gathering all the ingredients, she started on a new batch, this time adding more butter and whisking harder to thicken the paste. Laying the mix in the window, she began waiting for it to harden, and when it did, she was happy that she couldn't dig a spoon into it. Snapping off a piece from the edge, she let it melt in her mouth. She had achieved the colour, consistency and taste. But something was still amiss. She must add a local whiff to it and make it distinctly Mexican. Nutmeg perhaps. Or vanilla. Orange peel maybe. Na-uh, she thought. They were much too commonplace and muted. She must try something braver, give the chocolate a kicking aftertaste.

She started making a new batch, whisking harder still and just before pouring the mix onto a tray, she debated between throwing in ginger, sea salt or liquor but driven by a sudden impulse, added a dash of cayenne flakes. Placing the newest batch in the window to harden, she smiled. Her creation would no longer be flat but flirty and flavourful. She could hardly wait to see her father's reaction.

And when he bit into the chocolate, Antonio indeed let out a quiver. Open-mouthed, Sophia stared at him, waiting for him to say something.

A huge smile spread across Antonio's face. "It is one of its kind. The cayenne lends it a univocal punch. I hadn't ever known chocolate to have a bite. Just the thing to rouse the Mexican spirit. Sophia, you are a connoisseur like your grandfather!" he said.

Sophia looked far out at the ocean and smiled. The mind was paramount. It could not just conjure ideas but actualise them too. Life was an experiment.

Antonio and Sophia had the seven-layered chocolate-laced cake and the chocolate slabs packed and ready on wooden platters when Senora Guzman sent her attendant to pick up the confectionery the day before the soirée.

What followed after became the talk of the town.

"Everyone loved the chocolate slabs," Senora Guzman wrote in a note that was sent with the payment soon after the soirée. "They were exceptional, unmistakably local. Thank you! I will come to buy more very soon."

"Will you make Chocolate Cayenne for my summer party?" a lady from across town came and asked.

"I'd like for you to make me several chocolate slabs, similar to the ones that you made for Senora Guzman," a town merchant said, rushing into the bakery one afternoon. "I want to keep some as snacks around my house."

"I want to order twenty slabs of Chocolate Cayenne for a picnic that I will be hosting on the beach," a lady said, stepping off a large horse-drawn wagon. "I will serve them with lemonade."

The bakery was flooding with orders for chocolate. While Antonio continued baking bread and conchas, Sophia began making large batches of chocolate, not just Chocolate Cayenne but also Chocolate Mint, Chocolate Coconut, and Chocolate Sea Salt, working tirelessly from sunrise to sunset to keep up with the heavy flow of orders. Who could have thought, Sophia wondered, that work could be so achingly delightful? When done spiritedly, it became an overriding passion, pulling one through long days, past months and seasons towards yet newer, greener dreams.

Every now and then, her mother pushed her to consider one or the other local young men for marriage. "I know for a fact that many young men in the neighbourhood are deeply fond of you and would so like to propose to you if only you show an interest," her mother said assertively one early autumn morning as Sophia was heading for the bakery.

"Deeply fond of me? Why?" Sophia asked.

"Because you are beautiful and comely, tall and attractive, because you come from a decent home, because they hope to build a life with you."

Sophia was enraged. "Those blokes!" she exclaimed referring to the young men in the neighbourhood. "No way will I even let any of them tread close to me."

"Sophia!" her mother gasped, completely appalled.

"Ma, I mean it. Not long ago, I beat them in swimming and now I will whack their heads if anyone so much as comes smiling at me."

"But Sophia, you have to marry someone!" her mother persisted.

"Yes, someone, but not one of the neighbourhood fellows," Sophia replied heading out, chocolate orders dangling over her mind. In the distance, she spotted a hummingbird flapping over flowering shrubs. The green and red around the bird's neck shone in the morning light, flashing in her eyes, filling her head with visions. She knew that hummingbirds travelled to Acapulco from the north every autumn. How extraordinarily beautiful the hummingbird was, Sophia thought. The place where it came from must be enrapturing too. Far horizons were alluring, layered with miracles and romance. And they were always receding farther, arousing the urge to sprint to newer haunts, braver ideas and infinite dreams.

KISHAN SINGH

Kishan couldn't have left without seeing Roop. Bhuri, a girl who'd grown up with them, said she would ask Roop to come by the old serai, the day before Kishan left. Walking towards the serai, Kishan plucked a yellow lotus from a pond for Roop, hoping that so long as the flower bloomed, at least until then, if not longer, Roop would have a reason to think of him. Reaching the serai much before noon, he waited on the steps by the well. The sun shone high and bright. He heard the piping song of a bird. Turning around and spotting a sandpiper, he smiled. It was delightful to have the sandpipers over every autumn. They were unique birds, happy on both land and by water. He liked that they were adventurous, exploring new places, scampering around the fields and the bursting canals, nibbling on insects and cooing. Closing his eyes, he was trying to soak up the fluting tune when the sandpiper stopped singing. He opened his eyes and looked around. The serai was desolate, suddenly bereft of sound. In the boggling silence, many questions came to jab him.

"How would Roop feel about her upcoming wedding?"

"Would she be upset about their last meeting?"

"Would she cry?"

Shunting those questions, Kishan turned to the serai's imposing minarets for comfort. Taking in their beauty, he thought of how Empress Noor Jahan was an example that by a stroke of destiny, a girl from a modest home could rise to embrace royalty and art. In that instance, he was not sorry for having lost Roop. Forgetting his pain, he rejoiced that a wonderful life awaited her. Truly, a charming girl like Roop was destined for beautiful things. But the very next moment, it struck him that Roop was his lifeline. When she was not beside him, he breathed in and out thoughts of her. How would his heart that beat with a boundless passion for her allow him to take off for a place far away when he so badly wanted to be with her, see her, hear her laughter and feel her touch?

Then she came, his Roop. He wondered if he could still call her his. He gave her the lotus. Holding it awkwardly, she sat by him on the steps.

"Is it true?" she asked. There was dew in her eyes, agony on her face.

Kishan, too, had been asking that very question time and again in his mind since hearing the shattering news. "Is it true? Is it true that you have agreed to marry the landowner's son?"

"Is it true, Kishan, is it?" Roop nudged again.

"Is what true?" Kishan asked back.

"That…that you are going far away?" she asked.

He nodded.

"I am coming along with you." She was firm, definite.

"Coming along with me? Where?" he asked.

"To wherever that you are going, I am coming too," she replied with an unwavering stance, as though there was nothing to worry or ponder about, as though there could have been no other way.

"I'll be taking a long and hard road to a distant, unknown place called California. You can't come with me. Why would you put yourself through peril? Besides, you will be…getting married soon," he said turning the other way.

"No, I am not!" she replied quickly. "I have told Bibi, I am not. I am telling you as well that I am coming with you to wherever this California is. If you can risk that hard road, I can too. And Kishan, you won't be able to leave without me. I know you won't."

Kishan was dumbfounded. He had planned a flight and here she was, so clear about what she wanted to do. "Come along" with him. He wanted to tell her that he had considered all possibilities, even seeking her hand in marriage from the village elders, but realising that no one would take a landless, homeless, jobless waif seriously, he had tossed aside the idea. He wanted to tell her that he had even thought of eloping with her but again the awareness had hit him that they would never make it far, not even a few miles. Her people would kill them both. He wanted to tell her that it was for her life that he worried. To keep her safe, he wouldn't take her along, so that she may dash to a happy future far from the ambiguity woven thick around him. But not wanting to distress her, he didn't mention any of it.

A heavy rock settled on his heart when he said, "Roop, what your parents want is for your best. By marrying the landowner's son, you will live the life that most village girls can only dream about. You will be surrounded with beautiful things. And he will love you too. Who wouldn't love a girl like you? It seems the most perfect thing to do," he said and sighed, unable to say any more.

"And the best thing for you to do is to go away, leaving me behind? What about your plans for college, your plans for us? Don't tell me about nice things. All I want is to be with you," Roop said.

Kishan knew then that the parting would be harder than he had thought. "Roop, I have no plans anymore. I must go, and I can't ask you down a perilous road to an indefinite future when your family has a well-laid-out one for you," he said, his heart shredding to bits.

"Kishan, it feels as though you don't know me anymore. You ask me to choose luxury, not knowing where my happiness lies," she said, giving up. "I hope that in the new land, you'll find what you are seeking."

Kishan could see that Roop was distressed. Grief stricken, she was hardly the giggling, chortling girl that he knew and loved. He couldn't bear to see her sad. "I can picture you as a happy, fat landlady with three handsome sons. Why, I can even see you eating a plateful of sweets and ordering the maids around!" he said, faking a grin.

It was a gimpy joke, but she smiled for him.

They were quiet for a long while.

Then suddenly, she said, "Kishan, tell me about the serai's secret mesmerising spot. You can't go without finishing that story!"

"Oh yes! The serai's secret spot!" he said, surprised that she had remembered. "To think, it is almost noon. Hurry and follow me!"

They rushed to the gateway. Pointing to the high roof, he said, "Now, everyone smiles when the gypsies sing the song, "Noor Mahal di Mori." Very few, however, know about the mori, the slight slit in the roof of the serai's gateway. It's a beautiful coincidence that we've made it here just before noon. Now look up and keep looking."

Breathless, they looked up at the towering roof. Right at noon, when the sun was the hottest, an array of light slid through a nook and hit the floor, spreading across the red surface in a flash. Roop jumped up, her mouth ajar, her eyes wide. It was unbelievable. The magnetic cluster of colour had run right beneath her feet. Lasting a few fleeting seconds, it was a sight to behold and cherish forever.

Kishan leaned back. He had finished telling her the story of the secret slit in the serai's gateway even as his love story lay abruptly aborted.

"Kishan, I'll miss your stories," Roop said. "And I'll miss those dimples on your cheeks and… I'll miss you really bad." Tears streamed down her cheeks.

Kishan thought of how he had waited for her to say it. For the first time, she had said it in words. She would miss him. He smiled at the cruel paradox. It would also be the last time that he would hear her say it. "Wipe those tears and tell me you will always smile," he said. "That's how I will remember you — smiling. It will keep me alive."

"Only if you promise me that you'll always tell stories," she said. "Every time you finish telling one, no matter where I am, I'll know, and I'll be sure to smile."

He nodded.

Wiping her cheeks, she smiled her most splendid smile. Squatting on the red floor, slowly she removed the anklets. "These will look very nice on another girl. I know they will. Kishan, I wish you love and luck. Now go," she said, handing the anklets to him.

In that moment, Kishan died a thousand deaths. Perhaps, Roop was right in returning the anklets to him. Now she could tread towards her new life without the burden of old memories, his memories. He knew a part of him would remain forever trapped in that parting moment, under the serai's glorious gateway. Clenching the anklets, he walked away. Reaching the turn, he looked back. Roop was now standing in front of the serai. The pink of her salwar-kameez flickered in the sun. She raised one hand while her other held the yellow lotus. Kishan waved back. Turning around, he walked on, an excruciating pain boiling over from his chest to where he was hardly himself.

Kishan's last hours in Noor Mahal were hazy as he walked around packing his life into three small sacks. In one sack, he put his clothes and in the other, a weathered blanket and a pair of slippers in case his old shoes gave way. Knowing that he wouldn't find Indian novels in America, he put three of Sarat Chandra Chattopadhyay's novels — *Bordidi, Parineeta* and *Biraj Bou* in the third sack along with Roop's silver anklets. Putting the three sacks in a corner, he wondered if three or any number of sacks could hold all his memories of walking the alleys of Noor

Mahal in his grey kurta and pyjama, of reading and dreaming outside Ramdeen's sweet shop, of growing up in Baldev Mama's house, of living there yet always being the "other," of thinking about his mother and piecing together her story from all that her people would say of her until she came back to live in his mind. Some days, when Roop got him lassi as he helped Baldev Mama on his fields, in her concern, Kishan sensed his mother. But now he was leaving them both behind, his mother and Roop. Were they ever with him to begin with? One was long dead and the other was only a mirage of happiness in his life.

Up before sunrise, Kishan said goodbye to Baldev Mama and his cousins. Unable to grasp where Kishan was going, the boys thought he was leaving for some place near Rawalpindi or Peshawar.

"Kishan, if you see a kurta with red and blue stripes, buy it for me right away, will you?" Khushwant asked Kishan as he stood with his three sacks in the doorway, ready to leave.

"Kishan, get me one too, with purple and black stripes. I know you'll never leave me out!" Lakhwant said, not chancing to be left behind.

"I will," Kishan replied, realising that this wasn't the time to give the boys lessons in geography or distances. Somehow, he knew that his gifts would reach his cousins, but he would never see them again.

Like Kishan, Baldev Mama knew that it was the last meeting. The night before, pulling Kishan into the barn, he had asked him how he had come by the fare for the ship and Kishan had assured him that he had managed the fare without killing or stealing. Baldev Mama hadn't probed further. Now saying goodbye, Baldev Mama broke down. "Kishan, when you came to this house as a baby, I never thought that your leaving would break my heart so. May your new life be happy," he said, holding Kishan's arm.

Tears blurred Kishan's vision. From carrying him around when he was a child to walking him to school and teaching him the ways of life, Baldev Mama had tried to fill in as best as he could for Kishan's missing father. Thank God for uncles like him, Kishan thought, who alongside their own fended for deserted children whose fathers moved on without ever stopping to think of the children that they had sired.

Baldev Mama clasped Kishan's arm tighter before saying, "Son, remember always that our clan, the Jats, are farmers. A Jat must have a piece of land. When your father abandoned you, I worried about you being landless. Then I thought that once you became a government employee, you'd be able to buy land, but now you are leaving for a new world. I hear many things are possible there. When you've earned money, promise me you'll buy land."

Kishan nodded. He was proud of his clan. Jats were a fearless agrarian community that upheld farming as a ritual holier than any other, honouring land over all else. Not only did land provide them with their livelihood, it was also their identity. They would go any length — obtrude, fight and even kill to defend their land. "Rest assured that in the new world, I'll buy a farm," Kishan told his uncle, "and carry forth our tradition of tilling and nurturing land, of growing crops and hopes." He gave Baldev Mama, his cousins and the little house that had sheltered him through the years, a last lingering look and said, "May Waheguru watch over you. I'll write on reaching America."

His cousins offered to walk him to Jaspal's house but Kishan chose to walk his last walk in Noor Mahal on his own, breathing in the odours of its earth. All his growing-up memories were soaked in them. He knew he would never forget the smell of rising dust, of flowering sheesham, of yellow acacia blossoms winking in the sun, of juniper berries ripening farther away along the river, of manure sprinkled across the fields where perspiring farmers sowed mustard, of careless childhood, of throbbing adolescence. Lapping up the smells of the village, Kishan walked on.

He stopped by Master Imtiaz Ali's house and shoved a letter for him under the rickety gate so Master Imitiaz Ali would know that he had taken off on an adventure different than the one that he had been toiling for all along.

On reaching Jaspal's house, Kishan saw a horseman waiting by the gate, who said that Basanto Bhua's husband had sent him to take Jaspal to Jalandhar. Nodding to the horseman, Kishan stepped into the courtyard where greeting him, Basanto Bhua led him inside to a divan. Jaspal joined them there. As soon as Kishan told them that he had the fare for the journey, their eyes burst out of their sockets. "How did you come by such hefty money? Nobody in Noor Mahal has any money even to get by, let alone to lend?" Basanto Bhua asked.

Kneeling down and holding Basanto Bhua's hand, Kishan said, "I've not stolen the money, nor have I killed for it. The money is rightfully mine. Don't ask me anymore. Waheguru knows I am telling the truth."

Basanto Bhua sensed that Kishan was not lying. Jaspal looked at Kishan and then at Basanto Bhua. "I know Kishan. He can do no wrong," Jaspal said, walking over to the adjoining room to gather his stuff.

Kishan got up and sat by Basanto Bhua. She grabbed his hands and said, "Son, it is a blessing that you are going with Jaspal. During the journey and in foreign land, stand up for each other like brothers and all obstacles will fall!" She began to weep. Jaspal walked in with his two sacks, and food for the train. Basanto Bhua was bawling but Jaspal remained calm. When Kishan handed him the fare, he carefully placed the money in the inner pocket of his pyjamas alongside his own.

All three stepped out into the courtyard one after the other. Jaspal rubbed his cow's nose for a long time and patted the oxen. Then he bent down and touched Basanto Bhua's feet. Snatching a fistful of soil from the ground, hurriedly he mounted the horse and sat behind the horseman. Kishan followed and sat behind Jaspal. The horse began to trot amidst shouts of "Sat Sri Akal." As the horse broke from a trot to a canter to a full-throated gallop along the still drowsy fields, Kishan's heart beat loud. At the thought of never seeing Roop, his body convulsed in an agony more acute than any he'd known. The last of the soil that Jaspal had picked up from his courtyard was slipping through his fingers. Sensing that a storm was raging inside Kishan, he turned for a moment and then, looked ahead again. Soon they were galloping past the bazaar of Jalandhar. Thinking of the loud buying and selling at the bazaar, Kishan wondered if there was a way one could buy and clasp a dream. Then he thought that even if there were a way, for him, it was much too late, his only dream having eluded him, leaving him clanging like an empty vessel.

Leaping off at the railway station, they walked to the ticket counter and purchased the tickets. "It is time we talked. Look at me, will you?" Jaspal asked as they sat down on a bench.

Kishan turned towards him.

"Kishan, forget the girl," Jaspal said matter-of-factly. "It has cost me everything that I had to pay for this trip. You probably have done the unheard of and the unthinkable to collect the fare. Oye, I will not ask you how you did it, but I am asking you to forget the girl."

Kishan was quiet. It was hard to even imagine a life without Roop.

Jaspal tapped his knee. "Kishan, I may not have been smart at school, but one thing I know — a beautiful girl is a mountain of trouble. Yes, that's what she is. God knows how many blokes are crying their broken hearts out now that she is going to marry the landowner's son. She probably always had her eyes on the moon and that's where she is headed. And a lovelorn feller like you is taking off to bury her memories in a foreign land," he said. Handing Kishan a roti, he began eating one himself. Kishan started chewing on the roti to save face. He wanted to tell Jaspal that he wasn't a fool who fantasised about Roop. She loved him and would've gladly married him if fate and her family hadn't meddled in the matter. But remembering again that "If" was the greatest traitor of all, he stayed quiet.

Finishing the roti, Jaspal opened the pack of maroondas. Popping one in his mouth, he handed one to Kishan. "I never shared this with you before," he said, his mouth full of maroonda. "But today, I must. There was a girl in Ramewal, Preeto. I loved her, even begged my bibi to talk to her parents about marriage. But then one day, her father, a soldier, returned and they packed up and left for the Lyallpur Canal Colony. The British had given her father some land there. I was sad for a day or so, but then I let the matter go. And today, I wouldn't know her if I saw her. That's how you deal with these girls — forget them." He placed the pack of maroondas back in his sack.

Preeto? The name had Kishan wondering. Ramewal was a village not far from Noor Mahal. He hadn't heard of any girl called Preeto around there. Nor had he heard of any soldier from there who had been granted land in the Lyallpur Canal Colony. He let the matter go. If only he could put Roop behind and move on as Jaspal was suggesting — painlessly, effortlessly.

SOPHIA

As Sophia went panicking in the bakery on a December afternoon about how she was going to fulfil so many orders for slabs of her newest, instantly popular Chocolate Jalapeño, in walked a young, dark-eyed, well-built Mestizo man with short cropped hair, his eyes dancing to a tune that only he could hear. Sophia noticed that there was a euphoria around him and a restless abandon too. His stance was friendly and his smile easy. "My name is Giovanni Romero. I am a visiting officer from Guadalajara. I heard of your bakery's famous chocolate-laced cake. I will have a slice with coffee," he said looking into her eyes and smiling.

Sophia felt a sting, a tingling, obscurely thrilling sensation as though the officer were looking right through her eyes into her heart. Dual emotions swept through her. She couldn't recall ever feeling that way before — bold and frightened all at once. Faking calm, she introduced herself, thanked him, cut him out a slice and poured him coffee. As the officer sat eating and sipping coffee on the patio, Sophia could sense his eyes following her everywhere as she went about her work.

After he had finished, the officer flashed a smile at her again. Sophia wasn't used to men showering such attention on her. She rolled her eyes. The officer was audaciously flirtatious, lacking in propriety. Such rashness was appalling. Guadalajara may be a large, vivacious city, but its people sure lacked prudence. She was mumbling in disbelief when unknowingly a smile spread across her face, warming her body, making her gleam with happiness. No one had looked at her like the officer was looking — as though he couldn't look away from her face, as though his life depended on it. She was still trying to figure if she was angry or excited when she saw that getting up from his chair, the officer was walking right towards her. "The cake is delectable," he said smiling again. "And Senorita Morales, if you don't mind my saying, you are beautiful beyond belief."

For a few seconds, Sophia froze, and her vision clouded. Quickly straightening her apron, she decided to say, "Thank you" and move away but much to her embarrassment, she noticed that she was reddening and missing heartbeats. The man was doughty but strangely empowering. Something about him made her want to believe in the unknown, the unfamiliar.

The officer's smile grew into a grin. "Perhaps you could show me around the zócalo for a bit in the afternoon," he asked.

An old song about falling for strangers who fled like shooting stars began to play in Sophia's head, but she wanted to break all rules. Smiling back at the officer, she nodded. The novelty and the uncertainty about the man were gripping, promising the far pavilion, the runaway moment, the fugitive idea that she so loved to chase.

Strolling through the zócalo that December afternoon, Sophia looked up at the frothy blue sky. It was invigorating as if painted by an inspired artist with quick, coarse strokes. Birds flew swiftly under the copper sun and despite the soft breeze, the mango trees were astonishingly still, as though deep in thought. Everything around seemed to have drawn closer — the sky, the sun, the birds, and also a few dimmed out-by-the-sun constellations, making her wish that everything around would always stay that way — remarkable, resplendent but close, waltzing ecstatically to a subliminal celestial tune. She studied her shadow walking alongside Giovanni's in the waning sun. She quite liked the sight of them together — her wavering walk alongside his even, balanced steps. For once she did not mind the shouting vendors or the screaming children in the zócalo. Life was beautiful, the impossible attainable.

Giovanni told her about his impoverished childhood in the deep south, about losing his parents early on in life, about how thankful he was for the government sponsored programme that gave him an education eventually enabling him to become an officer. Sophia found his story fascinating, happy, sad, twined with adversity, purpose and promise. She wanted to touch him, his happy and sore spots, soothe him. It felt as if her life had an objective other than taking on challenges. "It must have been awfully hard for you after the death of your parents," she asked.

"I don't know," he said. "I just kept going. I had to — for my brother's sake and mine. On looking back, I think the tough days really helped me know myself. Tell me about your life?"

Sophia told him of her careless childhood, about swimming in the ocean on stormy days, her chocolate experiments, about believing in miracles. "I know of rare bugs, spices, old Mayan traditions and Aztec secrets," she said winking.

"Do you really? What else?" he asked.

"I have conjured a spunky recipe for Chocolate Habanera, which I'd so like to try out but I'd rather not," she replied.

"Why?" he asked.

"Why? Because Habanera is the hottest pepper in the world. It could make a man hit the ceiling! That's why," she said. "Would YOU want to try some?" she asked.

"I would be doomed before I do," he said.

They laughed till their sides hurt. Sophia was surprised at the familiarity that he evinced. She hadn't laughed like that since childhood. She thought about that sublime time when it took so little to be happy, when there was no angst about the future, when songs didn't stir memories, they only made her jump up and twirl. He was interesting, she thought. He'd made her travel back in time and revisit a happy space from the past.

He told her he felt privileged that she was letting him into her past and her present, sharing with him her quirky hopes and dreams. He knew for a fact that dreams held enormous power, making people move mountains, swim across oceans. "If I didn't dream, I would be back in the south, struggling to make a living off a little patch of land in my village," he said smiling.

Sophia liked how his lips parted to form a smile, how he flinched when he was thinking, how he watched her attentively as though he were the only one who really understood her, as though she were flawless. She wasn't sure as to what was happening, all she knew was that she wanted to talk to him forever. "Do you want to see the old fort?" she asked, yearning for the meeting to linger. "You can't visit Acapulco and not see the fort, you know."

"How could I not, especially if it means spending more time with the gorgeous guide. I would be a fool to say no. Today, sure is my lucky day. I am all ready to burst into a song."

Sophia bit her lip. He had echoed her thoughts. The truth was she could hardly keep herself from breaking into a song and dance herself. Suddenly, it made sense why people sang serenades. "Was this love?" she wondered. "I grew up playing along the old fort," she said as they neared the fort.

He looked her over and smiled as though imagining how she may have looked when she was little — happy, sunburnt, her brown hair flying in the ocean breeze. She looked into his dark eyes and was stunned to see her entire childhood playing out in them and on gazing some more, she could see his life miraculously unfolding before her eyes and then she saw herself standing alongside him, hand in hand by blooming lavender.

"Don't look into my eyes. You will fall in love with me just as I am fast falling in love with you," he laughed, snapping her back to the moment.

Sophia turned red. "I, I meant to tell you a little about the fort," she said, hiding her self-consciousness as colour deepened

on her cheeks, making her blush wildly. "It was built to protect
Acapulco from pirates."

"Oh! I know all about the fort. I may not have come to
Acapulco before, but I have read about the fort. I know about its
unique five-point star geometrical design. I also know that this
old fort is a testament to our history, from the first inhabitants to
the European settlers, trade with the east to the Mexican War of
Independence. There is something else instead that I'd want to
do in our time together — ask you something important."

"Like what?" Sophia asked.

"I want to ask you to be mine," he said turning grim. "To be
my wife, to be with me forever."

Sophia's stomach flipped. Everything was moving too
suddenly.

"Sophia, if you consent, I will ask your father," he said.

Sophia stopped and stared at him. Though she didn't say
anything, she knew that he could read it all in her eyes. She was
completely taken with him. She wasn't sure when it happened
— when he had walked into the bakery, when she had flushed
and smiled back at him, when they'd walked around the zócalo
that afternoon or when she had gazed into his eyes and seen a
future of togetherness. She smiled. It didn't matter when, the
fact was that she was buzzing with an overwhelming ecstasy. She
hadn't sought to toil with love, but it had struck her nonetheless
without announcement like spring flying in early on a February
morning to splash life with dazzling colours. And even though
her heart beat as though it would split open her chest and drop
out, she was happy like she had never been, oblivious to time,
space, herself.

Walking back home that evening, Sophia knew that her
days in Acapulco were numbered. Her future was interlaced
with Giovanni's and as stupefying as it was, for that uncertain
future, she was willing, and gladly so, to move away from her

parents, the bakery and Acapulco. Looking up, she saw a seagull attempting to soar high up in the sky only to stumble and start trying again. To fly far was to risk stumbling, but there was no grander adventure than probing new spaces. It made life worth living. Something new and exhilarating awaited her. She wanted to savour it, swim in it and steep herself in it. A million butterflies began whizzing in her mind, dispersing fear, making her want to soar far away to discover herself anew. Being in love was being free.

KISHAN SINGH

When the Hooghly Express chugged into the station, grabbing the sacks, Kishan got in and sat on a berth by the window. Jaspal sat across from him and smiled, his confident manner not in the least giving away the village lad who had trouble reading or writing. Fidgeting around, he was both restless and excited. Kishan could tell Jaspal's mind was elsewhere, perhaps on the ship or already in California. They were still getting a feel of the berths when the train started off. "Kishan, we must remember to always hold tight to the sacks," Jaspal said.

Jaspal was silly, Kishan thought. Who in the world would steal their sacks? What was there to steal? Old clothes? Worn-out slippers? Then he remembered the silver anklets. He couldn't lose them. Pulling the sacks closer, he looked out of the window and saw green fields rush past. He could hardly believe he was aboard a train. Since he was a little boy, he had always wanted to ride a train. Trains triggered his consciousness, fired his imagination, sent him flying to distant lands. Watching trains speed by, he would stop and stare with awe at the smoking engines and the carts trailing behind them, his whole being responding to the promise that trains held out — of taking him out into the vast world that lay beyond Noor Mahal. And here he was on a train. He should have been leaping with joy, but he sat sulking, no longer charmed by trains or cities. In losing Roop, it was as though he had lost his soul. The great poet, Bulle Shah, had called love both anguish and elation.

> *Your love in my heart*
> *Has come to abide*
> *The bristling cup of poison,*
> *By my sweet choice, I have drunk.*

Living the anguish in the train that day, Kishan was marvelling at the mystic's sagacity when he saw the River Satluj gliding away. Growing up around the river, he had cherished it for its bounties. Now it was time to bid his beloved river goodbye. His dry, unfocused eyes tried to trap the blue of the river as it slipped out of sight. As the train made its way through Ludhiana and Ambala, Kishan decided he would lay watch by the window to catch glimpses of the other lively rivers that would run past. Nothing in nature was as entrancing as a river. It charmed him how the snow on mountaintops melted and ran down to become rivers and how those rivers swung through valleys turning dry land into fertile fields before jumping into alluring masses of water called oceans. Mingling with the oceans, they would evaporate and come down again as snow to start the cycle anew. Rivers were preeminent, Kishan believed. In fact, all life evolved out of water.

Outside, the sun had started to wane. Jaspal pulled out the rotis and maroondas. He handed a roti and a few maroondas to Kishan. Just as Kishan took a bite of roti, he saw frothy waters. "Pali, look! The River Ghaggar!" he shouted.

Everyone around stopped what they were doing and began staring at him.

Jaspal nodded. "Much smaller than our Satluj," he said and went back to eating and twitching while Kishan watched the Ghaggar bounce. The red evening turned ebony and a full moon came to illuminate the skies. Soon Jaspal fell asleep. Kishan remembered watering the fields on full moon nights in Noor Mahal. Those breathtaking nights had inspired him to immerse himself in life, to revere it, and now he was going so far away from those scenes. He looked at the sleeping Jaspal. With everything gone — familiar people and sights, he felt grateful to have at least a friend to mourn losses with, to walk down unfamiliar roads with and to discover new worlds with. Then celebrating the quiet dignity of the River Markanda that came to flow along, he let the sight of its cool waters soothe his tired eyes as he drifted off to sleep.

In the early morning hours, the train panted into Delhi, nudging Kishan awake. Even so early in the day, the Delhi railway station was abuzz with the sound of goodbyes, of heavy luggage being dragged around, of vendors selling tea and snacks, of children laughing and shouting. But most of all what Kishan heard was the bluster of life that edged along despite death, disease and denial. If and if alone, he could flow past his heartache. A horde of questions came to prick him. Would Roop miss him? Would she remember the games they played together in the meadows when they were children? Would she remember the year that they entered teenage, their clandestine meetings by the trees behind her house, and all the stories he had told her? Would she recall that kiss in the rain? Or would she forget him and drown her modest past in the rippled folds of silks and the lustre of gold and gems? Kishan sighed. Those questions would forever remain questions.

Jaspal woke up. "The train will be stopping here for a while. I will bring us tea," he said yawning.

He was back soon with two clay tumblers. Taking a sip, he looked at Kishan who was holding the tumbler and staring into nothingness. "Kishan, I told you how I felt for Billo. When her family chose a drunk from Bathinda for her, I was shattered but I moved on, didn't I? You, too, must forget Roop," Jaspal said.

Kishan was fuddled. "Who's Billo? I thought you said it was Preeto that you loved and that her family moved to the Lyallpur Canal Colony?" he asked.

"Did I say Preeto?" Jaspal said hurriedly. "How does it matter? Billo or Preeto? She may have gone to Lyallpur or married a drunk from Bathinda. The point is that I got over her."

Kishan knew then. Jaspal hadn't loved any girl. He shook his head and sighed at how poor a liar Jaspal made.

Jaspal slapped Kishan's thigh. "Kishan, laugh! You are headed to California! I can already see a brown-eyed, golden-haired girl swooning over your dimples. And once she hears your stories, she wouldn't even mind your blunt nose," he said, snickering.

Kishan pushed Jaspal away. How lucky Jaspal was, he thought, for not knowing love or the pangs of separation, for soaring like a swift bird in the open skies, for not having to worry about mending a tattered heart. When the train pulled out of Delhi, Kishan solemnly watched the Yamuna dance its way to Agra and later as the train steamed past Allahabad, he took to admiring the pale blue waters of the Ganga, at once both agile and calm. The profundity nudged him. By hitting dents and bumps, receding and rising through the narrowest of furrows to reach the driest of lands, rivers sustained life. The Ganga continued to leap and bound for hours, green plains gradually turning brown and rugged. Then gloriously, the river swung and assumed the name Hooghly, bringing Kishan and Jaspal to their train journey's end, Calcutta.

The railway station in Calcutta was inconceivably crowded. It was impossible to walk down the platform without knocking someone or the other. Frail-looking, dhoti-clad coolies scuttled around like mice, carrying heavy luggage in and out of trains. Vendors walked around selling everything from steaming, aromatic food and fresh fruits to hairbrushes, locks and soap. Clutching their sacks, Kishan and Jaspal waded through the crowds and found a bench. Jaspal pulled out the last of the rotis. They had two each. Jaspal walked over and asked a vendor how far the Calcutta port was. When told that there was no way that they could walk that far, Jaspal began thinking. Sitting down on the bench, he said, "Kishan, since the ship will be taking off late tomorrow evening, we can sleep a little on this bench tonight and take a tonga to the port early tomorrow morning."

"Yes, Pali," Kishan replied, "it is better to spend the night here than out on the port."

Jaspal slouched and shut his eyes. Holding on to the sacks, Kishan looked around. He saw dark and short men with somewhat curly hair rush by. Women in red and green saris with big red dots on their foreheads trailed behind with bright-eyed, dusky children. Then he saw some men carrying a palanquin. He figured that an aristocratic lady was being carried to the ladies' compartment, so she may escape the lowly gaze of commoners on the platform. Not far from the bench, thin men lay curled on straw mats. Farther up, he saw bare-footed children running along the platform and then dogs, barking and chasing after one another. Trains were leaving and arriving. Their shrill whistles soon lulled Kishan to sleep.

Hailing a tonga the next morning, Kishan and Jaspal reached the Calcutta port. It shone pristine in the morning light. Kishan gazed at the scintillating Bay of Bengal. The colossal mass of water was hypnotising and endless, holding out possibilities that were equally limitless. Unlike the rivers, the ocean was formidable not playful. Giant ocean-liners stood lined up at the port. After asking around for the agent's office, Jaspal and Kishan walked into a small room, where the balding agent was writing at a desk. Two other men were arranging papers in files. Jaspal referred to his agent in Jalandhar and introduced himself and Kishan. The agent asked them to sit. "Steerage tickets are a little cheaper, two hundred and fifty rupees per person. Sailing in the steerage will save you some money," he said.

"What is the steerage?" Jaspal asked.

"The lower deck of the ship, next to the steering apparatus," the agent replied.

"Yes, yes, we will be fine in the steerage," Jaspal said, handing the fare to the agent, glad that they would have some money left over after paying the fare.

"You will be interrogated at California's Angel Island Immigration Station," the agent said. "To make it past immigration, you must present yourselves as potential assets to the new country."

Jaspal nodded. "Sure Babuji, we will do our best to not come across as uncouth liabilities," he said.

Penning their name, age and other details, the agent asked them to return in a few hours to collect their tickets and papers. Strolling along the port for a bit, Jaspal and Kishan had a meagre dinner of fish and rice. Then haggling with a vendor, they purchased sweaters and slipped them on. Snug against their chests, the sweaters made them feel well equipped for the trip. Up ahead a man was selling brightly-coloured sweet golas. So enticing were their colours that Kishan insisted on having one despite Jaspal telling him that it was cold and late in the day to be having a gola.

Kishan chose a purple gola. Just as soon as Jaspal paid the gola man, Kishan quickly grabbed the dripping gob of colour and bit into it. The gola's tangy, exhilarating taste had him humming and tapping. Even as he smiled, he had an eerie foreboding of something terrible.

SOPHIA

"Who is this young man anyway? Where did you meet him?" Antonio asked when Sophia mentioned over breakfast that there was someone that she'd like her parents to meet.

"He is an officer with the government. He is visiting from Guadalajara and came by the bakery yesterday when you were out delivering an order," Sophia said excitedly.

"Guadalajara? I guess that he will be returning there?" Antonio asked.

"Yes."

"Then the story closes right there." Antonio was resolute.

"Pa, I would just like for you to meet him," Sophia implored.

"Meet him for what?" Antonio asked.

"I quite like him Pa," Sophia whispered.

"Like a man from Guadalajara? Whatever does that mean?" Antonio pressed.

"She'd like to marry him is what she means," Sophia's mother said putting her coffee cup down and staring into her husband's face. "Antonio, do you not understand anything?"

"But he is from Guadalajara!" Antonio said.

"So?" Sophia's mother asked.

"What has our Sophia got to do with a Guadalajara man?" Antonio asked back.

"Guadalajara is a city where thousands of people live. Our Sophia will live there too. With this man, after they are married of course," Sophia's mother said matter-of-factly.

"Really? I take it that mother and daughter have their minds made? I am only being informed." Antonio shook his head.

"Pa, I haven't made up any mind. I only met him yesterday," Sophia said.

"You met him yesterday and today you are talking of marriage! What do you know about the man anyway?" Antonio asked.

"Pa, he told me everything. I know all that I need to. He grew up in the south, is well read and works for the government. He is a good, honest man and he asked me to be his wife. All you have to do is to meet him to know him," Sophia insisted.

"And what about the bakery, Acapulco and us?" Antonio asked in an effort to hold his darling daughter from moving away.

"Antonio, do not humiliate the girl for choosing life. Let her go. Every girl must grow up to find her love and make her home with him. It would be a wretched thing to have her live with us her whole life and run the family bakery," Sophia's mother said with a finality that Antonio couldn't counter.

That afternoon, Sophia's parents met Giovanni at the bakery, his reflective smile and thoughtful manner instantly calming their doubts, drowning their trepidations. That the young man was besotted with Sophia and she equally anxious to be with him was clear to see. Happiness was having someone to share the future with.

Giovanni knew he was asking the old father for much more than his daughter's hand. "Senor Morales, I fell for your daughter the moment I saw her," he said. "She is fascinating, charming and compassionate, a captivating reflection of the values that you and Senora Morales have instilled in her. I see in her the wife of my dreams and the mother of my future children. The seriousness of this commitment is not lost on me and I promise to love, honour and cherish her forever. If you consent, I would like to make the pride of your home the treasure of my life."

Sophia could see that her father was moved. Stepping closer to Giovanni, Antonio placed his hands around Giovanni's shoulders and nodded. In seeking La Pedida, Giovanni had not just honoured Antonio but also revealed how deeply rooted he was in the Mexican ethos and how city life had not effaced his southern values. Sophia also saw that her father was proud of her for choosing a man both affable and honourable. She saw Antonio brace himself for the day every father of a daughter had to prepare for — giving away his daughter. It was a gushy feeling, a fusion of happiness, love, nostalgia. Even as her parents walked about smiling and rejoicing at the beautiful turn in her life, Sophia could see their unseen tears. She could sense their fears, too, for the unknown that lay ahead. Somehow, she knew their prayers would see her through just as they had all her life. Prayers of parents were not mere wishes but longings of the soul, resounding in the universe till they met their outcome. She was soaring in the high skies. There was nothing braver than to love and to be loved. She felt courageous and strong, ready to take on the new and insurmountable.

KISHAN SINGH

Majestic and enormous, the *New Frontier* was mountainous in stature, its stately build striking. Jaspal was tipping with excitement at the sight of the ship. Kishan smiled at how Jaspal had embraced every step of the trip with a pert enthusiasm. They lined up beside the two hundred steerage passengers. Unlike the first and second-class passengers who had elaborate luggage, steerage passengers like Jaspal and Kishan, carried cloth sacks. Looking around, they saw many Punjabi men. There were men from Uttar Pradesh and Bihar as well. Most of the passengers, however, were Bengalis, coming from Hooghly, Cooch Behar, Baharampur and Midnapore, their restrained style contrasting with the loud Punjabi men.

After the first and second-class passengers had embarked, the steerage passengers stepped aboard. As they walked past the first-class living and dining areas where pretty flower arrangements decked up tables, a crew-member instructed them to keep going. They walked all the way to the bottom of the ship, jamming in the dark pit called the steerage. Kishan flinched at a horrific smell. The lavatories were dreadfully close to the bunkers. The steerage, a dingy hole, was a shocking contrast to the glamorous first-class living and dining areas that they had passed by.

"None of you must be seen in front of the deck," a crew member instructed loudly. "Those areas are reserved for the first class to stroll."

Kishan and Jaspal found their bunker and laid down their sacks. There were four berths — two at the bottom and two on the top. They put their sacks on the top and bottom berths on the left side. Two Bengali babus came along and took the top and bottom berths on the right. They said their names were Bankim and Ram. Jaspal introduced himself and Kishan. Then stretching on his berth, he smiled broadly. "Kishan, twenty-eight days will glide by fast," he said. "The ship will stop for a day in Singapore and then head straight for San Francisco." His eyes gleamed as he said, "San Francisco."

When the ship left the harbour, shouts of joy echoed in the steerage. Some passengers were jumping and shouting, others were waving their handkerchiefs and dancing. Acclimatising to the waters, the ship started rocking slowly as the Calcutta shoreline began retreating farther and farther away. "Let us kneel together in prayer," Bankim said.

Kishan, Jaspal, Ram and Bankim bent down and with closed eyes, asked of God to deliver them to their destination safely.

Returning to the berths, Bankim disclosed that he was somewhat nervous about the trip. "One never knows," he said, "after what happened to *Titanic*, the greatest ship ever made."

Intrigued, Kishan turned towards him. "Whatever happened to the greatest ship ever made?" he asked.

"You don't know?" Bankim gasped. "It sank. In 1912. On hitting a glacier, it broke, and water gushed in, pushing the ship down to the bottom of the sea. Fifteen hundred people met their death."

Kishan had never before heard of *Titanic*. All at once, his brain was churning images of the sinking ship, its passengers and crew. Bankim said he had read about *Titanic* in a magazine back in Calcutta. He was headed to study history at the University of California in Berkeley and intended on writing a detailed paper on *Titanic* there.

Soon it was time for dinner. Not in the least hungry, Kishan was in pain instead. It was his stomach. Something about it was not right at all but when Jaspal insisted, he agreed to accompany him to the very crowded steerage eating area. Jaspal warned Kishan to stay clear of the contaminated saltwater that was served with the meals.

Kishan agreed. They would only drink hot tea on the voyage and no water ever.

The ship was drifting along rapidly now. As they sat eating curried rice, Jaspal called Bankim a fanatic who told a story about a sunken ship when he should have been thinking of making it safely to San Francisco. "How do we even know there was a ship called *Titanic*? It could all be his whim!" Jaspal said.

Kishan knew well that Bankim was not a liar but a lettered man. He wanted to tell Jaspal that he was in fact glad that Bankim had shared such a pulsating story, but he didn't. Jaspal had a point too, about dwelling on happy thoughts during the voyage. "Pali, this ship is going to make it to San Francisco just fine. I know that," Kishan said. Even as he smiled, he could feel the pain in his stomach shooting. Simmering all evening, it now surged with a vengeance, kicking up a storm inside him. His throat felt dry, his head heavy. He dragged himself to the side of the bunkers where the water containers lay and even though he knew it was bad, hurriedly pouring water into a tumbler, he drank it.

The next thing Kishan knew he was shivering and shuddering on the narrow berth of the jerking ship, down with a terrible, ghastly fever, the likes of which he had never known before. His eyes were aflame, his heart pounded, his forehead throbbed. Smouldering in a blaze, he floated in and out of consciousness, the dark stench of decay flooding the air.

Cramming about him, many voices spoke at once.

"Brain fever."

"The saltwater poisoned him."

"Skin and bones, and all of seventeen!"

"He has barely any money."

"The doctor won't attend to anyone in the steerage."

A hurried cry bellowed, "He is fading fast!"

Kishan continued to quiver, muttering mindlessly. In a flash, he pictured himself back in Noor Mahal walking along a canal and Roop in her pink salwar-kameez, singing and splashing in the bubbling waters, a flock of sparrows cheeping around her. Then he saw himself walking on only to see her again, this time standing by a sugarcane field decked in magenta bridal clothes. He saw himself becoming edgy at that sight and moving away but Roop caught up with him. "Kishan, are you really going away?" she asked.

He told her he was, to California.

She asked to come along. No matter what he said, she wouldn't give in. She would go with him, she insisted. Steeped in delirium, Kishan rose from the berth with a start, breathless and agitated. "Roop, I won't put you in harm's way even if that means never seeing you again!" he shouted.

His feverish scream echoed in the deck. Rushing to his side, Jaspal laid him down. Kishan kept mumbling Roop's name. The night plodded on. Violent waves shook the steerage. The heat from Kishan's body and the chill from the deck collided and repelled. Jabbering fanatically, Kishan told Roop that he loved her more than she would ever be able to fathom. Then he shouted over and again that he couldn't live without her.

Bending over Kishan, a raspy voice cried, "He is dying. He won't even make it to Singapore."

"No," Jaspal said. "Kishan will live! I have money. I'll get him medicine, good food and clean water. We will set foot on California together."

Kishan wanted to get up from the berth and say, "Pali, don't mention the money. Someone will steal it!"

He also wanted to say, "Don't spend the money on me, not a leaf will stir if I die. There is no one and nothing to live for!" His frenzied brain, however, wouldn't let him form a coherent sentence.

Seeing that Kishan's mouth was parched, Jaspal said he would get him clean water. As he ran out, Kishan wanted to yell, "Pali, don't leave the sacks unattended. At the bottom of a sack lie Roop's silver anklets!" Yet again, unable to speak, he turned and twisted instead.

Lifting Kishan's head, Jaspal offered him water but Kishan turned his face away. Colours flashed in front of his eyes — blue, green, yellow, flaming orange. All night, his body heavy like a log, ached and shook. Morning brought with it a flitting white light. It shone bright on Kishan's face, refusing to leave. Staring at the light, he became astonishingly calm and stopped shaking. Stricken with it, he had an urge to follow that light but a pull from below held him down hard. The light and that pull battled, tugging and stretching him in opposite directions. In the background, he heard Jaspal say, "Kishan, the California fields are waiting to be tilled. We will plough them together!"

A part of Kishan yearned to follow Jaspal to those beauteous fields but caught between the light and the pull, he swam in the middle, memories of Roop vividly playing out before his eyes.

Smelling death, people stepped back. Not only did he smell it, Kishan saw death too. Hanging over his face, it wanted to strangle and suffocate him to lifelessness. Jaspal tried to shoo it away. Bringing in the doctor, he told him that Kishan was suffering from the wretched, incurable fever of love. Waving his hand, the doctor dismissed that as rubbish. Calling the condition food poisoning, he enquired after what Kishan had been eating. When Jaspal furnished details, the doctor nailed the blame on the contaminated gola that Kishan had at the Calcutta port and the filthy saltwater of the steerage. He gave Kishan three injections. "If he responds to the drugs, he might live," the doctor said.

All night, Kishan sensed Jaspal by his side, fussing over him like a mother hen. When the sun peeped out of the skies the next morning, Kishan saw that the deathly light that had loomed over him had faded to where it was hardly even bright, dissolving in the air soon after. The pull from below having won the battle calmed down as well and let him be. Sleep came along and cloaked him. When he woke up, it was late evening, the setting sun having painted the sky a deep maroon. Jaspal was sitting by his side. Kishan looked at Jaspal and whispered that he was sorry to be so much trouble. Shushing him, Jaspal heaved a sigh, looked up at the sky and thanked God.

SOPHIA

Sophia Morales married Giovanni Romero on a sunlit Sunday
in the early spring of 1902. The air smelled of sweet peas and
wisteria, forsythia bushes blazing in the wilderness. Neighbours
and friends came laughing in with whatever they could find
around their homes that could pass for a gift — flowers, candles,
sweets, embroidered linen. Some brought bunches of well
wishes. Sophia wore a Mantilla veil over her face, her flowery
white dress flowing in the breeze, her exuberant eyes rejoicing
in the potential of the future. Before she set out for church,
her mother pinned a bow of blue, yellow and green ribbons to
Sophia's dress for wealth, passion and luck.

At church, Giovanni and Sophia offered prayers to the
Virgin and Sophia's parents threw a lasso of orange blossoms
around them, symbolising a fruitful union. During the vows,
Sophia's eyes met Giovanni's. He loved her fully, completely with
all her flaws, freckles and imperfections. Basking in the glory of
that miracle, she was resplendent, the cosmos smiling upon her.
When it was time for Las Arras, the priest blessed the thirteen
silver coins that were an exultant Giovanni's present for his
blushing bride. Receiving the gift, Sophia glowed in happiness,
her mother and father watching on with joy. Everyone drank on
the way back from church, singing soul-stirring tunes, imbuing
the air with romance.

Feasting on pulled pork, spicy rice, beans and tortillas by
the beach, the crowd sang folk songs as they relished the rum-
soaked fruit cake garnished with pineapple bits, pecans and
coconut flakes. As Sophia's mother handed out almond sweets
and sweet-tart tamarind candies, the crowd took to dancing.
Sophia and Giovanni danced too, as though they were the only
ones who could hear the music, swinging with zesty abandon
as the afternoon turned to evening and an anxious moon rose

up in the horizon way ahead of time even as the sun was still setting. Someone said such an occurrence was rare. Sophia laughed at the moon's audacity and the sun's insolence. She loved their dare and her own too. It felt wonderful to be living her truth. To dance the dance of life, one had to be a great dancer. To be a great dancer was to possess great passion. And courage. Turning the page was never easy. Rising to the moment, Sophia geared to leave the place that she had known all her life and loved wholly. As safe and fulfilling as the past was, it was over. It had to be left behind to make room for surprises, new endeavours and feats. Bidding a grateful adieu to the past, she stepped up to new beginnings.

KISHAN SINGH

As Kishan lay recuperating, a young Punjabi woman came to his berth one afternoon when Jaspal and the Bengali babus were having lunch in the steerage eating area. She said she had brought khichdi and tea for him. Kishan thanked him. He presumed she was about twenty years old. After he had finished eating and drinking, clearing the dishes, the young woman left. Later, when Kishan asked Jaspal about her, he said she was a kind co-passenger who wanted to help.

The next afternoon, the young woman came again. She was always upbeat as though humming to the song of distant thrushes. When Kishan finished eating the khichdi and tea, she asked him if he felt better. He nodded and thanked her, and she left.

The third day, he noticed her gold bangles. "I guess you're married?" he asked, finishing the khichdi.

"I am. I am going to California with my husband," she said, and handed him the tea tumbler.

"I haven't seen any Punjabi women onboard. Are you the only one?" Kishan asked.

"Yes," she replied.

"Are you afraid? California is far away — a new land," he said.

"No. My husband has been all over — Singapore, Hong Kong. He served the British, even worked in Canada. He has seen California. He says it's the best. The days are long, the land heavenly," she said.

"Won't you miss your people?" Kishan asked.

"My husband says I will miss nothing in the beautiful land," she replied.

"What do YOU think?" Kishan asked.

"I think so too. Besides, I will have my own family soon. Children, you know?" she said, lowering her gaze.

Gulping down the last dregs, Kishan thanked her. She took the tumbler from his hand. "I'll get you more tomorrow," she said and left quickly.

She came in again the next day and watched on quietly as Kishan ate the khichdi she had brought him. He liked the khichdi. It was even better than the one Nihalo Mami made. "Thank you," he said.

She nodded; he continued eating. After a while, she asked softly, "Did you love someone?"

"Yes," he replied taken aback. Thanks to his illness, everyone in the steerage knew of his wrecked romance, he thought.

"It's hard being in love," she said.

"You wouldn't know. You've not loved anyone," he said, studying her face.

"How do you know I've not?" she asked.

"You have? You mean your husband, don't you?" he asked back.

"Yes, I love him. We got married a month ago. I had never seen him before that," she replied.

"Did you love someone else before?" Kishan asked, his voice wavering.

"Boy! You are forgetting yourself!" she snapped.

Kishan bit his tongue, ate the last of the khichdi and handed her the empty bowl. She gave him the tea tumbler. He slurped the tea.

"The past is like another lifetime. Dead. It has no meaning in the now. But today matters. Colour it with purpose." She looked at him and smiled.

Kishan tried smiling back. He managed. She got up to leave.

"What's your name?" he asked.

"Bhahalo," she replied. "The papers say Bhahal Kaur, but I like Bhahalo." Taking the empty tumbler from his hand, she walked away.

Kishan never saw her again. Two days later, her husband, a tall, burly man, came in to check on Kishan. His talk was loud and laced with adventure. He said he had heard of Kishan's sickness and asked the cook if his wife could make khichdi and tea for him in the steerage kitchen. "A Punjabi feels instantly better after having Punjabi food. Why, Bhahalo tells me you are much better now," he said laughing.

Nodding, Kishan thanked him.

The man started to talk about California. "One can't be sad in a place like California — warm and sunny all year long. It's truly golden!" he said.

The man was a romantic, Kishan thought. Later that evening, when Jaspal brought him dinner to his berth, chewing on a big bite, Kishan smiled. Gazing far out at the boundless ocean, he could hardly wait to partake of what lay ahead.

The air was abuzz with excitement when the *New Frontier* docked at the Singapore harbour for refuelling. Kishan wanted to pull out of the berth and gaze at the city, but Jaspal insisted that he rest some more. Watching over Kishan closely, not only did Jaspal bring food for Kishan to his berth but sometimes fed him too. A few days later when Kishan was strong enough to walk about, Bankim let him in on the truth. Jaspal had spent every paisa that he had on the doctor's fee and the English medicine to get Kishan back on his feet. Kishan was dumbfounded. Jaspal had never so much as mentioned a word of it to him. That evening, he asked Jaspal about it. Jaspal looked him in the eye. "We left home as brothers," he said. "I would never let my brother die if I had it in me to prevent it. No more talk about that. But if I even see you anywhere close to that saltwater again, I will beat the life out of you."

That day, Kishan's world took on a new meaning. Jaspal went from being his hero to becoming his brother in the truest sense. In resurrecting him, Jaspal had given Kishan not only life but also a purpose. In his new life, Kishan vowed to be his brother's keeper, to fight for Jaspal's cause, and to go any length for him and his happiness.

New Frontier sailed on for two weeks. Bankim yelled one morning that they were only ten days away from California. Everyone jumped up. The magic of California was yet unknown to Kishan but every now and then, he would let his mind take off and fly wild over California's green valleys and tall mountains. Then one morning, as he stood by the steering apparatus, Kishan saw California. The splendid San Francisco Bay beckoned with the promise of a brighter, happier life. He didn't know whether to shout or cry. For once, he didn't have words either to express his elation. Since he was born, he had been pushed around. Right after his mother died, he had been shunted out of his father's house. In Baldev Mama's house, he was a family member and yet not. He had heard of paradise since he was little. Now it seemed as though he would reach it. He remembered, however, that one needed to make it past the Angel Island Immigration Station to embark upon the golden land. Fearful, Kishan worried for what lay ahead. What if he and Jaspal were not accepted and forced to return? Holding tight to hope and dreams, Kishan straightened up for the trial at Angel Island.

SOPHIA

As much as Sophia had looked forward to it with an abounding eagerness, the move up north to the government encampment in the old Spanish colonial city of Guadalajara was disconcerting. Sophia had never seen such astounding buildings infused with history, nor encountered such an enormous sea of people in her life. She missed running into familiar faces and places, haggling with friendly vendors, knowing secret routes and comforting paths that led to habitual spaces. The street names didn't kindle affinity, only an all-encompassing wonder. She missed the mountains, the palm groves, the mango trees and the green ocean. Most of all, she missed her parents and the bakery. Though nothing about Guadalajara rang familiar, she knew she belonged to the place, to Giovanni. His love for her was without beginning or end, without hesitation, without expectation. Revelling in it, she began growing roots in the city, getting accustomed to the newness around her, befriending neighbours and passers-by, relishing her little house with the brick porch where she hung dark green curtains in the windows and planted gardenias along the fence in the backyard on pink afternoons as Giovanni carried out President Diaz's initiative of building roads and railroads and the laying of the first telephone lines across Mexico.

She waited breathlessly by the door for him to return home in the evenings, rejoicing in their insatiable hunger for each other, their mindless chatter, their impassioned kisses. Leaning against him by the fire on the patio, she lolled in the heartrending serenades that he sang to her, visions of everlasting spring playing in her mind.

Imbibing Mestizo traditions, she took to celebrating all the holidays with gusto, her favourite being Las Posadas when she enthusiastically played host to the neighbourhood children who enacted the parts of Mary and Joseph, even singing the Las Posadas versos with a perky zest all the nine days leading up to Christmas. And on Christmas day, wearing her very best dress and smile, she joined the neighbourhood to adore new-born Jesus. Except for the sudden memories of her parents and Acapulco that came to pound her every now and then, life in Guadalajara held out a dizzying promise. She visited her parents as often as she could, and upon each visit, she found them older and weaker but happy that she had found someone to walk along life's paths with. As for the bakery, her father now ran it his way. Far from serving chocolate-laced cakes or chocolate confectionery, he now served only bread. No longer a touted café, her family bakery was now one of the many panaderías in town where people purchased bread. What was gratifying, however, was that the bakery continued to churn out a tidy little income for her parents.

As Sophia discovered the eclectic faces of effervescent Guadalajara, Acapulco and the bakery slowly began to ebb away from Sophia's mind. Drawn by the local art, she started visiting the splendid Cathedral in the heart of the city on many a morning, agave bushes lighting her path as she went about shopping for crafts and ceramic pottery at the pretty boutiques along the way. Walking back home by the beautiful Hospicio Cabanas, she would admire with awe the intricately carved chapel as mariachis played haunting tunes, transporting her to a long gone colonial era enlaced with splendour, filling her heart with verve as also a wistfulness for what had passed and for what lay waiting to blossom. She wished for the City of Roses to bring her luck, sprinkle her life with golden dust. Charmed by the brave world that was unfolding before her, she reawakened her passion for chocolate. Tasting the varieties that were sold at mercados across the city, she discovered the world's great love affair with milk chocolate. There was nothing more seductive than milk chocolate. It was delicate and luxurious like velvet denoting love, aspiration, hope as well as fulfilment, gratification and completion. Lustily, she began making plans to launch her own brand of milk chocolate and was still trying and testing recipes when her twin boys, Giovanni and Seraphim were born in 1907. A daughter Isabel followed right behind in 1908. Knowing then that her milk chocolate creation would have to wait a while, Sophia immersed herself in motherhood.

KISHAN SINGH

At daybreak, on a cloudless September morning in 1916, the *New Frontier* landed in San Francisco. Kishan stared at the new embankment, California. It was bright to the point of blinding the eyes. Large, fizzy waves were caressing its vast, shiny shores. Spellbound, he stepped out of the ship, Jaspal and the Bengali babus walking beside him. He thought of how they had all landed on the coast of hope driven by a dream as fantastic as it was desperate. Jaspal hoped to grow roots in the new land; Bankim, to attend the university at Berkeley and Ram, to find work in the lumber mills. Kishan hoped to immerse himself in the colours of California, find his place under the orange California sun and be his brother's keeper through night and day, light and darkness, winter and spring.

An officer led the steerage passengers to the ferries that would take them to Angel Island. Sitting on the ferry, Kishan remembered the harrowing stories of detention. His stomach tightened. It had been a long and difficult road to the edge of the gilded land. Having come so far, they must endure in the face of trial. Wading across the foaming Pacific, they reached the daunting isle where Ram and Bankim joined a bunch of fellow Bengalis who stood huddled along the shore. The immigration papers for their group would be processed together, they said. Kishan and Jaspal wished them the best of luck for their onward journey. Taking a flight of steps, they reached the entrance to the two-storeyed white building called Angel Island Immigration Station. Kishan looked up at the menacing wooden structure. It exuded indifference.

Stepping inside the cold hall, they lined up behind scores of Asian immigrants — Chinese, Japanese, Filipinos, Indians and others — who like them were fresh off the ships that had sailed into the San Francisco harbour that day. Bowed down by sleep, Kishan and Jaspal leaned against the damp walls. The line moved slowly. Finally, when they made it to the front, an officer verified their papers, assigned them bunk bed numbers and asked them to proceed to the Asian Men's dormitory. Going up the steep stairway to the second floor, they made their way into the dark and crowded dormitory. Squeezing through the narrow aisles, they found their bunk beds and put their sacks down. There were about forty men in that dark space. Some were shuffling through papers while others were folding clothes. Strange languages echoed in the dimly lit, tightly packed room. Suddenly claustrophobic, Kishan rushed to the lone window at one end. It was a brilliant green outside, red sunbeams sneaking in through the window. Tall, lush trees stood on plush hills. In the far distance, he saw the barbed wire encircling the immigration station and still farther, the opulent Pacific. Though dog-tired, he wanted to stand there, bask in the sun and lap up the new and the unfamiliar that was uncoiling before his eyes. Soon, however, feeling unsteady, he walked back. And as soon as he sat down on the hard bunk bed, sleep knocked him out.

He was meandering through breathtaking valleys, peach orchards and orange groves when Jaspal shook him awake. An officer was calling out their names for medical exams. Shaking off sleep, Kishan followed Jaspal down the stairs to the hall where the officer directed them to separate cubicles. Inside the cubicle, a medical examiner drew blood from Kishan's finger and asking him to undress, checked his skin. Next, the examiner turned on a torch and scanned Kishan's scalp before flashing the torch in Kishan's eyes and ears and on his finger and toe nails. Turning the torch off, he tediously began to pen notes. Kishan put his clothes back on. A shocking silence pervaded the cubicle. Asking Kishan to proceed for the interview, the examiner continued taking notes, his facial expressions not giving away any discoveries that he may have made.

Kishan went and stood by the droves of immigrants waiting outside the interview room. Their anxious faces mirrored his own. A large clock hung on the wall, its hands loudly marking time, every minute adding to the angst. Morning gave way to afternoon, Jaspal was nowhere in sight. Perhaps his medical exam had been prolonged, Kishan thought. Just then he heard an attendant screech, "Kishaan Singh!" He followed the attendant into the interview room.

A stiff, blue-eyed Anglo officer was sitting behind a square table. Pointing Kishan to a chair in front of him, he asked Kishan his name, where he had come from and if he had been travelling with someone. Kishan answered the questions in his very best English. Next, the officer asked him what he planned on doing in America.

"I have come in the hope of a better life. I will work as hard as it takes," Kishan replied.

Again, the officer asked with emphasis, "What will you DO?"

Kishan knew then that the officer was looking for a precise answer. "I will work on the fields. About four thousand men from my homeland, Punjab, are farmhands, working across California. I will join them."

The officer gestured for Kishan to leave.

Kishan walked back to the dormitory, glad the officer hadn't asked him about personal assets or finances. Sitting on his bunk bed, he was waiting for Jaspal when he heard Punjabi being spoken. Turning around, he saw three Sikh men chatting in a corner. They may as well have been standing in a village alley in Punjab. The men saw him too and hollered at him.

They introduced themselves as Natha, Nishan and Mohan. Natha and Nishan said they had been at the Immigration Station for nearly six months while Mohan had landed two weeks ago. Kishan's heart staggered in his chest. Two weeks seemed dreadfully long. He didn't even know what to say or think of Natha and Nishan's six-month detention. The men told him that they were waiting for their approved immigration papers to come through. They wondered about the reasons for the delay, their eyes restless and uneasy. It was likely the medical results, Mohan guessed. It was the dreaded background check, Nishan thought. They told him story after story of people who had been stuck at the Angel Island Immigration Station for years, sneaking in the tale of the Chinese woman who after being detained three years had hung herself in the Asian Women's dormitory. Turning blue, she was dead in minutes. Then there was the Japanese man who after being confined too long, lost his mind and jumped from the top floor to death. Kishan moved back. He envisioned the Chinese woman hanging from the low ceiling, the Japanese man lying in a pool of dark red blood. He quivered. Surely, Jaspal and he didn't leave Punjab to be jailed inside that white wooden building.

Nishan asked Kishan about his plans.

"We will work the California fields and then when we have money, my brother and I will buy a farm," Kishan replied.

"Wouldn't we all like that?" Nishan said wanly. Looking down, he walked out of the dormitory, the other two following behind. Angel Island was far more sordid than Kishan had imagined.

The sun was going down on the golden coast when a very tired Jaspal returned to the dormitory. Kishan asked him about his medical exam and interview.

"Everything went well," Jaspal replied.

Someone said it was time for dinner. Eating cold rice and vegetables in an even colder dining hall, they returned to the dormitory and threw themselves on the bunk beds. Sleep knocked out Jaspal. Kishan stared at the roof. The traumatic stories of the detainees at Angel Island tore at his heart. His throat stiffened. He shut his eyes. He mustn't give in to despair.

He must hold tight to the aspiration that had brought him and Jaspal across the deep oceans to the land of promise.

The sun broke in with force the next day. At breakfast, as Kishan and Jaspal sat eating bread and sipping tea, Kishan saw that the Chinese, Filipino and Japanese immigrants sitting by them were looking around the room with unfocused eyes, their curbed hopes and dreams caught inside them like dormant volcanoes, waiting to erupt. He sensed a volcano festering inside him too and rushed back to the dormitory as Jaspal continued eating and shaking his legs.

In the dormitory, a Chinese man was carving letters next to an engraving of beautiful flowers on a wall. Curiosity got the better of Kishan and he asked the man what he was writing. The man whispered, "No English." Then walking to a teenaged boy who sat reading on a bunk bed, the man brought the boy along.

Running his fingers on the words etched across the wall and slowly translating them into English, the boy said, "My uncle has written a poem. It says that the flowers of honour, chrysanthemums, are in bloom in China now, and even though he is far away, he sees them with his mind's eye, and soon, he hopes to be greeted by newer flowers in this new land."

Kishan looked again at the carved letters and the flowers. His eyes brimmed. He told the boy that his uncle drew and wrote beautifully. The boy bowed. Bowing back, Kishan walked to his bunk bed, lay down and closed his eyes. The California dream quivered in the terrifying darkness. His eyes were shut and his breathing heavy when an officer walked into the dormitory and began reading out names from the release list. Detainees whose names were called would be able to leave right away. Scrambling out of bed, Kishan ran to where the officer stood. Torrents of chill ran up his bare feet, past his legs and stomach all the way to his chest but there was no way he would go back to his bunk bed and get his shoes. He began listening attentively as the officer read out name after name. Then he heard it — Kishan Singh. For a minute he went numb. Did the officer really call out his name? He didn't trust his wandering mind anymore. It was forever imagining things. He waited till the officer had read out the entire list. Then walking up, he asked the officer to confirm if the names, Jaspal Singh Dhillon and Kishan Singh had made the list. Glancing down and going over the list, the officer said Kishan's name was on the list. When Kishan asked about Jaspal, the officer scanned the list again and shook his head. Pinning the list to the wall, he walked away. Kishan rummaged through the list like a maniac but couldn't find Jaspal's name. Ruffled, he wondered where Jaspal could be, only to find Jaspal standing next to him. Together they went over the list again and still again, finding no luck. Kishan looked at Jaspal. Jaspal sighed. "The new list will be out in two days," he said.

Kishan took to wondering. Why had Jaspal's papers not come through? He felt a tap on his shoulder. It was the officer. Handing Kishan his stamped immigration papers, the officer said, "Get your things and be on your way!"

In the dormitory, some people were holding up their release papers and dancing. Others were laughing and quickly packing their bags. Nishan came and stood by Kishan. "So Kishan, you are on your way to the farmland," he said. "If God wills, I will see you there soon. Good luck!" His voice cracked.

Nishan's agony shook Kishan. "Don't ever give up on your dream. Having brought you so far, it won't let you down," he said touching Nishan's shoulder.

Nishan's lips curved to form a faint smile. Waving to Kishan, he walked away. Jaspal's pending paperwork came to loom again on Kishan's mind. Contemplating his course of action, he walked over to the officer who was still roaming the dormitory. "I will wait for my brother's papers to come through. I can't leave without him," Kishan said.

The officer raised his brows. "You don't understand, do you? This is Angel Island Immigration Station. People have been held here for years. If you had any sense, you would run out of here without blinking an eye," he said.

Kishan's jaw dropped. No way could he tread forward leaving his brother behind. The officer was losing patience now. "We can't keep people here for no reason and provide them with board and lodging. Leave immediately," he said.

It was the worst dilemma. The law demanded of Kishan to leave but he couldn't cross the bay and go out into California without Jaspal. But where would he wait? "May I work here at the Immigration Station? I will do anything for nothing. I just need to be around my brother," he said.

"Pack your things and talk to the Administrator in the front office," the officer grumbled.

Kishan felt upbeat. Walking over to Jaspal who stood in a corner, Kishan told him that there was a chance he could work at the Immigration Station. Jaspal was surprised. "Kishan, why don't you go out into the farmland and find work. I will join you there. If I were you, I wouldn't wait a minute!" he said.

Kishan looked at Jaspal. He remembered how Jaspal had tended to him when he was deathly sick on the ship, how Jaspal had spent every rupee that he had to get him back on his feet and how Jaspal had not moved on and left him to die on the deck. And now Jaspal was asking him to go forth. He would never take off without Jaspal, the friend and brother with whom his fate lay tied for all time to come. "Pali, the golden coast and the fields of wonder can wait a while. We will go explore them together! I will see you around," he said.

The Administrator, a stout middle-aged Anglo man, laughed loudly on hearing that Kishan wanted to work at the Immigration Station. "Young man, you are in America. It is a big country, a land of promise. Why would you waste your time at this Immigration Station?" he said.

Kishan insisted on working at the Immigration Station.

Flipping through a file, the Administrator said they were short of hands in the Asian kitchen. Kishan could work there. It would pay very little, he said. Kishan smiled. All he cared about was being there with Jaspal and as soon as Jaspal received his papers, they would venture out into California. His heart leapt.

Many odours greeted him in the kitchen, the most predominant being steamed ginger. Standing by the stove, a fat Anglo cook was ordering a frail oriental boy around. Glad to have another helping hand, the cook asked Kishan to wash the dirty dishes and thereafter boil rice and slice the vegetables for stew. As they went about preparing dinner, the oriental boy told Kishan that he was seventeen. He said he was from China and that his name was Han-Gan. Kishan shared with him that even though he had received his immigration papers, he was waiting for his brother's papers to come through.

"I am happy you came," Han-Gan told Kishan. "There is so much to do in the kitchen, but no one wants to work here. The jobs in San Francisco pay much more."

"Don't you want to go to San Francisco?" Kishan asked.

"I can't. It's my health. It wouldn't let me work in the factories or on the rail tracks," Han-Gan replied.

Kishan wondered about Han-Gan's health but didn't want to ask questions. Laying the table and serving dinner, Kishan washed and rinsed the dishes again. Just as he finished doing that, the cook abruptly asked him to leave and return at six in the morning. Picking up his sacks, Kishan stepped out into the cold dark and stood under a tree. He hadn't a clue where he would go. The woods were dense and cold. The tall trees seemed far taller and mysterious from up close. Then he saw Han-Gan running towards him, huffing and puffing.

"You have nowhere to go, do you? Wait for me here. I will finish my work and be back!" Han-Gan said running back into the kitchen. Wait Kishan did for close to an hour, admiring the beautiful San Francisco in the distance. It was glitzy, beating with life, twinkling in the darkness like a brilliant star. But for Jaspal's pending paperwork, the coveted land seemed well within reach.

SOPHIA

Sophia revelled in her children, rediscovering in them the
magic of childhood, of playing all day in the sun, of colouring
the world in hues of her choice, of chasing butterflies through
golden billows. They kept her on her toes all day long as they
ran barefoot through the patio on to the street, climbing tall
furniture and old trees, breaking dishes and spattering flower
petals, falling and bruising, crying and drooling, laughing and
blabbering all day long. Most days she fretted after them, on
others she let them be, free to touch, feel, mouth and experience
life, be themselves. What amazed her most was how Isabel kept
up with her vivacious brothers both in energy and in spirit.
Waking up to the pitter patter of tiny feet and sloppy kisses,
Sophia spun her life around her children, looking upon them as
a source of energy as well as exhaustion, irresistible bundles of
joy who egged her on to run longer, to strive harder and dream
more. She and Giovanni never had their fill of imagining the
children's future. The boys, they thought, would follow their
father and serve the government, and little Isabel would grow
up and make a perfect wife to a government official and perhaps
teach at a school as well. With that end in mind, shortly after
the boys started school, they enrolled Isabel at St. Theresa's
Academy, a leading school for girls in Guadalajara. Making the
best of that opportunity, Isabel began playing the piano. The
academy also kindled in the little girl an interest in the arts,
initiating her in horseback riding and introducing her to the
English language. Sophia and Giovanni looked forward to
the day when their daughter would learn fine housekeeping,
embroidery and cooking as well.

"Isabel sure has inherited the legendary looks of her ravishing
grandmother," Sophia whispered to Giovanni one evening as
they sipped tequila in their tidy little living room. "Her dark

eyes, lustrous hair, slender and tall frame are unmistakably reminiscent of my mother."

Interestingly, quite like her grandmother, Isabel had the profoundest faith in the Virgin of Guadalupe. She would sit quietly on her mother's lap without fluttering a lash as Sophia told her of the Virgin's abiding love for her devotees. "Isabel, what is most beautiful is the Virgin's immense love for children," Sophia would tell her daughter and Isabel grew up thinking of the Virgin as a close friend, sharing her many childhood joys and predicaments with the deity, even wearing her mother's necklace with the deity's picture in the locket at all times.

A diligent government employee, Giovanni was always thankful for the plenitude of work that made it possible for him to give his children avenues to grow. He could hardly stop extolling the President. "President Diaz is the harbinger of development in Mexico," he would tell his wife and children. "He will take the nation to unprecedented heights."

Giovanni's perception of President Diaz was far from how the rising number of Mexico's deprived and poor perceived him. Though the President sought to modernise Mexico by building factories, railroads, dams, and by laying telephone lines across the country, rural workers continued suffering unemployment and hunger. Opposition to the President grew by the day and in 1911, revolutionary groups from all over Mexico came together to overthrow the government and civil war broke out. Unable to suppress the revolutionaries, President Diaz resigned, and after a while, a liberal landowner, Francisco Madero, took over as President.

Giovanni continued building roads, railroads and laying telephone lines under the new government. But Mexico did not find peace under Madero either as violent control for power ravaged the country. Sophia and Giovanni hoped that eventually the fighting would cease but all they heard was how one or the other faction was planning to overthrow the government. In 1913, the government was indeed toppled, and Pedro Lascurain became President. But soon after, seizing power from him, General Huerta took over as President. The rebels forced him to flee as well, and a bloody civil war broke out again. Fear and anxiety marred the nation.

One rainy day, Sophia received a telegram that her father had suddenly fallen sick and died. She immediately boarded the train to Acapulco leaving the children with their father.

Reaching her parents' house after the rushed, perturbed train journey, Sophia found it raided and robbed. Not only was her father dead, her mother lay murdered too. The entire neighbourhood sat plundered. A shadow of its previous, happy self, the coastal community was torn by riots. It no longer looked anything like the place that she had grown up in, where she had relished the love of her doting family, where, laughing and waltzing, she had sold chocolate confectionery on warm, sunny days. Shell-shocked, she buried her mother and father and sold the old house and the bakery. Stung by recollections of her parents and her idyllic childhood, she broke down. Amidst muffled moans, it hit her hard that she was an only child, alone to carry a legacy both proud and painful, alone to bemoan, alone to keep memories.

KISHAN SINGH

Han-Gan's cough reached the shuddering-in-the-cold Kishan before he did. Han-Gan asked Kishan where he had planned on going if it wasn't for him. Kishan replied that he would have tried to find a warm nook under the tall trees.

Han-Gan laughed. "Those tall trees are the redwoods. There are no warm nooks under those trees! The nights here are freezing cold. I'll take you home with me."

"Do you live close by?" Kishan asked.

"Close enough," Han-Gan replied. Turned out, close enough was over an hour of walking through dark paths lined with thick grass, shrubs and tall trees, geese honking loudly in the wild. A gust of cold wind hit Kishan. Trembling, he held his sacks close to keep the icy wind out. By the time they made it to Han-Gan's room, Kishan was cold as clay. Han-Gan unlocked the room and lit a lamp. There was a bed, a chair and a little stove in a corner. A few other things — a mat, two towels, a blanket, some clothes and groceries were spread across the room.

Han-Gan brought Kishan nectarines on a plate. "They are from the tree outside my room," he said.

Kishan picked up a nectarine. Even the fruit in California was golden. He bit into it and smiled. The nectarine was divine, zesty, sweet and juicy.

When Han-Gan asked him to take the bed, Kishan insisted that he would be just fine on the floor, but Han-Gan wouldn't give in. Turning out the lamp, he spread out on the mat. Kishan lay down on the bed. It felt strange. He was in a foreign land, lying next to a seventeen-year-old from another part of the world and yet while everything was alien, there were a few things he had in common with Han-Gan — his uprooted state, his halting English, and his hopes for the future.

Han-Gan began telling Kishan about his bachelor uncle, a businessman from Shanghai who would be coming to California soon. "My uncle will be bringing in a lot of money," Han-Gan said. "Together, we will set up a store."

Kishan wished him luck. He wanted to continue talking to Han-Gan, but sleep overcame him. When he woke up the next morning, Han-Gan handed him a towel. Washing up in a corner of the room, Kishan walked into the open and saw the luminous sun rise over the San Francisco coastline. In a flash, he saw the sun rising in Noor Mahal, the roosters roosting and Baldev Mama shouting to his boys to get going. But before Kishan could fully take in that vision, it evaporated into the autumn breeze.

As they started back for the Immigration Station, Han-Gan kept coughing, often stopping to spit.

Soon they were back in the kitchen taking orders from the fat cook and preparing meals. Kishan was glad when Jaspal stopped by for a bit in the late evening. "Kishan, the next batch of approved papers would be released tomorrow morning in the dining room. We will take off right after for San Francisco and from there on a stagecoach to Sacramento Valley," Jaspal said.

Jaspal's unwavering belief that he would be able to leave the next day gave Kishan the jitters. As much as he wanted that belief to come true, he feared that it might not. That night as he walked back through the darkness with Han-Gan towards his rented room, Kishan was overrun with anxiety. What if the officer didn't call out Jaspal's name the next morning? A torrent of sweat rolled down his forehead as the incessantly coughing Han-Gan shivered in the cold.

Again, Han-Gan offered Kishan his bed. Again, Kishan told him that he would be fine sleeping on the floor, but Han-Gan refused to budge from the mat. Turning out the lamp, Han-Gan said he and his uncle hoped to sell woollen clothes in San Francisco.

"That's nice," Kishan said. Then suddenly, as though carried away by an impulse, he asked, "Have you been sick for long?"

Han-Gan was quiet for a long while. Kishan wished he hadn't asked that question. A loud sob broke the unnerving silence, followed soon after by wailing. Kishan was thrown off. Pulling out of bed and walking over to the prostrate Han-Gan, he asked, "What is it? If I can help, I'll not hesitate to do so."

Han-Gan continued to cry. Having dropped all defences, he seemed utterly vulnerable. "I am sick, very sick," he said. "Some days, I cough up blood. I came here to hit it big, but cough gripped me as soon as I landed and it refuses to go. When my uncle comes, he will take me to the doctor. Maybe it's tuberculosis?" He let out another sob, this time louder.

Kishan was sad. He would have never imagined that the smiling Han-Gan carried on his heart such a load of pain and fear. "When is this uncle arriving anyway?" he asked.

Han-Gan wiped his face. "A relative in San Francisco said my uncle is winding up business and would be coming by shortly. I wonder what shortly means," he said.

His grief tugged at Kishan's heart. Even though he did not understand Han-Gan fully or get the nuances in his speech, Kishan realised that night that there were many anguished souls in the world. "Han-Gan, write to your uncle and find out his plans. Then chalk out your path. But first, you must go see the doctor. If you can't go by yourself, I will go with you," Kishan said.

"I will go soon," Han-Gan whispered.

Returning to bed, Kishan continued looking at the puny Han-Gan in the dark until Han-Gan nestled himself to sleep. In Han-Gan's generously offering his bed to a stranger as he stretched his sick self on the floor, Kishan sensed affection that transcends language, race and nationality. Reclining on the bed, he thought of how Han-Gan's struggle spoke of the fortitude of the millions of immigrants who broke away from the familiar to seek a braver future in America. Was the journey worth the struggle? he wondered.

At the Immigration Station the next morning, the immigration officer began reading names from the release list immediately after breakfast. When several names were called out and he didn't hear Jaspal's, Kishan's heart hammered loudly in his head. Jaspal was standing next to him but they did not look at each other. And when the officer said, "Jaspal Singh Dhillon," Kishan grabbed his pounding forehead. He felt a hand on his shoulder. Turning around, he saw Jaspal holding his papers and sacks, ready to go.

"Kishan, must you make everything so dramatic?" Jaspal laughed.

Kishan embraced Jaspal. Together they would soon be farming the most captivating land in the world that sat waiting to be tilled.

Kishan collected the money that he had earned from the Administrator's office and told Jaspal that he had a goodbye to say. He found Han-Gan waiting for him in the kitchen, his eyes moist. Grabbing Han-Gan's sallow hand, Kishan thanked him and slipped the money into his palm saying, "Go see the doctor soon."

Han-Gan looked at the money. "I don't need this," he said. "I have money to see the doctor and don't you go thanking me. I am glad that you came to stay." He put the money back into Kishan's hand.

Kishan thought fast about what he could present to Han-Gan. He had three books but those were in Hindi. Just then he knew. He pulled off the kara from his wrist and slipped it on Han-Gan's saying, "This comes with the blessings of our fearless Guru Gobind Singh. It will sail you through every ordeal."

Han-Gan felt the sparkling iron bracelet. "Thank you," he whispered, flashing a wide smile at Kishan. That smile came to be imprinted across Kishan's heart. Han-Gan was the first friend that he had made in America.

"We will earn a few dollars doing an odd job or two in San Francisco and then take the stagecoach to Walnut Grove in Sacramento Valley in the evening," Jaspal told Kishan. "As many as two hundred Punjabis work in the fields by Walnut Grove. The Punjabi bossman there will help us find work." Jaspal had hatched up the plan after elaborately discussing details with the Punjabi detainees at Angel Island. In the face of an uncertain fate, they had gladly passed on their dreams to him.

A ferry streamed them to San Francisco. Three Anglo women were riding the ferry with them. They were baffled. Kishan knew it was his and Jaspal's dark skin, clothes and speech that made them stand out. It could also be the curious way that they were both looking around as though they had just started learning to see. The ferryman knew that Kishan and Jaspal were fresh off the boat. Smiling, he pointed out the landmarks in the distance. Nothing rang a bell. Kishan and Jaspal hadn't heard of Alcatraz Island. They hadn't the slightest notion of the Fisherman's Wharf. The luminous Sierra Nevada was just another range of steep mountains and the beaches seemed mere stretches of blue along the squiggly coastline.

Stepping off the ferry, they stared at San Francisco. Swift carriages as well as cars were rolling down busy streets lined with stores selling fruits, snacks, clothes and other goods. Tall buildings dazzled around them. Villagers from faraway Punjab, they were at once zapped and thrilled to be in one of the world's largest cities with a population of half a million. So captivating were the sights that Kishan wanted to sit cross-legged on the pavement and watch. But remembering the stagecoach fare, he began walking quickly by Jaspal's side, looking for work.

They saw workmen at a construction site. Jaspal asked them if they needed a hand but the workmen waved them on. Farther ahead, fruit sellers hadn't any work for them either but guiding them to the city centre, the fruit sellers said that they were sure to find some work there. At the city centre, a truck was dropping supplies at what looked like a grocery store. When Jaspal asked if they needed help, the shopkeeper gesticulated that he could use one person. As Jaspal started carrying the items from the truck to the store, Kishan began walking farther down the street in search of work. Golden-haired women in long, flowing dresses and fancy hats strolled by. Schoolgirls wearing frocks and laced boots walked happily alongside red-cheeked boys in shorts and bright sweaters. Up ahead, trolleys were speeding past. Kishan liked the sound that they made — like the ringing of a bell. Then he saw a soaring building at the corner of the street. The sign on it read Palace Hotel. Three box-laden wagons stood in front of it. A uniformed employee was carrying the boxes inside. Mustering confidence, Kishan walked up to the man. "Do you need help carrying the boxes?" he asked.

The employee looked at him curiously, then nodded. Settings his sacks in a corner, Kishan began carrying the boxes one on top of the other like the employee was doing and stacking them in a large storage room.

Carrying the last of the boxes, Kishan saw that the sun was going down, leaving orange streaks across the darkening sky. Grabbing his sacks, he walked to the main hall to collect his wages. Bright flowers, stately paintings and gorgeous silk carpets adorned the room. When an employee came along and handed him two dollars, Kishan was stunned. It was far more than what he was expecting. Walking out of the hall, he saw a straw-haired uniformed girl push a cart of fruits and cakes across the room. Kishan couldn't pull his eyes off the cart, not only because he was famished but also because the sumptuous food held out promise of all things better and beautiful.

Jaspal stood waiting for him by the grocery store. After helping with the inventory there, he said he had swept and mopped a barber's shop and a confectionery, making two dollars. He was thrilled to learn that Kishan had made two dollars as well. The four dollars added to Kishan's wages from Angel Island would give them more than the stagecoach fare. They sprinted to scramble onto one.

SOPHIA

Sophia's life in Guadalajara moved along in a somewhat stunted, hushed manner through the turbulent days of unrest in Mexico. In 1917, when President Carranza came to power with support from the United States, Sophia and Giovanni rejoiced at the change for the better. The grim-faced bearded patriarch would pull Mexico out of the quagmire of violence and unrest. Giovanni was thankful for not having lost his job with the change of government. The days following President Carranza's appointment were promising. Mexico maintained neutrality through the World War, focusing on stabilising and rebuilding the country, aspiring for peace and progress. Social and agrarian reforms were implemented. The Mexican constitution was formulated, granting rights to workers, peasants, and women, promising all the things that the Mexicans had been fighting for over the years. Things were beginning to look up for the civil-war ravaged country.

Stepping into the backyard one Sunday on a late November day in 1919, Sophia saw scintillating sunbeams peering through the lime trees and the orchid shrubs. Feeling a gush of euphoria, she ran to smell the gardenias, and soak up the hope that hung in the air. The twins were turning twelve the following week; she decided to bake a big chocolate-laced cake and buy the twins as well as Isabel, new clothes and toys. Christmas was around the corner. Toys would make the children very happy. It had been long since they had new clothes or toys. Throwing some pesos in her purse, she clutched Isabel's hand and took off for the zócalo, bidding a quick bye to her husband and the twins who were playing Catch on the patio. At a boutique by the cathedral, she bought pieces of vibrant, red pottery and yellow paper flowers for the house. Then she bought Isabel a doll with ocean-blue eyes. Isabel had just turned eleven and though outwardly she looked more like a young girl than a little one, over five-feet tall, her thick brown hair reaching her waist, she could hardly keep her hands off the doll. Never before had Isabel had a machine-made doll. Many girls from her school played with dolls like those. Delighted to finally own one, Isabel stared at the doll's crystal eyes, touched her curly eyelashes and stroked her golden hair.

Seeing Isabel happy, Sophia was glowing too. Fidgeting around the store, she bought blue-and-white sailor suits for the twins and had them wrapped in glossy paper. Then spotting a toy train set, she asked to try it.

"It is a craze with all little boys in town," the store owner said, placing the train set in front of Sophia.

She pressed a tiny button and watched enraptured as miniature trains began chugging on shiny silver tracks, whistling and puffing. She knew at once that the twins would drool over that train set, so she bought it right away. Mother and daughter stepped out into the plaza. Mariachis were playing music in the zócalo, their neatly fitted charro outfits and wide hats sparkling in the late evening sun. Looking around, Sophia spotted a man selling pomegranates and guavas and bought a dozen each. The shopping being done, she throbbed with excitement. Finally, tranquillity had graced Mexico. On reaching home, she thought she would first fry fish for the children and then sip tequila with her husband. Unmindful of the wallows of white dust swirling in the sky, Sophia and Isabel began walking back home.

KISHAN SINGH

The stagecoach screeched to a halt. It was large and beautiful, pulled up by six extraordinarily handsome horses. The fare to sit in the back was two dollars for a one-way ticket. Handing the fare to the driver, Kishan and Jaspal hopped on. Two Chinese workers came and sat across from them and a petite Anglo lady took the seat next to them. Just as soon as the stagecoach took off, the Chinese workers began munching on oranges, handing one each to Kishan and Jaspal. Accepting the oranges reluctantly, they gulped them down in seconds. The Anglo woman sensed that they were hungry. She reached into her bag and gave them both a bread roll each, which they devoured like two hungry wolves. Kishan thanked the woman. She nodded and began looking out of the window, not wanting to indulge them further. The stagecoach rolled out of the city into the countryside as Kishan took to admiring the endless stretches of green dotted by creeks and streams. Soon darkness dimmed all the scenes. Knocked out by sleep, the Chinese workers and the Anglo lady began snuffling. Kishan and Jaspal too, lay their heads back, their minds conjuring visions of shady orchards and thriving fields.

After ten tiresome hours, when they jumped off the stagecoach at Walnut Grove the next day, looking around, they were speechless. It was unbelievable. Even though no California landmark had seemed even remotely familiar, the farmland was the same. Flat and beautiful like in Punjab, the fields just as luscious, the River Sacramento serene and beautiful as the River Satluj and the way the waters ran through canals to feed the fields was exactly how they'd watered the crops back home. All at once, they fell in love with the California farmland, completely and frantically, and they knew that soon the land would love them too. The land always loved its tillers back.

Japanese farmhands were bending over the fields and singing as they picked weeds and dispensed fertilisers. Kishan asked one of them about Punjabi crews that worked in the area. The man looked them over from head to toe. "Some crews are picking vegetables on a farm farther up," the Japanese man said, pointing them towards vegetable fields in the distance. "Just follow the path, it will take you there."

Kishan and Jaspal took off, gazing in amazement at the immaculately sown fields around them with saplings planted at equal distances. Kishan spotted Sikh farmhands in the distance, their turbans setting them apart from the others. They ran and greeted their landsmen, who in turn shrieked upon seeing them. Just then a sharp whistle blew, cutting the meeting short. Someone said it was the bossman. Kishan turned around. A well-built, middle-aged, clean-shaven Punjabi man was shouting to the farmhands to get back to work.

Kishan and Jaspal greeted the grim-faced bossman most politely and asked for work.

The bossman had deep-set eyes. "My name is Arjan Singh," he said. "I came to California in 1900. Much of the California farmland was forest then."

Awestruck, Kishan and Jaspal smiled.

Arjan Singh didn't smile back. Getting down to business he said, "If people come to work the fields, they must work hard. This work is no easier than working on the railroads."

"Farm work is all we know, having done it all our lives," Jaspal said. "We will put our hearts and minds to it."

Arjan Singh pushed back his sparse curly hair. Wincing, he laid down the terms: he would claim a fourth of the money that the two of them would make each month. Kishan and Jaspal nodded.

Finally, Arjan Singh let out a smile. "I'll ask the men to take you both to the boarding house tonight and tomorrow, come and cut asparagus. Next, I will find you work on orchards. You are lucky; due to the Great War, California farms are busy supplying produce to Britain and France, and farmhands are in demand."

Kishan and Jaspal thanked Arjan Singh and began waiting by the fields for the Punjabi men to finish the day's work and take them to the boarding house.

The Punjabis who worked the California farmland comprised Sikhs, Hindus and Muslims, the majority being Sikhs. Walking Kishan and Jaspal to the boarding house, the farmhands shared that the Anglos did not understand the religious distinction. Confusing the word Hindu for Indian, the Anglos incorrectly referred to all Indians as "Hindus." To them, everyone who hailed from Hindustan was a "Hindu."

Reaching the boarding house, they led Kishan and Jaspal into a large room with rows of beds. Barely had they sat down on a bed that all the Punjabi men in the boarding house gathered around them, sharing their travails on farms across California's Central Valley. Many of them had been labouring on farms in the area for almost a decade, living in boarding houses as they moved about. "Like Punjab, California is a fertile haven — an inviting land of abundance. Everything grows here: grains, juicy fruits like peaches, grapes, oranges as also colourful vegetables like carrots, peas and sugar beets. Heaven on earth is what California is. And like Punjab, five rivers run around the area — Feather, American, Sacramento, Bear and Yuba," Man Singh, an exuberant man in his thirties said.

Kishan smiled on hearing about the five rivers that ran in the vicinity, sensing a deep bonding with the land. They had chicken curry, roti and daal in the dining area where Man Singh filled them in about life in the boarding house. Every morning the men split in groups, making tea and breakfast and packing the left-over dinner of roti, chicken curry and daal for lunch. Then returning from the fields in the evening, they began cooking again. "It is a good life, as good as it can get," Man Singh said.

Some Sikh men at the boarding house wore turbans all the time while others forwent wearing turbans to the fields, choosing instead to wear large sunhats. The following morning, taking a cue from the latter, Kishan and Jaspal threw on borrowed sunhats, trousers and shirts and started off for the fields.

From that day on, there was no looking back. Taking to the fields with vigour, they began labouring across farms, working their way through the dirt and manure, month after month — boxing vegetables, chopping wood, digging potatoes and sweltering in the wheat fields, the orchards and the vineyards. The hard, exhausting work left them with aches and pains, with calloused hands and bruised elbows and knees. It was best to make friends with hope, Kishan told Jaspal. It could pave their way to their dream of owning a piece of land. Besides, there was a joy in watching crops grow, in producing food that would feed men, women and children in places far and near. With the World War raging across Europe, the Allies looked upon America to keep them going. Rising to the challenge, California farms were booming. Throngs of tractors, trucks and combine harvesters zipped about the countryside. Abandoning their bewildered-in-the-new-land looks, Kishan and Jaspal, too, began pulling wheat drills and combine harvesters on sleek tractors across the endless California farmland, the blue sky above them tinted with the yellow and gold of the flaming sun. The new land was replete with astounding colours, each more enrapturing than the other.

SOPHIA

Barely had Sophia and Isabel walked a few feet from the zócalo when a policeman asked them to step onto the side of the road and join a crowd.

"Rebels have raided the south of the city and according to the Administrator's orders, people headed that way have to spend the night inside the cathedral," the policemen said.

The crowd grumbled.

"It is for your safety that you wait till the rebels are curbed," the policeman roared.

A ruffled Sophia and a baffled Isabel with the golden-haired doll in her hand followed a restless crowd as the loud officer guided them inside the dark cathedral. Reclining in a cold nook with Isabel, Sophia shivered, anxiety swirling through her mind like an unruly river. She worried for Giovanni and the boys but didn't utter a word of dismay for fear of frightening Isabel who had already been reduced to a dazed silence by the sudden events of the evening. Caressing her daughter's hair and kissing her softly, Sophia took to thinking. Riots could turn cities upside down. Again, she worried for the safety of her sons and husband but pushing fear aside, she told herself that the riots couldn't possibly impact the government encampment, where their house stood, guarded as the encampment was by armed men. Pulling Isabel closer, she looked at her daughter's face. Bowed down by fear, hunger and sleep, Isabel was looking around with listless eyes. Sophia handed her daughter a guava. "When your school closes for summer, your father and I will take you and the boys to the shrine of Our Lady of Guadalupe in Mexico City," Sophia told Isabel, trying to steer the little girl's mind away from panic. Snuggling with her mother, Isabel nodded and bit into the guava.

As soon as the sun rose the next morning, vendors from the plaza came to offer food to the stranded, hungry and tired people inside the cathedral. Though Sophia fed Isabel a few bites, she couldn't bring a morsel to her mouth. Her heart beat loud and a dreadful shiver came to jolt and shake her as soon as she thought of her husband and sons. Soon a police officer came and let the people out. "Be watchful as you head home. The riots of the previous evening have ended in unimaginable loss of life and property," the officer said.

Gathering her shopping bags, Sophia walked out of the cathedral with Isabel, the officer's words ringing loudly in her mind. Clasping Isabel's hand, she began walking faster. They were a few feet from the encampment when she saw a crowd gathered in front of it. Sophia and Isabel ran past the crowd to their house. They saw uniformed officers standing by the door. Stepping in, Sophia looked around. The house was ransacked, and the furniture broken. Bullet-punched holes marred the walls. Numb and groggy, she walked on, one hand holding Isabel's and the other the shopping bags.

When she saw three bodies lined up on the floor of the living room, Sophia let out a wail, releasing Isabel's hand and the bags. The red pottery crashed with a thud, splattering over the floor like gushing blood, and two toy trains zoomed across the living room into oblivion. Sophia fell to the floor in a heap.

KISHAN SINGH

On a biting cold March morning in 1917, Kishan and Jaspal jumped into the back of a red Ford oak-bodied truck headed for Stockton to pray at the gurudwara there. Joining scores of Sikh men in paying obeisance, Kishan liked the calm that spread across the building, the singing of the hymns soothing his mind and senses. After the services, as they sat eating langar, they began conversing with Harbans Singh, a middle-aged, stout man with friendly eyes who by hard work, pinching pennies and intelligent networking had come to own three restaurants in and around Yuba City. His affability drew Kishan and Jaspal to him instinctively. He, too, seemed drawn to their simplicity and ingenuousness, offering to drive them around and acquaint them with the area in his Chevrolet Baby Grand.

Kishan and Jaspal thanked him profusely. Lodged in the back seat, Kishan couldn't take his eyes off the pretty green car as it rolled down country roads along swanky vegetable farms, honking at farmers on horsebacks. Kishan's fascination for the car was not lost on Harbans. "Driving the Chevy is no different from driving a tractor. Why, you may try driving it if you so like," he offered, pulling the car to the side.

Kishan switched places with him. Pushing the pedal, he began driving slowly as a sprightly wind came to stroke his face. Indeed, driving a car was no different from driving a tractor, except the car could run much faster than the tractor, tendering a far smoother ride. Springing along fields, farmhouses and meadows, they drove to the post office where Harbans helped Kishan mail money to the Lala in Jalandhar after which, they stopped at Harbans's restaurant. Sipping tea from dainty floral motif porcelain tea-cups that they could hardly resist taking their eyes off, Kishan and Jaspal shared with Harbans their aspiration of being able to buy a farm one day. Immediately, Harbans offered to help them set up a bank account and show them ways that could fetch them the most interest on their savings. "Stay clear of the Punjabis who squander their earnings on liquor," Harbans warned. "Work hard, save religiously and live by the laws of the land. That alone will lead you to your goal."

Inspired by Harbans's example and remembering his advice, Kishan and Jaspal continued working through the heat and the cold, bumping and falling only to get up and start sowing grains, packing vegetables and picking fruits again. To get a feel of the country's pulse, Kishan buried his face in the newspaper every chance he got, eagerly reading about President Woodrow Wilson's agricultural initiatives, and Jaspal perpetually asked Kishan to teach him new and smart Americanisms which he loved to throw at the many Punjabi bossmen they met along their way. If ever a bossman said that the only work that he could offer them was to dig potatoes on farms down in Santa Clara Valley, shaking his head, Jaspal would say, "Tell it to Sweeney." And if on a favourable day, the bossman gave them work on vineyards or orchards in San Joaquin Valley, Jaspal would exclaim, "That sounds like berries to me!" The expressions left the Punjabi bossmen confused sending Kishan and Jaspal smirking. Befriending the sweeping California farmland, they went sowing and reaping in the green valleys of wonder and abundance, some days feeling more stimulated than on others.

All the Punjabi bossmen that they encountered were the same — rude and hostile. Only their names were different. In Kishan's mind, their selfish, domineering ways blended, and he began referring to them all as Arjan Singh.

The summer of 1920 flew in with promise. The farms were overflowing with strawberries, peaches, plums and apricots. Round red tomatoes peeked through the vines, streaming the long, colourful days with melody. Kishan and Jaspal's arms, legs and chests were more muscular than before, their sunburnt faces telling of the everyday struggles of farmhands. The end of the World War brought a bounty of opportunities. Back from the front, many American men were not interested in working the fields, choosing instead to work in factories in nearby towns and cities. Kishan and Jaspal embraced the abundance of jobs on the farms with gusto, aspiring to pave their way to their dream by sweat and toil. The only respite from the long working days was the occasional trip to Yuba City. Besides spending time with Harbans there, Kishan looked forward to meeting the Punjabi students from the University of California, Berkeley who gathered often at Harbans's restaurant, befriending a tall, young man with chiselled features and sharp eyes, Jeet Singh. He was a member of the Ghadar Party, an Indian political organisation in California striving to free India from British rule. Inspired by the great Indian patriot and poet, Kartar Singh Sarabha, who had also been a student at Berkeley, Jeet Singh sang Sarabha's poems with ardour.

I am a particle of ravaged India's ruins
This is the only name I have
The only hallmark, the only address.

Jeet Singh's fire kindled Kishan's enthusiasm. "Until India reels under slavery, there is no way that her people will be treated as equal citizens in their adopted homeland, America," he told Jeet Singh and began contributing money to the Ghadar Party's cause.

One windy morning, when Jeet Singh showed Kishan around the University of California, Berkeley, Kishan thought everything about the university was fascinating — the Classical buildings, the smell of books, but most of all, he was mesmerised by the ideas that meandered through its halls — of science and philosophy, of rebellion and freedom. "Kishan, you belonged in Berkeley too," Jeet Singh said. "Why, Jaspal told me that you were an outstanding student."

Kishan smiled. Letters from India had intimated him about his exceptional high school scores, but he hadn't mulled over them. "I am happy doing what God intended of me — tilling his most favourite land, California, where a resolute farmer can grow anything that the earth stands to offer man," he replied.

Nodding, Jeet Singh encouraged Kishan to visit the Elk Grove Public library and read something other than a newspaper. Kishan jumped at the suggestion. Taking the motor bus to Elk Grove the following week, he was dazed on seeing so many books in one place. Filling out a form, he got a library card and decided to borrow a novel but wasn't quite sure where to look. The front desk man asked him to consult with the Assistant Librarian. "She is arranging books in the far corner," he said.

Kishan walked over to the young lady who was kneeling on the floor, a stack of books by her side. She was twenty something years old. Pushing back her thick red hair, she got up, straightened her green dress and introduced herself as Amy McCarthy. Kishan noticed that she was tall and had strong, muscular legs. There were brown dots on her cheeks, the same brown as her eyes. He wondered about the dots and then he remembered. They were called freckles.

Shaking her hand, he said, "Hello, I am Kishan Singh." Her hand felt soft against his calloused one. She looked at him and smiled, shaking his hand firmly. He told her that he was an immigrant from India and needed help in picking out a novel.

"I am glad to help," she said, leading him towards the Literature aisle. "Maybe you will like *Moby Dick*?" she said. "It's about a big whale and a man."

"A man and a whale! Sure, I will borrow that one."

She knew exactly where the book sat and pulled it out. It was a beautifully bound brown book, the title imprinted across the front in golden letters. "When you've read it, tell me if you liked it," she said, issuing the book on his card.

He nodded.

"Do you hope to read English at a college someday," she asked.

"No, I am a farmhand. I hope to be a farmer someday," he said.

A big smile lit up her face. "Do you work close by?" she asked.

"I work on farms around Marysville, Vacaville, and Sacramento. Pretty much everywhere in the Central Valley," he said.

"You are a busy man, Kish'aan!" she exclaimed.

"Kish-an," he said, correcting her.

"Oh, is that how you say it, Kish-an?"

"Yes," he replied. "And yes, it is busy. But once my brother Jaspal and I buy a farm, we wouldn't be moving around so much." Her keen eyes and friendly demeanour were encouraging, making him spontaneously share his dream with her.

Kishan read *Moby Dick* slowly, intensely, several afternoons in a row upon returning from the fields. It unleashed an astounding tale about the mysterious sea, an obsessive man, a fabulous beast, at once demonic and sacred and a dissimilar yet deeply connected world. It was a strange story about life and the inevitability of death, about anguished men in search of themselves. This was perhaps what America was about — a still evolving mythology, a diverse reality so in contrast to India which had a mythology as old as the Himalayas.

When he met Amy the following week, kneeling on the floor, where she was organising books, the first thing he told her was, "*Moby Dick* makes a good story. Though it tells of a voyage to death, on finishing it, one is reflective but not sad. Perhaps you could pick out another novel for me."

"Sure, how about trying a woman writer?" she asked.

"Okay," he said, shrugging his shoulders.

She walked to the Literature aisle and returned with a tiny book. Issuing it on his card, she handed it to him.

Thanking her, he looked at the book. It was called *The Awakening*. "I'll be sure to tell you what I thought of it," he said. Waving her goodbye, he was about to walk out when she started walking by him, following him into the patio outside. "Tell me what's happening on the farms?" she asked.

"I am cutting and packing asparagus," he replied. He was surprised that she was interested in the farms, in him.

"I wanted to tell you something; I grew up on a farm in Tulare County," she said suddenly.

That explains those tough legs, he thought immediately. He was familiar with Tulare County, having picked fruits there. "What kind of farm?" he asked.

"A vineyard. My family grows Thompson grapes. Have you had those? They are green and stout. They make the best raisins," she said blushing. "My grandfather began growing them. He was friends with Farmer Thompson himself, the one after whom the grapes are named."

Kishan smiled. She had summed up so much in a few lines — history, raisin making and a romantic childhood. "Do you go back often?" he asked.

"As often as I can. I had thought I would teach at a school in Tulare County and live on the vineyard forever. But one September, I came down with severe asthma. Dust from the farms can trigger asthma, the doctor said. So, I came to the city and became a librarian instead," she said. "The asthma doesn't bother me much here."

"I have picked grapes in Tulare County," Kishan said recalling the mirthful smell of ripe grapes on sunny mornings, swarms of bees hissing over them.

"When you buy a farm, what will you grow?" she asked.

"Vegetables and grains. Some melons perhaps. And dreams," he replied.

"You are a dreamer!" she laughed. Waving to him, she started walking back to the library.

He wanted to follow her and tell her that his dreams were the colours of spring greens, ripe barley, plums, peaches and apricots, that he dreamed of swimming across the sparkling American River on a bright orange afternoon and that he wanted to drive a tractor through the emerald fields to the rims of the red California sunset. But he didn't for fear that she'd think he was mad and began walking to the bus stop instead. Along the way, he stopped. It was unbelievable. He was grinning again after so long. Pushing away stray hair from his forehead, he ran to catch the motor bus that stood waiting at the corner.

SOPHIA

The twins were buried in their new white-and-blue sailor suits alongside their father. The priest told Sophia that Jesus Himself had received the little boys who were waiting to receive communion. No explanation did anything for Sophia. She pined for her boys, yearning for their touch, their kisses, their senseless chatter, their incessant laughing. Deliriously, she began talking to her dead husband, detailing the happenings of their wedding day. Recalling her marriage vows, she cursed the rebels, shouting that it was not death, but murder that had parted Giovanni and her. In the next instance, she loudly cursed Giovanni as well for breaking promises, for betraying her, for leaving her behind in a world stripped of hope. Life had taken an unthought of, undreamt of abysmal turn. Thunder, lightning and convulsion had come raging in to shatter the lull and her little world had become the centre of that seething storm. The deadliest of storms was always the hardest to foretell.

Love had led Sophia far away from her hometown. It had also devastated her. She had been blighted on suddenly losing her parents but had somehow come to believe that her little realm in Guadalajara was safe, held together by an invincible God, never to shake or crack. How she had been proved wrong, startled and jerked out of that belief. The ground that she stood on had devoured her husband and her sons without caution or warning. Nothing was forever. Except grief. It refused to go, sucking her further and further into its folds. Her grief like her love was deep. She cried till she had no more tears left to cry. Then a deafening silence overtook her.

"Mama, say something. Please say something," Isabel said, shaking her mother.

Sophia gazed at her beautiful daughter. Walking along a flowering meadow, they had hit a mountain of adversity.

Crying or quietening couldn't move that mountain. They must climb it and cross over. Together. For each other's sake and their own.

"Mama, are you okay?" a terrified Isabel shook her again.

"I'm okay, I am fine," Sophia said. "I'm here. For you. You needn't ever be afraid," she got up and held Isabel in her arms. Life had let her down, but she wouldn't ever let her precious daughter down. She would stand by her Isabel through everything, protect and nurture her through rainy days and misty nights.

An officer who had been a friend of Giovanni came to see them. "Rebels are venting anger at President Carranza due to the growing economic inequality," he said. To defy the Carranza government, rebels had attacked the government encampment, shooting first the guards at the entrance. The only survivors from the encampment were the ones who were away. "It would be best that you join your family somewhere," he suggested. "With the rebels breaking wild and the government unstable, that would be the safe thing to do."

It dawned upon Sophia that she had no family to turn to. There was absolutely no one. The long and bloody revolution had gobbled every single person in her family, first her parents, and then her husband and little boys. Stumbling she fell into a chair. Where WOULD they go? Where COULD they go?

"Mama, don't you worry," Isabel said, reaching for her hand. "The Virgin will watch over us."

Feeding off of Isabel's hope, Sophia picked herself up, walked to the closet and took out an old box filled with pictures. Pulling some out, she put them in her purse. Then packing whatever of value remained in the house, she told the officer where she and her daughter would go. Bahía de Kino.

"Bahía de Kino?" the officer asked. "That's a faraway village by the sea. Is there no place close by where you could go first?"

"No, we have nowhere else to go but Bahía de Kino," Sophia replied.

The officer offered to put them on a train to Puerto Vallarta, from where they could board a boat for Bahía de Kino. Sophia asked Isabel if she wanted to take something along. Sifting through the rumble, Isabel picked up her school badge and fastened it to her dress as though to hold on to a happy memory to soothe her irreparable loss.

At the railway station, the officer bought Sophia and Isabel two tickets to Puerto Vallarta. Wishing them well, he slipped some pesos in Sophia's hand. On boarding the train, caught in fright and chaos, Sophia dropped the money. The seven-hour train ride to Puerto Vallarta was nerve wracking, sending Sophia sweating with fright. She thought of how love had come to be replaced by fear in her life. Swimming in the sea of love, she had tasted strength, passion, excitement. Now wallowing in fear, all she saw was a sweeping darkness.

Getting off the train at Puerto Vallarta, Sophia and Isabel made a dash for the port. Reaching there, Sophia removed her ear studs, ring and pendant. Then pulling out a few pieces of jewellery that she had retrieved from her torn-up house, she tried selling the items to the many vendors along the port. But no one would give a decent deal to a confused, breathless woman. Their unkept state was to blame, Sophia thought. She pulled Isabel aside, brushing Isabel's hair and then her own. Dabbing lipstick, she tried selling the jewellery again. After many attempts, quoting strongly and confidently, she managed, barely, the boat fare for two.

Walking towards the boat, Sophia thought about her house in Guadalajara. The gardenia bushes that she had planted in the backyard of the little brick house sprang before her eyes. The bushes stood stark against the fence. She couldn't see any gardenias. She stared harder at that vision but couldn't trace a single flower. There were no butterflies either. How could there be any? A flowerless downcast garden was no place for butterflies. Butterflies went where flowers bloomed, no matter how long the flight or how dangerous the path. She knew that she and Isabel had to travel far to seek out new gardens, to start a new life. The distance to the village by the sea was long. She must brave the journey. To meet the future, she must forget the past and walk firm in the present.

KISHAN SINGH

Kishan thought of Amy all the way home on the motor bus. There was something about the way girls smiled. It promised a perfect world, urging a man to dream and believe. He remembered then how he had entwined his life around a girl's smiles before and suffered. Now Amy's smiles were impelling him to fly once more. Even as a part of him was bouncing with ecstasy, he was afraid to fall in love again, to be happy and desperate again, to be shattered a second time over. But the very next minute, Kishan found himself musing about how Amy had stepped out of the library to tell him that she grew up in the country and that she had loved it there. Now, that was not part of her job. She must like him enough to share that personal detail. He remembered how looking at his face, she had flushed when talking about her childhood, imbuing the air with music. It was a flawless moment. He shook himself. He had no business thinking about a girl again, least of all an Anglo girl. Anti-Miscegenation Laws forbid interracial relations, stating clearly that brown should mingle with brown and white with white. Kishan sighed. If only laws could take his mind off Amy's large brown eyes.

Returning from the fields the following day, he began reading *The Awakening*. He had thought he would read for a while but pulled into the story, he couldn't put the book down. The protagonist of the novel, Edna Pontellier was arresting, eccentric, unpredictable and yet so vulnerable that Kishan fell in love with her. She kept him awake late into the night, carried away as he was by her moods and impulses. He applauded when she learned to swim, when she stopped making pretences and most of all, when coming into her own, she began to make art. He rejoiced in how love gave Edna wings to fly. He ached when her heart broke. Love and heartbreak, though all consuming, made one a stronger artist. Breathlessly, he read on, waiting for Edna to emerge as one but felt let down when instead of pursuing her passion, Edna went adrift, fighting herself and her desires. The end crushed him.

The next week when he walked up to Amy in a new shirt, with slicked back hair and smelling of cologne, she noticed right away. "Kishan, you look so very nice!" she said. "What a dapper shirt! And I like that cologne."

"Thank you," he replied, faking carelessness and handing her back the novel. "*The Awakening* is unforgettable. Edna Pontellier broke my heart. Why, I even dreamt one night that I had pulled her out as she was swimming away to her death," he said.

"Kishan, how deeply must you have internalised the story to dream about it in your sleep," Amy said. After a pause, she asked, "If you'd like to see the State Capitol someday, we could go together."

"Sure," he said. Then remembering the Anti-Miscegenation Laws, he asked, "Would it be okay for you to go with me?"

"It is okay by me," she said smiling. "We can go next Friday. I will take the afternoon off."

"All right," he replied. "I'll see you on Friday afternoon."

Heading home on the motor bus, Kishan recalled how Amy had been so eager at the prospect of showing him around the State Capitol, her smile was wider, she would even be taking the afternoon off to be with him. He mustn't imagine too much, he told himself and peeked out of the window to divert his thoughts. A Harley Davidson zoomed past. He liked those motor bikes. They were large, fast and beautiful. Like leopards. Just then a truck honked. The roads were particularly busy that day. It was amazing all the new things that were now running on the roads — fast cars, trucks, motor buses. He remembered the one time that he had ridden a new inter-city train from Sacramento to San Francisco to meet Han-Gan who now lived in the city with his uncle, where he was being treated for tuberculosis. The ride had glided like a fast-paced dream — smooth and speedy as he had sat on a cushy berth looking out of the window. Then thinking of Friday, of being around Amy, he smiled. It felt as though the glint from Roop's eyes had come to settle in Amy's, igniting his world again.

When Friday came, he ran into the library and looked around. He felt a tap on his elbow. He turned. Amy was striking in a dark green dress. "I'm ready," she said, tugging the strap of her black purse.

On the motor bus, he noticed that people were staring at them with disapproving eyes. Something told him that the well-meaning trip to the State Capitol was far from prudent.

"Kishan, the State Capitol houses brilliant art," Amy said as they stepped out of the bus. "The paintings, sculptures and murals inside it tell of California's story from the arrival of the Spanish all the way up to the historic Gold Rush."

Kishan stared at the State Capitol in the distance. The golden ball atop the Capitol's dome blazed in glory. Two Anglo men in jeans walked up to them. One of them was wearing a wrinkled red shirt and the other large, dark sunglasses. Stepping closer, the latter looked first at Kishan and then at Amy and then at Kishan again. "What are you doing roaming around town with her?" he asked Kishan, taking off his sunglasses.

Kishan juddered and stopped.

"Yes, I am talking to you. You have no business walking around town with an Anglo girl," the man snapped.

"Mister, you mind your own business," Amy said.

"Miss, do you not understand? He is dirty and brown."

One blow would knock his front teeth out, Kishan thought but remembered in time that in the new land, a man must keep his head else he would be lost forever. He had known that this could happen but had let the excitement of being around Amy manipulate him and here they were, an inch away from a racial riot. Looking straight at the man, he said, "You are right, I have no business being around her. We will take separate buses and go home."

He gestured to Amy to turn back. But instead of turning around, Amy stepped closer to the two men. Raising her pointer finger, she said, "Who are you to decide who roams around with whom? We came to see the Capitol and we will not return without seeing it."

"In that case, we are here to show you around the building," the man in the scruffy red shirt said, laughing. "Let the curry muncher go."

"Stop the nonsense and get out of our way," Amy said.

Kishan looked at the scornful men, their faces full of guile and intolerance. Then he gazed at Amy's brave eyes radiating with belief and camaraderie. The men and Amy stood for two opposing white factions against the backdrop of the historic State Capitol, the golden ball of opportunity for all searing on top of the magnificent dome. He turned to Amy, his resolute eyes conveying that she and he must leave immediately. Quickly, they began walking back towards the motor bus stop.

"Kishan, you know that it is a free land. Anybody can go anywhere," Amy said as they neared the motor bus stop.

"Yes," Kishan replied. "Anybody can go anywhere but not with just about anyone."

"That's not true," she started to explain.

"Amy, it is," Kishan cut her short. "Why, there are Anti-Miscegenation Laws in place. We should never have violated rules." His forehead creased. Talking of discrimination in the land of freedom felt shameful.

"Kishan, there are no laws that forbid friendship. And the Anti-Miscegenation Laws will be revoked too. It is only a matter of time."

A motor bus drove in. "Perhaps, you should take that one," he said, waving to her.

"I will see you soon," she said, waving back.

She walked to the bus and got on, sitting in the back by the window. Waiting for the next bus under a tree, he kept looking at her. When the bus took off, she waved at him again. He was about to wave back when a line of trucks came along, blocking the bus completely.

Lying in his bed at the boarding house that night, Kishan thought of how different his world was from Amy's. It was nice of her to let him into hers even if for a bit. He was glad to be offered a glimpse of the other side, of beauty, of knowledge, of history and hopes. Reality, however, was not as accepting of him as Amy's smiles. He had been so happy at the thought of visiting the State Capitol, but even before he could step into it, the disdainful men had taken a stab at that happiness. He must forget that he even came close to visiting the State Capitol. He must stay true to his world, to the fields, to saving money and buying a farm.

The next morning, he gave his new shirt to a young farmhand and announced that his large bottle of cologne was for everyone in the boarding house to use. He even put the hair gel away. What use was it to a farmhand who bent over and toiled in the soil all day long?

When he went to the library a week later, he tried to keep the talk with Amy matter-of-fact. She didn't mention the trip to downtown either. She continued to smile though. He had no business being beguiled by her smiles, not any more. Toughening to them, he remembered how he had been shown his place in front of the State Capitol. The very next minute, however, he hoped that Amy would always continue smiling. He liked it that she was always hopeful of what the world had to offer to her and to others. He wouldn't obsess about her, but he could share that happy hope. It would do him good, keep him moving.

SOPHIA

Sitting on the boat's deck, Sophia stared at the tall mountains and the blue water. Puerto Vallarta was achingly remindful of Acapulco. Frolicking through a divine girlhood surrounded by a loving family in Acapulco, she had come to be submerged in bottomless grief along the coast of Puerto Vallarta, devoid of family and home. As fatal as that truth was, she didn't let it punch her. Dry-eyed, she kept looking ahead as the boat began whisking the water, the coast slowly disappearing behind her. A tired and sleepy Isabel leaned against her mother. "Mama, will Uncle Milano know us when he sees us at Bahía de Kino?" Isabel asked softly.

"I hope so," Sophia replied. Never once had she seen her husband's brother Milano. She knew of him only through Giovanni's conversations about his brother. Would Milano step up to take them in? Would he help them to sail across the ocean of disaster that had come to flood their lives? Nothing seemed certain anymore, but the last thing she wanted was for her daughter to be anxious. She smiled reassuringly at Isabel. Just then her gaze caught Isabel's half-closed eyes. In a spark, she recalled that she had not fed Isabel even a bite since boarding the train to Puerto Vallarta that morning. Sophia trembled. Leaving Isabel on the deck, she rushed to the boat's cabin. With the few coins that she had on her, she bought tortillas and fed them to Isabel, who slipped into a delirious slumber.

Fear shook Sophia. It would be four days before they would reach Bahía de Kino. How would she feed her child until then without a peso in her pocket? Around her, the poor and destitute huddled on the dock, their eyes breathing disbelief and distrust. Where she hoped to catch a glimpse of compassion, all she saw was listless indifference. Unknown the faces were but unmistakably similar to hers, reeking of annihilation, stripped of

174 The Rainbow Acres

meaning, purpose, and hope. They were the faces of the hapless people of a poorly governed country where death and disaster had become a routine. Over a million people had died during the ten years of political unrest in Mexico. Strange, unbelievable things were happening everywhere. The sick and hungry walked the deck, grabbing and stealing, taking anything that they could lay their hands on. Death, loss, uprootedness no longer evoked worry or sadness in people. They had come to be accepted as life. Even if Sophia shared her tragedy with someone, she knew that it wouldn't make an eyelid flutter, much less win her sympathy. Removing her wrap, she covered Isabel with it. Then, quickly walking up to a boat attendant, she asked him if there was something she could do to earn a few pesos. Wash dishes, mop the deck, anything so she could feed her child.

The attendant asked her to wait as he went inside the cabin. Slouching on the deck, she waited, Isabel sleeping beside her. After a while, the attendant stepped out. Handing her a piece of old bread, he told her there wasn't any work for her. Sophia's face fell. Then looking at the bread, she shook Isabel awake, asking her to eat it fast. Watching a distraught Isabel eating the dry bread, the attendant who had begun to walk away, stopped.

"Is this the hungry child...daughter...girl that you had spoken about?" he asked.

Sophia nodded.

"Come and talk to me in the corner," the attendant said.

Sophia followed him to a nook, Isabel trailing behind.

"There are wealthy men on board. They are having cocktails at the bar inside the cabin. If your daughter goes and serves them drinks, she could earn quick money. The tips could buy you meals for the rest of the trip," the attendant whispered.

Alarmed, Sophia stepped back. "No, no," she said. "My Isabel is a child, all of eleven. She just looks all grown. I can serve the men their drinks."

The attendant shook his head. "Na-uh," he said. "The men liked to be served by young girls. I just made you the offer thinking that you were hungry and cold. It is your choice."

"Thank you, but no," Sophia said, turning away and leading Isabel back. Hunching on the hard, cold deck, she draped her wrap around Isabel again. The evening turned colder and darker still. Soon a damp night descended. Sophia looked at the stars and then at Isabel, whose weary eyes were losing focus. Her body felt very warm against Sophia's. The boat was rocking slowly towards Bahía de Kino. Sophia convulsed with agony. Four days seemed like a dreadfully long time for Isabel to be cold and hungry. Sophia's eyes blurred, a heavy murkiness falling over her.

Isabel began impelling her to let her go and serve at the bar. "Mama, I will be gone only for a bit and run back as soon as I have enough money to buy us food," she said.

Sophia shuddered. "No, child, no. You mustn't go. There is danger in men," she said.

"Mama, don't you worry," Isabel said, getting up and brushing her hair. "I will be back before you know."

"But Isabel, you have a fever!" Sophia exclaimed.

"Mama, you are the one who is feverish and famished! You haven't had even a scrap of food since morning. You can hardly even sit up," Isabel replied. Sophia was still arguing when Isabel left.

Helplessly, Sophia watched her daughter walk inside the cabin. Shaking with trepidation, she waited for Isabel in the chilling dark, her brain conjuring dreadful sights and sounds. Her mind imagined vile men drinking and laughing. Then she visualised a drunken man touching Isabel's hair. Gathering her meagre strength, Sophia pulled her semi-conscious self up and lashed at herself for putting her daughter in harm's way.

Slowly, she began walking towards the bar to bring Isabel back. Her head spun, sparks of light flashed in her eyes, her breathing was heavy, and a stinging numbness spread across her feet, but she stumbled on. Stepping inside the cabin, she collapsed.

When she regained consciousness, she was lying on the deck. Stars shone in her face, almost blinding her.

"Mama, I am okay. I told you I would be okay. You needn't have come for me," Isabel whispered to Sophia. "I had hardly served a drink or two when a tall lean man at the bar noticed the badge of St Theresa's Academy upon my dress and asked me about it. When I told him that that was my school badge, a sudden seriousness befell him. He said his daughters too, attended St. Theresa's Academy. Sighing at my dishevelled state, he hung down his head, wondering aloud how much more misery lay in store for Mexico. Then reaching for his wallet, he pulled out some money and handed it to me, asking me to leave."

"Did he really?" Sophia asked widening her eyes.

"Yes, Mama. And when I started to thank him, he waved me off, asking me again to leave at once," Isabel said, her eyes flooding. "He was a good man. The Virgin sent him our way."

On hearing of the man's kindness, Sophia's eyes welled up too. She imagined the man to be solemn and gentle, the kind that wants to make every situation better. Goodness dispelled wrong, reversed misdoings, restored humanity. In the face of her eleven-year-old daughter that night, Sophia saw faith in God and man that she was beginning to lose. Before eating pork stew and rice under the starry sky, Sophia thanked the Virgin for her love. Never would she forget that traumatic night even as she knew that far more dreadful and preposterous occurrences were unfolding across the length of Mexico.

KISHAN SINGH

Kishan and Jaspal were working in San Joaquin Valley one January afternoon. It was a particularly harsh winter that year — 1921. Fastening their jackets and putting on mittens, they were packing almonds when Harbans stopped by with news.

"Beautiful chunks of flat land are up for sale down south in Imperial Valley. A hundred miles east of the city of San Diego are six-hundred thousand acres watered by the River Colorado. So many Punjabis have bought farms there after drawing loans. There is no better time than now to become farm owners," he said.

"Pali, Harbans is right. Land in Imperial Valley is much cheaper than the land in the Central Valley. We should tour it immediately," Kishan said.

Jaspal shook his head. "We will buy land in the Central Valley even if that means waiting and saving more. The south is a rugged strip. Only a fool would go that way. I wouldn't be surprised if the land is for free there," he said.

Kishan knew it would be a long while before they would have enough money to buy even a small farm in the Central Valley. Confused, he looked at Harbans who got up to leave, insisting again that they give Imperial Valley a thought.

Months passed by. Kishan couldn't stop thinking about the desert valley. One afternoon, he suggested to Jaspal that they could buy a small farm in the desert and gradually add to it. "One has to take a chance," Kishan said.

"Imperial Valley is the driest stretch of land! Why would anyone leave Central Valley and its wonders — grapes, peaches, apricots, almonds and wheat? What in God's name can one grow down there in the desert?" Jaspal asked.

"We could grow vegetables and melons. And cotton, the most marvellous of crops. A few harvests could change our lives," Kishan said.

"Growing cotton is riskier than you think. The most marvellous of crops has also caused the most bankruptcies," Jaspal said.

Kishan kept prodding Jaspal every so often to get at least a feel of the south but Jaspal refused to give in. Then one day, a Japanese farmhand told Kishan that he was headed to Imperial Valley to pick melons with his crew. Kishan prevailed on Jaspal to join them. Jaspal finally relented and they jumped on a truck headed south.

Going so far down and then east, Kishan wondered if he were still in California. The blue Pacific was nowhere in sight. The green hills had given way to brown ones. Going farther along, he saw those brown hills turn to rocky mounts and treading deeper, the mounts swayed into rough ridges. If someone came in looking for the California of the gorgeous green fields or the California of the famed white, sandy beaches decked with gutsy swimmers and artful surfers, they would be astounded on seeing Imperial Valley. It was a valley like no other in California — home to a dusty, desolate, bewitching desert, where the sky was a brilliant blue in the morning and a burning red in the afternoon.

In the heart of the desert valley lay nature's miracle — luscious farmland, nurtured by the River Colorado. Down there, picking melons, Kishan and Jaspal heard the story of a famous Punjabi farmer from there — Ajmer Singh Gill, who had come to Imperial Valley with an invincible will to till the ruthless desert, starting out with a small stretch of land, a mule and a horse. Taking a chance on cotton, he had struck gold, going on thereafter to buy a large belt of land that spread from Imperial Valley all the way east into Arizona. Gill was now the proud owner of a fleet of cars and tractors and so resounding was his success that children had started to read about him in schools.

It was a story like no other, stirring Kishan and Jaspal's dream, reminding them that they came from a proud clan of farmers; it was not their lot to be mere farmhands. "I had a feeling all along that we belonged here. Now, I am convinced that our destiny lies right here with this beautiful yellow earth, with the melons and the lettuce, with the carrots and cotton, with the crimson sunsets and the howling coyotes under the splendid glimmer of the moon," Kishan said.

Jaspal agreed. The lush fields had kicked up in him a reverence for the desert. "Kishan, the land rakes up memories. The River Colorado reminds me of the River Satluj flowing through the canals along Noor Mahal," he said.

Kishan smiled. Had they really come home? Had life come full circle?

They returned to Sacramento with the searing hope of buying land in Imperial Valley but the prospect of finding partners was dim. Even the Imperial Valley success stories couldn't rouse interest in the desert. Harbans was the only one it seemed who saw the scope of the desert valley. If only Harbans had not put all his savings into buying a vineyard in Fresno with his brother. Partner or not, Kishan let Harbans know that he and Jaspal relied on him for everything — from finding them partners to negotiating the deal and cracking it.

And sure enough, one balmy summer morning as Kishan and Jaspal were boxing lettuce on the outskirts of Sacramento, Harbans drove down to share that he had met two men, Amrik and Joginder who were willing to partner with Kishan and Jaspal to buy a farm in Imperial Valley. The duo, Harbans said had landed in California over a decade ago, gradually investing in three farms in Central Valley and were now looking to buy land down south. Harbans said they were well connected too, even offering to arrange Jaspal and Kishan's meeting with the duo at his restaurant in Yuba City the following week.

Kishan and Jaspal jumped at the offer. Reaching Harbans's restaurant on the scheduled day, they prepared themselves to answer all possible partnership questions.

Soon the duo arrived. After the introductions, they began talking about themselves. Speaking of his deep love for farming, Amrik called California a farmer's paradise. Joginder joined in saying that there couldn't be a better place under the sun than California and that farmers formed its heartbeat.

Kishan couldn't believe it. The men's thinking was in line with his and Jaspal's. Both looked strong and agile. Amrik was in his forties and Joginder in his late thirties. Medium-statured, coarse-haired and severely tanned, it was shocking how similar the two were in appearance. They even wore identical shiny shirts. Like twins.

"All the big-time farmers in Imperial Valley, Punjabi as well as Anglo are our friends," Joginder said. "Cotton is the jewel of the desert valley. A few good harvests can turn men into millionaires."

Kishan's face glowed. The men were well connected and well informed.

Amrik began talking about back home. He said he and Joginder had lovely memories of their village Nawanpind, a cosy hamlet in District Hoshiarpur in Punjab. Then subtly packing away the nostalgia, he was back to talking business, asking Kishan and Jaspal how much money they were hoping to invest.

Jaspal told him that he and Kishan had about eight thousand dollars saved up.

"We are looking to invest more than double of that. Harbans thinks highly of you two and we value his opinion. Forming a partnership, we can pool resources, borrow from the bank and buy a farm. Drawing a loan would be easy," Amrik said. "The Director of Imperial Bank in Holtville is known to us. With a loan, we can buy a large farm."

Joginder said that Kishan and Jaspal needn't worry about the California Alien Land Laws either.

"What exactly do the laws imply?" Kishan asked Joginder.

"Indians have been deemed ineligible for American citizenship, and hence forbidden from owning land," Joginder replied.

Kishan sighed. The California Alien Land Laws were a barefaced manifestation of racism, of the white man's claim to superiority over other races, his attempt to assume full and complete control of the California land.

"The laws are hurtful indeed, but there is nothing that can come between Punjabis and the farmland. Why, Punjabis are already skirting the laws and buying land across the length of the state," Joginder said.

"How?" Kishan asked intrigued.

"They buy the land and register it in an Anglo's name. It may seem surprising but many an Anglo eagerly steps up to help Punjabis."

The juxtaposition was bewildering, Kishan thought. On the one hand were Anglo statesmen who passed laws that were shamefully discriminatory, and on the other were Anglos who were helping Punjabis to surge past those laws and become landowners. Opportunity managed to slink in and light up the darkest of places.

Joginder said a retired Anglo judge named Arnold Brown had happily agreed to help them skirt the laws by holding the land for them in his name. The judge was on old friend, he said.

Kishan and Jaspal were now completely swept off. Their cherished vision was coming to life.

"We will pick out a nice stretch of land in Imperial Valley in a week or two and call you two over," Amrik said before the duo drove away in a Rover 8.

Kishan gazed at the twin cylinder car as it was speeding away. The men sure were resourceful. If it were not for the identical, shiny shirts that they wore, he would have thought them well dressed too.

Two weeks later on a lyrical morning that smacked of hope, Jaspal and Kishan took the motor bus going south to sign the papers on a hundred-acre stretch of foreclosed land that Amrik and Joginder had finalised in Imperial Valley. Breaking the journey in Valencia, they decided to spend the night with a Sikh farmer, Jagat Singh who had once worked with them in the rice fields up north. Jagat now grew oranges on fifty acres that he had purchased not long ago. Ecstatically, Kishan shared with Jagat that he and Jaspal had found farming partners, Joginder and Amrik, and that together, they would be purchasing a large stretch of land in Imperial Valley.

Jagat said that he knew Amrik and Joginder, having picked grapes with them up in Fresno, and wondered why on earth the duo would want to partner with Kishan and Jaspal when they had both money and contacts.

Kishan was quick with an answer. "The duo wants to partner with us because they want to farm large tracts of land. They want us to run the farm in Imperial Valley so that they can move on and explore more prospects elsewhere," he replied. "Look at it this way: we need them for their resources and they need us for work."

The next day, borrowing Jagat's truck, Kishan and Jaspal drove down to Holtville in Imperial Valley. Holtville was a small desert town with barely a few thousand people. It had several stores and a restaurant or two, adobe homes making way for frame houses. As scheduled, they met Amrik and Joginder at the Imperial Bank after lunch. Amrik and Joginder wore dress suits. Kishan hoped his and Jaspal's polyester shirts and trousers would make the cut. The duo led Kishan and Jaspal to the Bank Director's office. The name outside the office read Timothy Williams. Even though his English was awkward, Amrik confidently introduced Kishan and Jaspal to Mr. Williams. Trim and very tall, around forty years old, Mr. Williams had a contagious smile. He said he had been in conversation with Amrik and Joginder for a few days and that his bank had agreed to loan money to them to buy the foreclosed stretch near Holtville. Compiling papers, he set them on the table. "We'd do the paperwork just as soon as Judge Arnold Brown comes along. The judge believes in the potential of Punjabis," Mr. Williams said. "He is holding land in his name for a few in Imperial Valley."

Kishan and Jaspal smiled. Things were moving at an incredible pace. They had been waiting only a few minutes when a man came to say that the judge was running late. Mr. Williams offered everyone tea. As they sat there, waiting and sipping tea, curiosity seized Kishan. "Wouldn't it be better if Jaspal and I saw the farm before signing the papers?" he asked hastily.

Joginder shuddered as though someone had poked him with a nail in the middle of a beautiful ride. "The judge would be coming by any minute," he said. "Surely, you don't want to keep him waiting."

Kishan was bothered to see him hesitant. He pulled Jaspal to the side. "Pali, we are not transferring our money to Imperial Bank or signing a thing without surveying the land," he insisted.

"Kishan, where do our eight thousand dollars figure against their twenty?"

Kishan didn't relent, walking over to Mr. Williams, he told him that he and Jaspal would be comfortable signing the papers only after seeing the farm. Mr. Williams said that it seemed viable indeed for them to see the farm first. Clearly annoyed,

Joginder said he would take Kishan and Jaspal to see the farm and Amrik could stay behind with Mr. Williams and wait for the judge.

On the way, Joginder commented that he had selected the most exquisite hundred acres.

Hundred acres. Joginder's words echoed in Kishan's mind. Back in Punjab, he didn't even know anyone who owned a hundred acres. He had heard of big-time landowners but being small-time tillers, neither Jaspal nor he had ever rubbed shoulders with them. He wanted to shout out to the world that he and Jaspal were going to be co-owners of a hundred-acre farm but didn't. The last thing that he wanted was to be thought of as a naïve, illiterate farmhand, incapable of becoming a farm owner.

Walking the prospective farm, Jaspal bent down and snatched a handful of soil and fondling it, let it escape through his fingers. His smiling eyes met Kishan's. The land indeed was enrapturing, the river running rapidly through the canals. Kishan envisioned melons and lettuce, carrots and beets sprouting out of the brown earth in the future, and thickly spread cotton too. He chuckled. Joginder started walking back to the car in long, quick strides. Lingering a little longer and feeling very satisfied, Kishan and Jaspal joined him.

Back at the bank, Mr. Williams had news. "The judge has come up with unforeseen work. He says he will come by tomorrow," he said.

Kishan stomped his foot. It felt like someone had halted a speeding train well on its way to its destination. Agreeing to seal the deal the next afternoon, he got up to leave. He and Jaspal would have liked to roam their future farm all evening but Joginder and Amrik insisted on taking them to spend the night with them at the house of a farmer friend of theirs. "It will take less than ten minutes to drive there," Amrik said, adding that his friend Rattan Lal was a big-time farmer who owned several hundred acres in Imperial Valley and two large ranches near Yuma, Arizona.

Kishan was hesitant. He wanted quiet time with Jaspal, so they could ponder aloud about their would-be farm. Jaspal would have liked the same but not wanting to displease their future partners, they agreed, following the duo in the truck to their friend's farmhouse.

Kishan and Jaspal had never seen a house like Rattan Lal's before, so large and luxurious. Orange trees and dainty fountains adorned the driveway. Two attendants walked out of the house and greeted Amrik and Joginder as Kishan and Jaspal waited by their truck. Amrik told Kishan and Jaspal that Rattan Lal was away to Arizona, but it didn't matter. He and Joginder were always welcome to all of Rattan Lal's houses, the two in Arizona and this one in Imperial Valley.

The attendants led them into a grandly done-up guest suite comprising a living room, kitchen and a bedroom with a bath. Amrik and Joginder soon made themselves comfortable, pulling out a Jack Daniels from a bag, pouring large drinks for themselves. It was a day to celebrate, they announced. Tired from the long day, Kishan and Jaspal excused themselves and prepared to sleep on the living-room sofas, but Amrik and Joginder led them to the bedroom and insisted that they slept there.

The room had two sprawling beds and a fancy lamp lit up the space. Slumping on a bed, Jaspal said, "Kishan, let's get a goodnight's sleep. Another long day awaits us tomorrow." He yawned and shut his eyes.

Kishan turned off the lamp and reclined on the other bed. It was very comfortable, by far the nicest that he had ever rested on. He thought about their prospective partners. Though the duo could be forcefully insistent sometimes, there was no way he and Jaspal could buy a farm on their own since they had neither

186 The Rainbow Acres

enough money nor the relevant connections. Then closing his eyes, he turned this way and that but couldn't get himself to sleep. Half an hour passed. He got up to get water. Passing through the living room on his way to the kitchen, he noticed that Joginder and Amrik were not on the sofas. He heard laughter. Peering out of the window, he saw that the two were sitting on the patio, drinking. It was Joginder who was laughing. Kishan leaned by the window. Just as he had feared, the laughter was at his and Jaspal's expense.

"What fools! Jaspal picked up a handful of dirt and caressed it and that other buffoon, Kishan, who presents himself as being well-informed, an emotional madcap he too is," Joginder jeered. "Well, the judge will hold the land for us and these two can work their backs off without knowing that they are no more than our farmhands!"

Kishan's forehead furrowed. He clenched his fist. Outside, Amrik guffawed. "Have you seen the look on their faces — like they are out to conquer the world. Jaspal behaves as though he comes from nobility. That other intelligent buffoon Kishan plays humble to suit his purpose but fools they both are," he said, downing a gulp of whiskey.

Kishan wasn't angry. He was sad. A Chinese farmhand had fooled him once, taking off with his painstakingly earned one hundred dollars, promising to bring bejewelled watches, one each for him and Jaspal from Nevada only to be never seen again. Now, his own countrymen, from his beloved Punjab were out to thug them. Quickly, Kishan walked back to the bedroom. Jaspal now lay sleeping on his side, breathing deeply. Leaning over him, Kishan said, "Pali, wake up!"

Up in a second, Jaspal looked around. "Is everything okay?" he asked.

"No," Kishan replied. "Nothing is okay! It is all a hoax and these men are frauds. Let's get out of here."

Picking up their things, they hurried to the truck and sped off. Racing past sleeping San Diego and Orange Counties that night, Jaspal was shocked to hear what the scoundrels thought of him and Kishan. They were lucky that the thieves hadn't snipped their hard-earned savings. It would be a while before they could trust anyone again. "If I were back in Punjab and someone had tried to cheat me, I would have beaten the man to pulp. But doing that in California would mean rotting behind bars for the rest of one's life. Amrik and Joginder are not worth giving up one's life for," Jaspal said gritting his teeth.

"Yes, we must always stay on the right side of law. God knows that we have many obstacles marring our path already," Kishan said, driving towards Valencia.

It was past midnight when they reached Jagat's farm. Learning of the fiasco, Jagat was not surprised. He had doubts about Joginder and Amrik to start with, and after Kishan and Jaspal had left for Holtville, he had enquired about Joginder and Amrik from a Sikh farmer in his area who had worked with the duo and discovered that the two were crooks, infamous for their shady deals. "You were not going to be their first victims," Jagat confirmed.

Kishan and Jaspal sighed in dismay. A few days later when they shared the shocking story with Harbans at Yuba City, Harbans hung his head in remorse. In wishing to help Kishan and Jaspal, he had unknowingly almost pushed them down a ditch. For a long time after, Kishan avoided talk about buying land. And whenever a Rover 8 sped by, his spirit dampened and quickly, he'd look the other way.

SOPHIA

Sophia had thought that because Bahía de Kino was a coastal village, it would be somewhat similar to Acapulco. Landing there, she discovered that it was nothing like she had imagined it would be. The warm, arid village was astonishingly quiet, lacking the bustling exuberance of Acapulco. Placid and sparsely populated, it was hauntingly beautiful though, its coastline enrapturing, its sights and sounds comforting. Tall cacti grew in clusters along the coast. Birds chirped in desert willows and the air smelled of marigolds. Men walked around selling hot chilli peppers. Shirtless children ran about on the streets, horse playing and giggling. Tucked away from the turmoil of mainland Mexico, Bahía de Kino oozed affability, the cool sea breeze ruffling Sophia's hair, soothing her face and calming her mind.

Though Giovanni had wanted very much for Sophia to meet his brother Milano, political instability had rendered that impossible. She had imagined Milano often in her mind, visualising him to be thoughtful and good humoured like his brother Giovanni. Landlessness had driven both brothers from the south soon after their parents' death. While Giovanni had gained employment with the government, Milano had ventured far north in a quest of a vocation, settling in Bahía de Kino and making a living by fishing in the Sea of Cortez.

"Milano is restless, an intrepid voyager. The sea speaks to his soul, and he responds by sailing far out into the horizon every day," Giovanni had said.

Sophia wondered if Milano would match his brother's description of him. Shuffling through her purse, she pulled out one of the pictures that she had brought along from Guadalajara. The faded sepia showed her husband and Milano wearing white shirts and dark shorts. The brothers stood with their hands in the pockets of their shorts, smirking as though at a joke that would always remain hidden from the world, confined securely within the tight enclaves of their hearts and minds. The picture left Sophia yearning to be let into the lost world of the brothers, to hear the clever joke, to laugh. If only the past could be recreated, if only people could be brought alive, if only jokes could travel time to regale her uninspired, abstruse life.

Showing the sepia to a man selling prickly pears, she asked him if he knew of Fisherman Milano Romero. The man shook his head. Walking on, she showed the picture to a group of men who stood talking. The men looked at the picture and then at Sophia and Isabel. "You sure have come a long way," one of them said, leading them to a wooden bench. Even in their tousled state, there was no mistaking that Sophia and Isabel were city folk.

The man ran to get Milano.

Sitting on the bench in that unknown village, Sophia was not the least bit afraid. She had buried loved ones, seen hunger, homelessness and near prostitution. There seemed nothing to be fearful of anymore. Instead she looked at Isabel who was reclining against her. Her daughter was a twinkle of starlight breaking through the confounding darkness. Surely not everything was lost. Her lovely Isabel would see her through the ocean of despondency. Together, they would find their way through the ambiguity.

The afternoon gave way to an orange evening. Isabel slipped into sleep. Sophia continued sitting upright, her blank eyes studying the unfamiliar landscape. Birds were flocking home through the darkening skies. She saw men with fish baskets walk by. She assumed that the fishermen were returning home after the day's work. Milano, too, must be on his way, she thought, straightening her hair. She was trying to stay alert but felt light headed, her eyes heavy in the sockets. The exhaustion was getting the better of her. Just when she thought she would be blown out by sleep, she saw a man walking swiftly towards them. She knew at once that the man was Milano. Though he carried only a slight physical resemblance to Giovanni, he had his brother's unmistakable poise. Wet from sailing and fishing in the waters, his feet and legs were smeared in sand. Coming close, he contracted his eyes, looking inquisitively first at Sophia and then at the sleeping Isabel.

Sophia sighed and smiled. Resting Isabel's head against the bench, she got up to introduce herself. Before she could, Milano knew. Smiling big, he embraced Sophia and then Isabel who spread her arms around her uncle eagerly despite having been woken up with a jolt.

Milano led Sophia and Isabel to his bamboo shack, street dogs trailing behind them.

"It is the fishy smell around me," Milano said laughing. "The dogs are sniffing for the fish."

"Where is the fish?" Isabel asked, suddenly curious.

"Today was a lucky day," Milano said. "All my baskets were full. I handed over the fish to the sellers in the mercado after saving a few to eat tonight. Come close if you want a peek."

Isabel crept closer and peeped inside the pocket of her uncle's shorts. She saw six pairs of fish eyes looking back at her. She let out a laugh. Sophia smiled. It was the first time in many days that she had seen Isabel laugh.

They were greeted at the door by Milano's wife Carina, a very tall dusky woman with long dark hair and a broad smile. She introduced Sophia and Isabel to her six-year-old son Phillipe, who said a quick hello before hiding behind his mother.

Sophia looked around. The small bare house was solacing. Sensing the warmth of family, of belonging, of hope, she felt a surge of relief. With help from Milano and his family, she and Isabel would make it to dry land. She saw Isabel was cuddling her little cousin. Infatuated with Isabel, the little boy watched her enamoured as though a fairy had flown into his house. Sophia watched on as the cousins began playing El Yoyo together, Isabel tickling Phillipe's little hand, sending him warbling with laughter.

Later down on the mat, little Phillipe told everyone his favourite story — La Tortuga. "La Tortuga, the old dancing and flute-playing turtle belongs to our village," Phillipe whispered.

"Really?" Isabel asked.

"Yes! She hides in the trunk of the old acacia that stands on the far end of the street, playing her flute all day long, refusing to come out of her hole because she is afraid that the village children will cook her into soup. But one day, the children did trick her into stepping out."

"Was she cooked into soup?" Isabel asked.

"Oh no! La Tortuga is much too clever for that. She fooled the children into watching her dance and slid back into her hole where she continues playing her flute. I can walk you to the acacia in the morning," he offered. "Will you come?"

"Sure! You are my little cousin. I would go anywhere with you," Isabel said, kissing his cheeks.

After dinner, the cousins nodded off on the mat.

The adults, however, did not sleep. Learning of the shocking death of his brother and nephews, Milano wept incessantly. As a southern uprooted peasant, he looked upon the rebels as the saviours of the poor. The irony of the killings of his brother and nephews by rebels left him perplexed. "A city man my brother Giovanni may have become," Milano said, "but at heart, he was still a southern peasant — upholding the rights of the rural poor. How could the rebels attack their own? Hell has broken loose. Surely, it isn't a world for the likes of me anymore."

"A massacre doesn't discriminate," Sophia said. "In the wake of one, sons of peasants and sons of landlords wind up bathing in blood together. If it wasn't for my Isabel, even I wouldn't have thought this world a place worth living in anymore."

KISHAN SINGH

The sudden death of President Harding on August 2nd, 1923 shook the nation. Vice President Calvin Coolidge was sworn in as President shortly after midnight on August 3rd, 1923. The simple demeanour of the new President promised calm and integrity to offset the indulgences of the roaring twenties. Suddenly very hopeful, Kishan took to chasing his dream again. The orange and the jade of the melons and the lettuce in Imperial Valley began calling out to him and in the dead of the night, he even saw the glittering white of the cotton. The impulse to own a farm began coaxing him harder than ever. He was tired of living in boarding houses, he told Jaspal. Spending the night in Rattan Lal's cottage in Imperial Valley had planted the idea in his mind that it was possible to own a house. But, first they had to buy land. Despite the bad experience with the scoundrels, his heart yearned for Imperial Valley. They must take a chance again with the desert. Imperial Valley didn't belong to Amrik and Joginder. It held promise for anyone brave enough to till its rugged land and combat its heat and dust. At Kishan's behest, Harbans contacted Allah Baksh, a forty-year-old established farmer in Imperial Valley to help Kishan and Jaspal buy a farm there.

Kishan took off with Harbans for Imperial Valley one morning on a weekday in early September of 1923, Santa Ana winds blowing ferociously in their faces as they drove along the tottering paths towards the desert while Jaspal stayed behind to work on a peach orchard in San Joaquin Valley. Making it there in the late evening, they began probing possibilities of buying land with Allah Baksh who said that he had first come to Imperial Valley as a farmhand, but working hard, he had progressed to farming over a hundred acres. "Farming is a vocation that brings one close to God," Allah Baksh said as they sat talking over dinner. "In farming a piece of land, a farmer takes upon himself God's work of feeding the world. I feel lucky to be stepping out every morning to carry out God's purpose."

Kishan smiled. He fully abided by Allah Baksh's belief. Farming meant attuning one's self to the changing hues of nature, arousing the land, no matter how obstinate, to bear crops and make those crops available to men and women across the world.

"I like to see Punjabis taking on the California farmland," Allah Baksh said. "I'll help you find a fertile strip in the valley." Then cheerfully, he shared that he would be marrying a Mexican girl who had been introduced to him by a Punjabi farmer's Mexican wife and that they would be wedded in a Catholic ceremony in Yuma followed by a nikah in Los Angeles.

Kishan was swept off. Up north in the Central Valley, rarely did a Punjabi talk of marriage. Some had been married back in Punjab and spent their time dreaming about their sons crossing the oceans to join them and the bachelors seldom mentioned marriage, toiling mechanically in the fields day after day as though they were wedded to work. He congratulated Allah Baksh.

Allah Baksh thanked him. "I will be by no means the first to marry a Mexican woman in Imperial Valley," he said. "Since Punjabis and Mexicans are both brown, Anti-Miscegenation Laws can't bar such alliances. Quite a few Punjabis — Hindus, Sikhs and Muslims — in Imperial Valley have married Mexican women. English connects the couples. Many have children too, with such interesting names as Frieda Sidhu, Estefan Singh Punia, Jose Bilawal Khan and Anzo Chand! Why, not only that, the children are ingenious bundles of joy tattling on in Punjabi, Spanish and English with equal fluency!"

Kishan clapped. The children's names were interesting indeed as was their linguistic proficiency, revealing the children's exotic bi-ethnic identity in a multicultural California. "And what would you name your son?" Kishan asked Allah Baksh. "Fabio Allah Baksh Khan?"

"Sure," Allah Baksh laughed. "Sometimes, life is about going with the flow!"

Surveying the valley for a few days, Kishan zeroed in on a fifty-acre stretch near Holtville and with Allah Baksh and Harbans's help, he successfully struck a deal with the Anglo farmer who was selling the farm. It was time now to draw a loan. Allah Baksh, Harbans and Kishan planned the trip to Imperial Bank. Harbans asked Kishan not to bad mouth Amrik and Joginder to the bank Director, Mr. Williams. "We must never let the Punjabi farmer's image be compromised in California — be it a Sikh, Hindu or a Muslim farmer," he said.

Even though he could never bring himself to get over Joginder and Amrik's treachery, Kishan agreed to keep that matter buried. But as soon as they drove to Mr. Williams's office and sat down, turning towards Kishan, Mr. Williams asked, "Mr. Kishan Singh, the previous deal that you were striking with Joginder Singh and Amrik Singh did not pan out. May I know why?"

"Yes Sir, my brother Jaspal and I got cold feet. We realised that we just wanted each other as partners. And because with our slim savings, we could not buy a grand hundred acres, we waited until we found this ideal small stretch that the two of us can buy with help from your bank," Kishan said, smiling.

Backing him, Harbans and Allah Baksh assured Mr. Williams that hard-working as they both were, Kishan and Jaspal would certainly pay back the loan instalments on time.

Mr. Williams agreed to take the chance on Kishan and Jaspal if Judge Arnold Brown agreed to hold the land in his name for them. Allah Baksh hastened to tell Mr. Williams that he and the old judge were friends.

"That's wonderful," Mr. Williams said. Kishan could hardly believe it. Their beautiful dream stood waiting around the corner. Star-struck, he wired Jaspal asking him to come down to Imperial Valley immediately.

"Fifty acres is enormous land if one has a mind to grow crops," a jubilant Jaspal pondered aloud on jumping off the motor bus.

At Mr. Williams's office, Judge Brown stared hard at Kishan and Jaspal. Greeting him, Kishan thanked the judge for helping them skirt the discriminating California Alien Land Laws.

"Your faces are compelling. You are what America is about — working hard to realise dreams. I'm glad to hold the land in my name for you because of your promise and also because of the good names your friends Harbans and Allah Baksh enjoy in the Punjabi community," the old judge said.

Kishan and Jaspal thanked him again after the paperwork was done. It was a day to write home about. They were walking on clouds and could hardly wait to begin tilling their land, but before that, goodbyes had to be said up north, so they took off with Harbans to quickly wrap things up for good in Central Valley.

Their farmhand friends at the boarding house were elated to hear that Kishan and Jaspal had now become farm owners. The older men took pride in Kishan and Jaspal's progress and the younger in their aspirations. Helping them pack their things, the men said that they knew this day would come for the duo, hard-working and ambitious as the two were. Bidding goodbye, Kishan and Jaspal wished the men well, promising to keep in touch with them. It was time for the duo to board the bus for their new home — Imperial Valley. Harbans offered to drive Kishan and Jaspal to the motor bus stop. Just as Harbans stepped on the gas, Kishan asked him to stop by Elk Grove. "I must say bye to someone at the library in Elk Grove. I can't leave without doing that," he said.

"Who is in Elk Grove?" Harbans asked.

"Kishan has made friends with the pretty Anglo librarian in Elk Grove," Jaspal laughed.

"She is the Assistant Librarian," Kishan said curtailing a smile.

"Oh yes, the Assistant Librarian. I must mention that she is brown-eyed, red-haired and ravishing. Kishan can't take off for the desert without saying bye to his heartthrob. Why, his heart flounders every time he even thinks of her," Jaspal said laughing louder still.

Kishan punched Jaspal's arm, wishing at once that he hadn't shared so many details about Amy with Jaspal. Then looking far out at the nut orchards, he smiled. Jaspal was right. It was true that his heart jiggled at the very thought of seeing Amy. It was also true that he could never leave without bidding bye to her, without letting her know that he was headed south to farm his own land.

Harbans stopped by the Elk Grove Library. Kishan ran inside the building, restless and excited. He found Amy just where he had hoped she would be, in the back, arranging books.

"Hello," he said, relieved to see her there. Whatever would he have done if she weren't there? he wondered.

"Kishan!" she said smiling, her eyes shining like stars. "How delightful to see you! And after so long! Where have you been?" He thought she sounded like she had missed him and had waited for him to come by.

"Down south," he replied, out of breath. "The other day, my brother Jaspal and I bought a farm in Imperial Valley. Our very own."

"What?" she asked. Her smile grew wider. "Congratulations!" she said.

He saw her face reddening. She truly, really was happy for him. "Thank you," he said quickly. "I came to say bye. I will soon be taking the motor bus going south."

"What? You are going?" she asked, surprised. Then quickly pulling herself together, she said, "Yes, yes of course, you have to go now that you own a farm down there. Well, I am glad you stopped by. Good luck!"

"Thank you again," he replied. Something told him that he wasn't the only one whose heart was fluttering. Leaving was hard he thought, always so darn hard.

"You could write you know." She grabbed a pen and a bit of paper. Scribbling fast on the paper, she handed it to him. "My address," she said, still flustered.

"I will," he said, folding the paper. "I have to go now. My brother and a friend are outside, waiting."

"Bye," she said.

"Bye," he whispered.

He was about to turn when she stepped up and embraced him. He was stunned, never having thought that she would do that.

"Thank you," he said and felt stupid right after. In the car, he thought of how Amy had played an enduring role in his life at a defining point in time when he was seeking moorings, hoping to discover America and his place in it. Connecting with him over incredible stories, she had helped him align his past with his present and make sense of his life as it was unrolling in the amazing new world.

The car joggled and braked.

Kishan looked up. They were at the motor bus stop and the motor bus stood waiting. Gathering their things, Kishan and Jaspal stepped out. Kishan recalled how difficult and long a stretch Central Valley had been. It would have been harder if it weren't for Harbans. His unconditional support and goodwill had deeply moved Kishan's heart. Thanking him profusely, he and Jaspal jumped on to the motor bus. Jouncing along twining roads going south, they turned towards each other and smiled. They had moved up from owning cloth sacks to leather bags. Grasping them tight, they looked forward to their greatest adventure yet.

SOPHIA

Milano helped Sophia build a one-room shack a stone's throw away from his own. In time, Sophia divided the room into two, living in the back and setting up a colmado in the front, where she began selling fruits, vegetables, soaps, baskets, beans, rice, spices, hairbrushes and other little things.

Waking up to the trilling of larks each morning, she would pack Isabel off to her tiny, informal school and arrange items in the colmado before villagers began slopping in to purchase this or that, staying on to talk about new-born babies, sick neighbours, secret romances and upcoming weddings, even asking her occasionally to read an old newspaper aloud to them so they could know what all the commotion in the capital was about. Though everyone knew how Sophia's world had come crumbling down all in the course of one harrowing day, no one mentioned any of that, smiling at her instead as if to convey that life was too short to cry one's way through. Sophia gladly returned their smiles and if a villager was particularly engaging, she would even offer the person a tumbler of tequila and talk on through the afternoon. The world's deep desire to fall back into normalcy even after the most horrific of storms came to nudge Sophia, impelling her to continue chasing butterflies.

Cooking beans and tortillas on the front patio in the evenings, she would regale in the present, in the chance to start afresh far away from the politics at the centre. The legendary revolutionary leader Emiliano Zapata had been long dead, but his myth continued to live on. Ousting President Carranza, many Zapatistas now held important positions in General Obregon's government. But the comings and goings of Presidents held no meaning now in Sophia's life. Her days only circled around Isabel, who had grown to be a tall teen with glossy hair and translucent skin. Although Isabel's simple school in Bahía de Kino did not compare in any way to the renowned St. Theresa's Academy in Guadalajara, Sophia was happy that far from forgetting the English that Isabel had picked up at the Academy, she was now reading borrowed English novels from her teacher and helping her mother and classmates speak and write English as well. Having received only but a rudimentary education in Acapulco, Sophia was nonetheless aware of the power of books. They could not just change lives but also save lives, connecting people to the wide world. She was glad that Isabel felt loved, rescued and comforted by books. The Mexican Revolution had robbed her daughter of a childhood, but not of beauty and wonder. On many days, however, Sophia worried about the limited choices that Bahía de Kino had to offer her daughter. But Isabel disagreed. "Mama, there is a lot that I can do in Bahía de Kino," Isabel said one day, brushing off her mother's concern.

"Like what?" Sophia asked. "Run a colmado like your mother? I would want for you to do better than that, my child."

"Of course," Isabel said with a wide smile. "I could teach or sell embroidered clothes. Tourists are flocking to the village all year long. And they quite like the fuchsias that I embroider on blouses and skirts. Smitten by the flowers, they buy the items immediately."

Sophia knew that her daughter was wise beyond her years, choosing to draw happiness from flowers even in the most austere of times. Inspired by Isabel's zeal for life, Sophia began seeking silver linings in dark clouds, working hard for a future that she hoped would be a colour other than grey. The past was a story packed away in the attic but on some days, the tart pomegranates, the warm sea and the frolicking fish woke up memories of another time when life sang the song of spring, when kisses from two little boys floated in the air, when she danced intoxicated by the love of a man called Giovanni. But hardened as she was by time, life and poverty, Sophia knew not to welcome that long dead story back into her life. So, whenever the past knocked, heartlessly folding it, she would pack it away again.

In the spring of 1925, a jaunty young fisherman came to buy pomegranates at Sophia's colmado. A smile spread across his sun-kissed face as he ran his fingers through his wayward hair. "I had gone fishing far north along the coast to *El Dorado*, the fabled land of gold," he gushed.

"Really?" Sophia asked. "What is it like?"

"Fascinating. It's a place of lucky beginnings, where a resolute man can work his way to wealth, get all that he wishes for and more," the fishermen said, grinning from ear to ear.

The man was an amorous dreamer, Sophia thought remembering a time long ago when she, too, spoke in a shrill voice coloured with aspiration before destiny sent her life helter-skelter, desolating and dismaying her. It was reassuring to see that the rapture lived on in others, that it still ignited minds, making them believe in places and possibilities. "Why did you not stay on in the glitzy land?" she asked.

"I have many friends there. I will soon go back," he said, his eyes flaring with hope.

"What is the magical land called?" Sophia asked.

"California," he whispered, bursting with exhilaration.

"California," Sophia murmured. "The name itself promises the impossible."

The fisherman laughed. "It is the coast of gold and opportunity, of dauntless dreams and sunny skies," he said, grinning yet again. Impishly, he scanned her face as though devising a plan to retrieve all her lost smiles. Then slipping his hand into his pocket nonchalantly, he pulled out a little brown packet. "For you," he said, handing it to her.

"What is it?" she asked, gazing at the shiny brown packet.

"A treat from the golden land! Open it," he impelled.

She tore off the wrapper slowly and pulled out an enticing brown slab. Quickly, she bit into it. Tears rolled down her cheeks. It was her beloved chocolate. She had forgotten her romance with the dark sliver of ecstasy. Recalling that long fizzled stint, she thought back about the passion that was born in Acapulco and lay buried in Guadalajara. Wiping her tears, she was rejoicing in the silky wedge of delight when from a deep crevice in her mind, she recalled that her maternal uncle and cousins had moved to a city called Los Angeles in California. Reaching for a piece of paper, she quickly scribbled on it. "An uncle of mine moved to California with his sons many years ago. I have jotted down their names," she said, handing the bit of paper to the fisherman. "Please do enquire about them for me the next time that you go fishing along the golden coast."

"I will, you have my word," the fisherman said, folding the paper and slipping it down his pocket. Winking and waving to Sophia, he hustled out.

Sophia never forgot the meeting with the happy fisherman nor the chocolate in the brown packet. Most of all, she thought about the prospect held out by the land of gold — of opportunity and success, of aspiration and fulfilment, of sunny smiles and climes. It seemed just the place to live out one's promise, to spread one's wings in and fly.

Months passed. She heard no word from the star-gazing fisherman.

"Fishermen are wanderers," Milano said. "They pursue the sea in every direction. Who would know better than me? It is not likely that the romping fisherman who had stopped by your colmado will return anytime soon. It is also possible that he may have taken off in another direction, not having even gone to California."

Sophia shook her head. "He couldn't have gone to any place else but California. I know it. It is the way he spoke of California as if he had left his soul there."

And she was right. A month later, the rhapsodic fisherman barged in again, tipsy from his newest adventures at sea. "Guess what," he said, handing her a bag, "I have brought you chocolate, not just one but several bars."

Sophia thanked him.

"And I have brought back something else besides," he said grinning.

"What?" she asked breathless.

"A letter," he whispered, pulling out a white envelope from his back pocket.

Clenching the envelope, Sophia ripped it open with trembling hands. It was from her oldest cousin, Santiago.

"'Poor Mexico, so close to America, so far from God,'" Santiago had written from Los Angeles. "I am very disturbed to hear of your ill-fated story from the fisherman. I promise to help you settle down in California and marry off your daughter, if you manage, somehow, to cross the border into America."

Sophia's heart soared. A door had opened to the coveted land. A slew of butterflies came to dance around her. They would lead her and Isabel to the coast of promise. Colour and hope, life and love would come to vitalise them again.

In the days that followed, Sophia began writing to Santiago regularly. The sun was beginning to shine on her again, the dust was settling. She started drawing spectacular butterflies on paper. Creatures as ethereal as butterflies were best etched on paper and not on sand. The wind could not wipe out a butterfly sketched on paper. She would hold on tight to her paper butterflies, never to let aspirations flounder again.

"If Isabel and I cross the American-Mexican border, my cousin Santiago will help us start afresh in California. He and I have been writing to each other. We would do well in as opportune a place like California. Please devise something, help us cross over to the other side," Sophia asked Milano when he stopped by one evening to drop off a basket of fish.

Milano nodded. "Numerous Mexican workers cross the border in search of work all the time. California is the green haven that it is because of Mexican workers. If you are so keen to go, you and Isabel can join a farming crew that is headed there," he said.

"Yes, it would be best to cross over informally because Santiago mentioned that entering America through a formal port of entry is a long drawn uncertain process," Sophia said.

Before he took off for home, Milano promised Sophia that he would ask around about farming crews that were leaving for California and she eagerly began awaiting a braver dawn to clasp a second chance at happiness, to start a new life in a new land. American tourists, out on boating and fishing adventures in Bahía de Kino often stopped by Sophia's colmado to buy produce and desert blooms. Sophia thought there was something suave about them. They were generous, courteous and thoughtful, paying for items without haggling, sometimes even leaving generous tips. Looking at them with longing, she recalled that not only was America home to those magnanimous people, it was also the original abode of the charming butterflies and elusive hummingbirds that had always beckoned her. Drawn by the dream, she began imagining a future for herself and Isabel in California. "California is the place where everybody is from somewhere else. English binds the immigrants together. Read it, write it, think in it and speak to me in English. Your Uncle Santiago says with English, you will immerse seamlessly into California," Sophia began telling Isabel over and again.

A few months later in January of 1927, Milano introduced Sophia and Isabel to a black-toothed foreman named Miguel Guzman, who happened to be a distant cousin of his wife. Miguel had been going back and forth across the American-Mexican border for years and planned on leading a farming crew into Arizona and California soon. He promised that he would help Sophia and Isabel reach their family in Los Angeles.

With stars in their eyes, Sophia and Isabel bid Milano, his family and Bahía de Kino goodbye. Thinking of Milano's extraordinary generosity in helping her regain her footing, Sophia broke down. "By offering me refuge and helping me to walk again, you have done what only family could. You have been your brother Giovanni's keeper in the truest sense. The universe shines in you," she said embracing him.

"Sophia, you are your own light. May you continue to sparkle!" Milano said, wiping his tears and smiling.

Sophia and Isabel took off with Miguel and his crew for San Luis Rio Colorado, a town on the American-Mexican border. Miguel attempted to lead the crew members across the border on many a night but failed due to border patrolling. So, he led them a little farther where the border wasn't under scrutiny and on a dark endless night, the crew took off for the other side, watchful of snakes and scorpions, walking on and on through the wilderness and tall grass, resting under trees and against boulders, eating wild berries and stale bread, the croaking of frogs and the hooting of owls shattering the quiet of the night. Fatigued, hallucinated, famished, thirsty, bruised, blistered, muddy but hopeful, Sophia and Isabel tread on until they saw a purple sun rising over swaying alfalfa and long melon fields.

"We are on American soil. This is Yuma, Arizona!" Miguel exclaimed.

Standing beneath the American sky, an exhausted Sophia sighed with relief. Dusting off the debris from Isabel's clothes, she decided that she and Isabel would work with the crew for a bit, make a little money and then take off to meet their family and future in the Californian City of Angeles — Los Angeles.

The crew settled in a shelter in Yuma and   Sophia immediately resumed contact with Santiago in Los Angeles. He assured her again of his unfailing support, even writing to say that he had found a great marital match for Isabel, now almost nineteen. Sophia was ecstatic. Happiness hollered to her from around the corner and she wanted to coddle it. From having lived extraordinary stress, she had grey hair and aching knees, making her look older than her years. Some members of the crew called her, Old Sophia. Old or young, driven by the impulse of buying pretty things for her Isabel's wedding, Sophia decided that she would work tirelessly in Arizona regardless of the scorching sun because nothing but the very best things would do for her beautiful Isabel.

Miguel found work for the crew on the orange groves of an Indian farmer known around Yuma as the Hindu man. Sophia thought the farmer strange, just plain strange. There couldn't have been another word for him. Speaking a strange language, he was loud and brash and what was worse, she caught him staring at Isabel many a time. Then one Sunday, she saw him with a long piece of cloth draped around his head.

Miguel told her that the Anglos incorrectly referred to all Indians as Hindus. "Not every Indian is a Hindu. This Indian farmer is actually a Sikh and that headgear is called a turban. He wears it when he goes to his Sikh temple on Sundays," Miguel said.

Never having heard the words "Sikh" or "turban" before, they didn't register with Sophia.

The crew picked oranges for quite a few Sikh farmers in Arizona. But Sophia's opinion of them didn't change. Their gazes made her cringe. "These uncouth men with equally uncouth glances make me want to disappear," Sophia told Isabel one afternoon as they sat eating lunch under a tree.

Isabel refused to have any of it. "Mama, please shed this terrible bias — once and for all. We are all immigrants. If anything, we should all be coming forward to support each other due to our shared experience of taking difficult journeys to reach America. And just so you know, Sikhs are hard-working farmers. They don't bother anyone."

"I don't care if they are hard-working or not. I only wish that they didn't stare the way they do," Sophia said waving her hand. It was her duty to protect her daughter from unwanted advances and outlandish men and no way would she relinquish that responsibility come rain, shine or brazen-faced Sikh farmers.

"Tomorrow, we will head west to Imperial Valley in California," Miguel said one afternoon as the crew was walking back to the shelter after picking and packing the last of the oranges at an orchard in Yuma. "Imperial Valley is a haven in the middle of the desert with thousands of acres of fertile land watered by the River Colorado. This being carrot picking season, we will find abundant work there."

Sophia cheered. They would finally set foot in California. "How far is Imperial Valley from Los Angeles?" she asked, her eyes gleaming.

"Barely a few hours away by bus. Five hours, perhaps," Miguel said.

Sophia gushed. She and Isabel would work for a week or so in Imperial Valley and then take the bus to Los Angeles. "My cousin has found a great marital match for my Isabel in Los Angeles. The man owns a house and a store. He even has a Cadillac, you know," she told the crew excitedly.

"A Cadillac? Whatever is that?" Ernesto, a young farmhand asked.

"A big car," Sophia replied, her face beaming with satisfaction.

"Yes, it is a big, comfortable car. I know the man that Sophia is talking about. He is much older than Isabel and a widower. But how does it matter? He is a wealthy Mexican to say the least," Miguel said raising his brows and smirking.

"He was married only for a bit before his wife died of pneumonia leaving him childless. He is a good man," Sophia said hurriedly. "My cousin would choose nothing but the very best for Isabel. She will live a life of plenty in the City of Angeles." Slipping into a reverie, Sophia imagined Isabel happily married and living in a cosy furnished house driving about town in a big car, flowers in her hair, pearls around her neck.

"And what about you, Old Sophia? Will you continue working on the fields with us after Isabel's wedding to the rich man?" Ernesto asked abruptly as though he had read Sophia's thoughts.

Sophia was caught off guard, "Ah me? I guess, I will find work and live in Los Angeles somewhere," she whispered quickly.

"My mother will live with me wherever I live, always and forever," Isabel said, fiercely wrapping her arms around her mother.

Sophia looked ahead, glad that Santiago had helped her find a husband for Isabel. Now Isabel's future was secure. If she had sat around waiting for love to come by and splash Isabel's life with elation, there was no knowing when that would happen if it happened at all. Besides, what was love? A beautiful lie, a misplaced memory, a short-lived spring. Or was it a deceitful promise reduced to nothing more than a fuzzy picture in the mind, a melody that one eventually forgot? She would choose security over love for Isabel any day. Closing her eyes, she wished for Isabel's future husband to see and appreciate Isabel for who she was — brave, optimistic, beautiful — and shower her with happiness, wishing also that unlike her mother, Isabel's bliss would last till eternity, wiping out forever the memories of her frightful past.

Sophia's mind flew her to a sunny habitat, where large orange butterflies danced over merry verbena blooms under a magenta sun. Breaking into an unabashed smile, she blew a kiss of thanks to the sky.

KISHAN SINGH

Kishan thought Imperial Valley was a sister to him and Jaspal. Like them, she had learned to sparkle in the face of many a downer. Once dismissed as dry and infertile, thanks to the fabulous River Colorado, it could now be tilled for double and triple cropping, even yielding crops through the length of winter. Fifty acres was not large enough to take a leap at cotton. Cotton would have to wait till they bought more land. He and Jaspal decided that vegetables would be the ideal crops to grow on a fifty-acre stretch. The mild dry winters and the alluvial deposits from the Colorado flood plain would facilitate an abundant harvest of vegetables. Employing a friendly and well-meaning Mexican overseer, Cesar, to help them about the fields, they hired Mexican crews and began planting lettuce, cauliflowers, carrots, asparagus, onions and peppers on the acreage, following it up with the dispensing of fertilisers and pesticides.

One day at a farmer's market, Kishan purchased a race-injured stallion whom he and Jaspal began to call Stud. Though not swift anymore, Stud was diligent. Riding him about, they took turns to supervise the weeding and watering of the fields. Then as luck would have it, Allah Baksh put his old Ford truck up for sale. Kishan knew not to miss a chance like that. The truck was old, but it was holding strong. So, they purchased it for a pittance, cleaning and shining it for hours outside their rented rooms in Holtville.

Lying on his hard bed, Kishan began dreaming on many an evening of building a farmhouse. Rattan Lal's spacious state-of-the-art cottage with lush orange trees lining the driveway had come to form an ineffaceable image of affluence in his mind. On long, hot afternoons when he was run down from working on the farm, he envisioned himself and Jaspal living in a cottage like Rattan Lal's. One evening, as he and Jaspal were driving by Rattan Lal's cottage on their way back home to Holtville, Kishan took to thinking of it again. Right then, Jaspal who was quiet and fatigued, having woken up early that morning to water the vegetables, said, "Soon, very soon, Kishan, we too will have a house of our own. Like Rattan Lal's if not better!"

Kishan stared at Jaspal. It was incredible the way their thoughts had converged and melded together in their hope for a house by an orange grove. They burst into laughter.

1925 announced itself with a bang. Calvin Coolidge would resume office as President for a new term, having won with a popular majority vote of 2.5 million over his opponents' combined total. For the first time in American history, the President's inauguration would be aired on radio, the newspaper said. Kishan was excited. Huddling around the radio with Allah Baksh and his family, he and Jaspal listened to the Vermont farmer's inaugural address with wonderstruck eyes as the President stressed that agriculture must thrive independent of political control. Modernising farms instead of manipulating prices was the way to increase profits. Kishan agreed with the President. No honest farmer should ever have to manipulate prices because manipulation went against the very premise of growing and providing. Feeling a rush of energy and enterprise, Kishan began exploring new farming possibilities, applying to the Imperial Bank for a loan to buy a tractor. The tractor would surely help them pay back the loans from the bank sooner. A few weeks later, when they brought home a green John Deere tractor, Kishan couldn't stop raving about the gasoline-powered machine. It could cultivate intensely, increase yields manifold and decrease labour time to half. He liked the sharp turns that the tractor could make, reaching the far corners of the fields, making sowing, ploughing and harvesting easy and artful.

Loading crisp lettuce heads, cauliflowers and cabbages on railroad carts headed east, one bright morning in late spring, Kishan rejoiced in the beautiful harvests. Next, they would pick carrots and asparagus. Come summer, it would be time to pack off the sweet onions and peppers. The thought of profitable produces sent his mind whirring.

After grocery shopping at Holtville on Sundays, Kishan and Jaspal would do the cooking, making a large pot of chicken curry and rice to last them a couple of days. Kishan looked forward to cooking spinach every now and then, steaming it along with cabbage and broccoli, mashing all three together and spicing the mix with salt, pepper and roasted tomatoes. Then he and Jaspal would gobble down the dish with corn tortillas that the newly married Allah Baksh's Mexican mother-in-law, Margarita made for them in large batches. They'd reciprocate her favour by presenting cake and liquor to her often but getting wind of Kishan's storytelling, Margarita declared one day that she would only accept the cake and liquor if offered with a story or two. So, on Sundays when Allah Baksh invited Kishan and Jaspal over for dinner, Kishan began telling Margarita and the family stories before the meal. All stories sprang from his readings and experiences. He'd narrate different kinds — western fairy tales about goodness rewarded; eastern fables from the Panchatantra celebrating intelligent living; mythological stories about the three-eyed Indian God Shiva who was both the foremost artist and the supreme warrior; agrarian folktales from Punjab about the values of honesty and hard work; and sometimes, even the legend of Robin Hood's quest for justice.

On days when he was nostalgic, Kishan would also share the true story of how he and Jaspal had started from a historic Punjabi village, crossing the oceans to reach the coast of hope, California. And on enthusiastic days, he would tell a story just to live out his fantasy about a Sikh farmer who became so big a land baron in California that President Coolidge invited him to the White House for tea. The story didn't end there. Falling in love with a strawberry-haired Anglo girl, the Sikh farmer romanced his girl to the hilt, travelling with her through time and space, whizzing through constellations, counting stars. Consciously or unconsciously, Kishan's stories were now laced in the lore of America — resilient, hopeful, and celebratory.

"Imperial Valley tells marvellous stories to rival those of humans," Kishan wrote to Amy just as 1926 blew in. "Spruced by rain, it bristles with ecstasy. Popping out of their holes, hungry rattlesnakes hiss around looking for rodents. Dust rolls behind cars and tractors as scorpions and tortoises, rabbits and roadrunners pace around all day long. On a lucky day, one can even spot a buckboard or a stagecoach racing down the valley's unpaved paths. In the evening, the setting sun turns the pale sky to a fiery orange and gradually to a deep purple. Then the moon takes over, flooding the air with mystery, lighting the edges of the distant mountain peaks, twinkling over the trees and dimming out the stars with its phosphorescent glow. Most of all, I want you to know that there is no better place than the desert valley to spot the magical Milky Way."

Kishan hoped the Milky Way would catch Amy's imagination. Though they had been writing to each other frequently, he hadn't seen her since leaving Central Valley over two years ago. Finishing the letter and slipping it inside a stamped envelope, he wondered if she still smiled as much as she did before, if she thought of him even half as much as he thought of her, wishing deeply that she'd take a trip down to Imperial Valley soon.

A week later, when Kishan was walking around talking to the labour, the mail carrier delivered a letter from Amy. Kishan could hardly hold his excitement every time he heard from her. It was like backsliding to teenage, his heart joggling, his hands shaking. He liked her pale green stationery and her beautiful cursive. Quickly, he tore open the envelope and pulled out the letter. A big smile sprang up on his face on reading that Amy was indeed intrigued by the Milky Way and hoped to come down to Imperial Valley one day to catch a glimpse of it. And interestingly, she had recommended a novel too, *The Great Gatsby*.

"It is about a man in love," Amy had written. "The writer visited California recently. I heard him talk at the Sacramento City Hall."

The next morning, Kishan sped off in the truck for the town of Imperial, hoping the library there would have a copy.

"*The Great Gatsby* came out early last year and I ordered a copy right after," the grey-haired librarian at Imperial said, adjusting his reading glasses and issuing the novel to Kishan.

Rushing through dinner that evening, Kishan slouched on the couch with the novel, reading through the night. Jay Gatsby's journey from being a dirt-poor farm boy to a man of enormous wealth to win the love of a lost girl did not impress Kishan because Gatsby had acquired money not by hard work but by disgraceful means. Most of all, Kishan felt betrayed by Gatsby who was ashamed of his farm boy heritage. By making false claims to aristocracy, Gatsby dishonoured the working class of America — men and women who with their hard work were leading the nation to glory. Kishan would have rather had Gatsby be proud of his humble past, deriving strength from the untarnished honesty of that life.

"Gatsby's story ended sadly because nothing good can spring from disowning the past and pursuing a wrong goal by deceitful means," Kishan wrote to Amy the next morning.

The following week when the mail carrier brought another letter from Amy, Kishan could hardly wait to read her take.

"Though the novel has been received with moderate enthusiasm, I liked *The Great Gatsby*," Amy had written. "Who could have thought a little book could set off nationwide debates on class differences in America?"

Kishan smirked. It was nice to hear that the book had got teachers, librarians and others to discuss class differences in the country. To him, discrimination in an unequal American society had always been very real. He was suffering the California Alien Land Laws that kept him from holding the farm that he owned, in his own name. He was also a victim of the ridiculous Anti-Miscegenation Laws that prevented him from pursuing a romantic relationship with the girl he liked. He had neither high financial nor social standing and he didn't care. He was proud to be a hard-working farmer, proud of his underprivileged past, proud of his everyday struggles.

Cotton was God's greatest gift to Imperial Valley and Kishan could hardly wait to buy more land and try his luck with the queen of crops. As chance would have it one day, he and Jaspal met a friendly, red-cheeked Swiss farmer, Bart Aspen at a fertiliser store in Holtville. Bart invited Kishan and Jaspal over and showed them around his rambling cotton plantation outside the nearby town of Brawley. Watching them admire the flowering cotton fields stretching on for miles, Bart encouraged Kishan and Jaspal discreetly as was the way with his people to go for the cotton. "Growing the droplets of snow is a joy that I hope to relish for the rest of my life," Bart said.

Kishan stared at the soft, white cotton flowers looming in the horizon like clouds. That sight made him crave even more for a larger piece of land. "Pali, a large farm would be our door to not just a secure but also a prosperous future," he said to Jaspal on the drive back home. Then thinking awhile, he whispered, "Plush melon harvests can pave our way to cotton."

Jaspal agreed. There was money in melons. Money could lead them to a large tract of land and eventually, cotton. Talking to successful Japanese melon farmers in the valley, they discovered that with the right combination of moisture, sunlight and heat, melon seeds sprouted fast, saplings running across the fields in weeks. They decided to rotate melons with vegetables. Kishan recalled eating melons by the splashing waters of the River Satluj running through the canals by the wheat fields in Noor Mahal. He remembered especially the incredibly delicious melon that he had shared with Roop — how he had saved its seeds, how he had tried to grow those seeds along Baldev Mama's fields and how those seeds hadn't taken root in Noor Mahal.

In Imperial Valley, Kishan was glad for the melon seeds. They sprouted fast, the saplings decking the fields with yellow, red and orange flowers, which were followed soon after by melons. Staring at the golden balls, Kishan rejoiced in the fulfilment of that wish for growing melons which was made back in Noor Mahal but came true in Imperial Valley. Packing the melon crates off for the east coast in the late summer of 1926, Kishan chuckled in anticipation of sowing the next melon crop.

Encouraged by the profitable vegetable and melon harvests, he and Jaspal began working harder and longer still, hoping sooner than later to buy more land and grow cotton. Though they saved painstakingly to buy more land, Kishan decided that it was imperative to buy a car. "The old Ford truck is great to be driving around the farm, but a Model T is what we need to drive to the city," he told Jaspal. Together they decided on the Ford Model T Tudor Sedan, purchasing it through a dealer in Holtville. Driving it around, they couldn't stop marvelling about the smooth black exterior and the roomy interior of the sturdy car. "It can even pull a plough across the fields," Kishan told Jaspal excitedly.

"With its large four-cylinder engine, it can probably pull a combine harvester too," Jaspal laughed.

"Now all we need to do is to drive to Los Angeles and buy new clothes," Kishan said.

They bought button-down shirts and suits similar to what men were wearing in the city. And even though Jaspal was sceptical about spending any more money on clothes, Kishan persuaded him that they must buy hats and ties as well. "We are no longer farmhands but farmers," he reminded Jaspal. "Look at the Swiss farmers in the valley. Always impeccably dressed, they wear fine suits with fedora hats when driving to the city. We should be well dressed too."

Thereafter, they began driving to Los Angeles once every month for a day of fun. Kishan thought the city thundered with life and liberation. His mind could hardly keep up with the staggering visions and sounds — people pacing around, street cars honking and girls in flapper dresses smoking and swaying to jazz. Most of all, Kishan admired the streetlights. It was one thing to read about electricity and another to see lights connected by wires, twinkling in mid-air. It wouldn't be long, he told Jaspal, before electricity would make its way to the countryside, lighting up farms, improving the living standards of farmers. In their suits and hats, he and Jaspal were often taken for Spanish men and they played along, mouthing phrases in Spanish. Merging in the madness and commotion of Los Angeles, they were pleased to evade discrimination. Kishan was aware, however, that racism was not dead. Many Punjabi farmers from Imperial Valley who lacked social graces were refused access to restaurants and rooms in Los Angeles' hotels. Fashionable clothes and social etiquette could ward off racism temporarily, Kishan told Jaspal, but it could pop up its nasty face anytime.

On one weekend trip to Los Angeles, they got themselves photographed at a portrait studio in downtown. Locking their exuberance forever, the photograph caught Jaspal's unhindered smile, Kishan's reflective gaze and their new slicked back, side-parted hair but more than that, it was Kishan's and Jaspal's self-assurance that resounded in the shot. Sitting on the mantel in their room in Imperial Valley, that portrait, lyrical like a poem, enfolding both their past and their present, began coercing them to risk yet newer roads.

Though Amy was always the one with recommendations for novels, it was Kishan who discovered Hemingway's *The Sun Also Rises* when strolling through the library. Caught up in the complex, multi-layered story that Hemingway had woven, he couldn't put it down, finishing it in a day and a night. "*The Sun Also Rises* is brilliant," he wrote to Amy the next day. "Do read it when you have a chance."

He heard back from her after a fortnight. "*The Sun Also Rises* left me aghast," Amy had written. "Filthy writing can sell but will never qualify as literature."

Kishan folded the letter. He didn't agree with Amy. To him, *The Sun Also Rises* was a fantastic specimen of great American writing. It was not filthy but real. He had come to deeply admire the protagonist of the novel, Jake. Despite being dented by the war, the man retained goodness, humanity and hope, toiling to earn his living like the multitudes of working men and women that were changing the face of America. An honest, hard-working man, Jake was the heart of the novel and of America too. Placing Amy's letter inside a drawer, Kishan decided that on his next trip to the city, he would buy his own copy of *The Sun Also Rises*. And if he could ever find Mr. Hemingway's address, he would surely write to him, thanking him for writing the great American story.

One day, on learning that an Anglo farmer who was moving out of the state had put his three-hundred acre farm up for sale, instantly, they began following that lead. The very thought of owning three hundred acres was exhilarating, an ambitious longing yearning for fruition.

Kishan met Mr. Williams to discuss the possibility of drawing another loan because even though he and Jaspal had saved as best as they could after having paid the previous loan instalments, their savings were not nearly enough to jump at the three hundred acres. Unsure of what Mr. Williams would say, Kishan waited for his response, his heart thumping in his throat. If Mr. Williams refused, he and Jaspal would cry over the missed opportunity for the rest of their days.

Thinking awhile, Mr. Williams asked, "What do you plan on growing on the three hundred acres if you come to own them?"

Kishan spelled out his well-thought-out plan. "Mr. Williams, my brother and I plan to take a chance on cotton. But the cultivating expenses being enormous and the risks high due to cotton's vulnerability to weather and pests, we intend to move with caution. To begin with, we will grow melons and vegetables on two hundred acres and cotton on the remaining hundred," he said.

Mr. Williams nodded. "It is best to be cautious with cotton, especially if it is one's first brush with it. Cotton has ruined as many farmers as it has hoisted." Then pausing for a moment, he said, "I'll try my best to help by personally overseeing the loan sanction. Due to your regular payments of the previous loan instalments, it is likely the bank will grant you another."

After eight long weeks and numerous formalities, when the loan came through, sitting by Judge Arnold Brown, as he signed the purchase papers, Kishan and Jaspal acquired the three-hundred acre farm in the winter of 1926. It was a day steeped in happiness. Swimming in ecstasy, they congratulated each other on becoming big time farmers, assuring one another that they would continue rising with the sun and labouring till the birds went home.

Updating themselves about the newest farming practices, finance and risk management, marketing and tax payment, they asked the Farm Bureau to help them buy two more tractors at subsidised prices, realising in time that farming large tracts was a business as dynamic as any other.

The newly bought three hundred acres sat thirty miles east of Holtville, a short drive from Kishan and Jaspal's previous fifty acres. A wiggly and dusty wagon-beaten path dotted with date and mulberry trees led up to the acreage, mountains looking upon it from the far west. A few old oaks stood along the fields telling tales of a time long ago, splattering the space with history. After some thought, leasing the previous fifty acres to a Chinese farmer, Kishan and Jaspal decided to focus on the three-hundred-acre stretch. A dilapidated house sat on the acreage crumbling fast, at the back of which was a shed and an outhouse for an overseer. Moving Cesar into the shed right away, Kishan and Jaspal pulled down the old house and started building four bedrooms, a bath, a kitchen and a living room upon the existing cinder foundation that was holding strong. It would be a year before they could move in, the builders said. Continuing to commute from their rented rooms, they sowed vegetables on the new acreage as they prepared to cast their lot with melons and cotton in the spring.

"Nothing but the very best melon seeds will do for the new farm," Jaspal said to Kishan one balmy February morning in 1927, speeding away for Los Angeles in the old Ford truck to purchase melon seeds, it being melon planting season.

Cesar and Kishan took to work. Everything had to be in place so that they could start sowing the melon seeds just as soon as Jaspal returned in a day or so. Driving the tractor across the dry and cracked fields, Kishan wished fervently for rain. It had been an unusually dry winter. October, November, December and January had come and gone with no sign of rain. The valley was dry. It even cackled. A little rain would make the fields laugh and put the dust clouds to sleep. The tilling done, Kishan and Cesar spread manure across the creased land. Exhausted at the end of the day, Kishan drove home to the rented rooms, had dinner and turned on the radio. It was an RCA Radiola 28. Kishan loved that radio. Seeing the mahogany wrapped desk-shaped box with large round knobs in the radio catalogue, he hadn't been able to resist it. The advertisement had called that radio an unparalleled feat and Kishan had at once believed it. He had seen radios before but nothing like that enticing brown box. It promised him the spunky unknown. Smitten, he had touched its shiny knobs in the picture, even laughed at the thought of turning them around. Then quickly he had ordered the radio from a dealer with the last bit of money that he and Jaspal had been left with after purchasing the new farm. They had set aside that bit for an emergency. There would be no emergency, Kishan had told himself, and in the case of one, they had Allah Baksh to bail them out. And when the box was delivered, tediously setting it up, he had sworn never to mention the radio's cost to Jaspal.

That day sitting alone by the radio, listening to the evening news, Kishan applauded the political initiatives for consistent irrigation rates and better seeds for farmers. Now farmers would be able to make more than just a few bucks. Numerous plans for upgrading the farm began sprinting through his mind. As idea upon idea churned in his head, he stepped into the open to breathe in the evening air. The sky seemed unusually dark and low. He stopped to smell the heavy clouds. Looking up, he saw impossibly quiet birds gliding through the calm air. Then suddenly he looked down. Worms had crept out and were crawling on the dry earth. His farmer's sense recognised that lull. Immediately, he rushed indoors. When he heard the first grumble, he was not surprised.

He had heard of desert thunderstorms. They could drench fields, sweep away cattle, wash homes down and in the worst case, drown people. Severe lightning could start bush fires that in a matter of hours could turn the valley to rubble. He had barely muttered a prayer when the tumultuous roar of the thunderstorm blasted the night. Kishan rushed to the window. Orange and blue streaks flashed across the dark skies, striking the mulberry trees, reducing them to ashes and stumps. Then the sand began billowing up. Before long, rain was thundering on the rooftop making Kishan fear that the roof would collapse.

He dabbled with the radio, but the transmission was lost. It was the worst night to be alone. He began pacing the room. The storm raged on past midnight. His mind ran to the fields. Too much water would turn the fields into a swamp. He had always been in awe of water. Water had a mind of its own. It did as it pleased — nourished or destroyed. He recalled the horrific monsoons that came to rain down havoc on him in Noor Mahal the summer before he sailed to America. Instead of feeding the fields, the rain had washed away the cotton crop, and left in its wake influenza, changing his and Jaspal's life forever. He remembered how farmers back in Punjab fought incessantly over water, water disputes running down generations. Farmers were even found murdered over water that they diverted from other fields into their own. In Imperial Valley too, water was often the bone of contention. As much as he and Jaspal had tried to avoid it, on a few occasions, they had wound up doing the Punjabi thing — physically tackled a few Japanese and one Swiss farmer all for water. Sensing a sudden quiet outside, he rushed to the window again. The storm was rolling farther away, charcoal clouds foaming along the horizon. Sighing with relief, he drove slowly in the dark dawn to check on the farm. Reaching there, he was glad that the under-construction house stood strong. The barn was leaking but hadn't crumbled. Cesar had led Stud into his shed, where huddling under the tin roof, the two had evaded the rain and lightning. Kishan looked at Cesar. They smiled awkwardly, thankfully. Stroking Stud's coat, Kishan told the panic-stricken horse that the storm had moved on. Then he stepped into the drenched fields. The day before the earth lay crying for water, and now here it was — in the fields, in the overflowing canals and in the mud holes. It was their good luck that the storm had been a passing one. It had likely buzzed in from Arizona and shaking up the valley, had drifted west into San Diego.

Kishan thought that in answer to his prayer, the storm had moved on. In passing through, it had left behind just enough rain to help them grow their dreams. Looking at the fields, he imagined an abundant harvest of melons in the future and just as he was about to smile at that happy vision, he felt the glorious morning glimmer in his face. The sun felt warm upon his back. Up ahead he saw a miracle so unforgettable that it came to be carved on his being. In front of him was a brilliant rainbow, stretching from one end of the sky to the other in a perfect semi-circle, all seven colours sparkling in the dimly lit sky. He had never seen anything as beautiful, as achingly pristine. He wanted to grab that happiness and hold it close in a clenched fist, never to let go.

Two days later when Jaspal returned from Los Angeles with the seeds, Kishan told him that he had a name for the farm. Standing by the fields, they were both amazed to see that the rainbow that Kishan had spotted in the sky after the storm had now descended to the ground. Within forty-eight hours of the rain, dormant wildflower seeds had hatched from the dry earth. A vibrant medley of yellow desert dandelions, golden poppies, orange verbena blooms, pink mariposa lilies, red lupines, purple primroses and blue cornflowers now formed a rainbow upon the land, turning what was a dusty plain a few days ago into a lush wonderland bursting with colour.

Jaspal agreed that there couldn't be a better name for their cherished farm. Braving the storm, they had reached home — The Rainbow Acres.

February 26th, 1927

Dear Amy,

I hope you are as spring-struck as I am.

I apologise for not writing in a while. You will be happy to know, however, that the past few months have besplashed my life with unbounded joy. Jaspal and I have purchased a new farm that spreads across three hundred acres. As we rejoiced in our dream fulfilled, a passing storm left behind the most unforgettable rainbow over the farm. That rainbow has come to be forged indelibly on my psyche to where I have named the farm The Rainbow Acres. True to its name, the farm is a dazzling motley of colours at all times, gorgeous wildflowers glittering along the edges of the fields. Flying in early this year, spring especially has lent it a maddening vivacity. Splattering the farm with perfume, spring has brought with it a bounty of lettuce, bell peppers and beets. What's more, it has decked the melon vines with extraordinarily large orange flowers. The Colorado is jumping all out of control, bouncing high in the canals. Songs of cuckoos fill up the mornings and butterflies and bees come to hover over the sweet onions at noon. While going down each evening, the sun leaves behind splashes of pink, which gradually meld into darkness. That's when swarms of fireflies come out to light up the night with their sparkles.

While everything about The Rainbow Acres fascinates me, I am most intrigued by the old oaks that stand like discerning savants along the carrot fields. Grown by the natives hundreds of years ago before the Spaniards came, the oaks have carvings on them. Story has it that a long time ago, a native princess fell in love with a passing Spanish trooper. She pined for him, night and day, etching messages on the oaks on lovesick afternoons. I can never have my fill of gazing at the carvings. Perhaps they are sayings in an alien language, perhaps songs of loss and betrayal. How lovely it would be to have you come over to The Rainbow Acres to breathe in the splendour of the desert wildflowers and to watch the fireflies dance with the moonbeams. But most of all, I am banking on you to unravel the secrets scribbled on the old oaks. I can even imagine you running your fingertips over the messages, wind ruffling your red hair. If my letter has in any way charmed you about The Rainbow Acres, please plan your trip soon.

Fondly,
Kishan

As mesmerising as the spring of 1927 was, it was also the time to take on the new and daunting project: the planting of cotton. Kishan and Jaspal braced themselves for the challenge. Cotton was risky, farmers around the valley warned them again. It was susceptible to weather changes. The pests didn't leave it alone. The growing expenses were stifling. They had heard of all the odds. Hardening to the test, they ran seed drills over ploughed fields and sowed the cotton seeds, following it up with weeding to ensure that the seeds got sufficient nutrients, sunlight and water.

A few weeks later when the seeds sprouted, and the saplings began to shoot, Kishan and Jaspal shrieked with joy, their eyes bristling. It would be two months before the flower buds would appear. Eagerly, they began waiting for cotton to send them spiralling forward, delighting meantime in the upcoming farmhouse. To keep things simple, they decided on colouring the outside of the house white and the roof a bright red like carrots growing by the house. Kishan was particularly happy about the carrot crop that spring. It promised a plentiful harvest. One morning as he sat estimating the gains that the carrots would likely be bringing in, a distressed Jaspal came rushing to him. "Kishan, the carrots are ready for harvest but the labour crew that we had hired has not shown up. It is most worrisome. We must hire a new batch quickly!" he said.

Kishan got up with a start. Perhaps the labour crew had left for up north to work at a higher paying factory instead. "Let me talk to Allah Baksh," he said. Speeding to Allah Baksh's farm, he knew Allah Baksh would surely step up to help. No way would Allah Baksh let their beautiful carrot crop be ruined. And sure enough, as soon as Kishan shared the dilemma with him, Allah Baksh came to their rescue. "A new batch of Mexican labour came in yesterday from Yuma. I can send it your way for a week. That'll give you time to arrange for more," Allah Baksh said.

"Thank you," a relieved Kishan murmured.

SOPHIA

"Pulling out carrots is not nearly as hard as picking oranges," Sophia told Isabel as their crew went about wiping clean field after field of carrots. "Besides, the wages are higher in Imperial Valley, this being California, you know."

Isabel smiled and adjusted her sun hat. "Mama, it's a beautiful farm, overflowing with wild flowers! I can even hear the cuckoos singing in the bushes. This colourful paradise is so different from the farms in Arizona!" she said.

"Didn't I say California is the hallowed land? Wait till you get to Los Angeles. It is a gem of a city by the ocean," Sophia said as her mind took to imagining Los Angeles again.

"Mama, may we have lunch along the far edges of the fields?" Isabel asked. "Clusters of poppies are dancing to the wind there."

"Girl, don't go getting too comfortable. You are here to pick carrots not to relish the scenes," Sophia said. The farm belonged to two young Sikh brothers, Miguel had told her, and Sophia had seen the brothers too. Both wore sun hats. The older went about riding a horse, overseeing the building of the farmhouse that was coming up not far from the carrot fields only to return every so often to check on the carrot harvest. Around mid-morning, he worked for a while alongside the farmhands, digging and packing carrots before riding off again. It was most unusual. Never before had she known a farmer to work alongside the labour. From how he looked at her and Isabel, it seemed as though he wanted to talk to them, but Sophia knew better than to indulge a stranger. The younger one walked about joking and laughing with the crew, waving at her and Isabel as well. He seemed way too happy as though crazed by spring. She couldn't help noticing that both the brothers were well dressed, not sloppy like some of the Sikh farmers back in Arizona.

"To think that Sikhs are here in California too. Never would I have thought that they own land here as well," Sophia whispered to Isabel.

"Miguel says Sikhs have farms across the length of California," Isabel said wiping her brow with her sleeve.

"We will be breaking for lunch now. We will eat under the oaks," Miguel came along and said.

Sophia nodded and gestured to Isabel.

"But Mama, I wanted to sit by the poppies over on the other side. The river too, runs through the canals over there," Isabel started to say.

"Isabel, the entire crew will be eating under the oaks," Sophia sternly cut her short.

"We will work here for a week and then head back to the farm where we had originally come to work at," Miguel said as everyone sat eating lunch. "The owners of this farm sure are lucky — they are reaping a bounteous carrot harvest."

"Lucky those brothers certainly are. It is a large farm and breathtakingly beautiful. The younger of the brothers who was walking about talking to us said he has named the farm The Rainbow Acres after a rainbow that a storm left behind over the farm," Ernesto said, scooping beans into a tortilla.

"The Rainbow Acres," Isabel said, breaking into a wide smile. "That's just the right name for a welcoming farm like this! The horse is friendly too. I fed him carrots and petted him and he let me!"

Sophia turned to look at the horse who stood tied to an oak as the owners sat eating lunch at a makeshift table a few yards away. "The Sikh brothers are fairly young to own as large a farm as this," she said curiously.

"Men from Punjab — Hindus, Sikhs and Muslims — are fast purchasing land across the Pacific coast. Not only that, they are also marrying Mexican girls. The law permits brown to marry brown. There are numerous Punjabi-Mexican couples now," Miguel said.

Sophia thought back about the Sikh farmers who farmed the orange orchards near Yuma. Now she knew. Every Mexican girl was a prospective bride to them. No wonder they would stare at Isabel the way they did. She was still recoiling at that memory when the older of the two Sikh brothers came to untie the horse, turning around to nod at the crew members before riding away. She thought he looked especially long and hard at Isabel. Sophia stiffened. The Sikh farmers in California were no different from the ones back in Arizona. "It is one thing to acquire land, quite another to amass decency," she said shaking her head.

KISHAN SINGH

Kishan saw that Jaspal had more than noticed the unusual girl among the labour just as soon as the new crew took to harvesting carrots, glancing her way over and again. She had a distant look in her eyes to where she would be talking to a person but Kishan could tell that her mind was somewhere else, seeking something that she had known and lost. With her upright posture and proud walk, there was no mistaking her for a farmhand. Conspicuously tall, she stood out in the crew, her mother chaperoning her as they walked about in their long cotton dresses and sun hats.

The girl's eyes, too, would find Jaspal every now and then. Kishan saw her watching Jaspal as he went about riding Stud and as he worked alongside the labour on the fields. And when Jaspal went to check on the builders working on the house, Kishan saw the girl look around every so often to find him. At noon, when the labour dispersed for lunch and Jaspal and Kishan sat down for a bite to eat, they saw that girl walk up to Stud who stood tied to an oak. Feeding him carrots, she petted him for a while before sitting down to have her lunch.

Somehow, Jaspal was not in the least surprised to see her petting the horse. Instead he smiled. Trapped in an elated angst, he was delving in wonder and beauty, leaping in and out of joy. Back at the rented rooms that evening, Kishan saw him admiring the sunset and crooning. At dinner too, Jaspal sang softly. Eating barely a bite or two, he left to walk outside for a bit before bed. The next day, Kishan thought Jaspal was quiet and introspective as he went about overseeing the labour, answering Kishan's questions in monosyllables. At noon, when they sat down for lunch, the girl came by again to feed and pet the horse, smiling irresistibly. Seeing her, Jaspal was buzzing again, continuing to laugh through dinner.

On the third day, when the labour went to lunch and Kishan sat down to eat too, Jaspal said he did not care for lunch. Just as they had expected, the girl came, fed and petted Stud, but before she walked away, Jaspal stepped up. Untying the horse, he handed her the reins. Perplexed, Kishan looked on as the girl hopped on Stud and took off in a full-fledged gallop around the fields. Stud was no easy beast to handle, but with the girl atop, he glided and floated around the carrots. She went around the fields a few times before halting by the oaks. Jumping off the horse, handing the reins to Jaspal, she looked at him and said, "Thank you," before sitting down to eat with her crew. Kishan went and stood by Jaspal.

"Kishan, like the horse, the girl, too, has seen better days," Jaspal said.

Kishan nodded. He'd known it from first glance. The girl and her mother did not belong with the crew. There was a mystery about them. It was provoking him with an overbearing curiosity to where he could hardly wait to discover their story.

Returning to the rented rooms that evening, Kishan and Jaspal ate dinner quietly. Tired from the long day when Kishan dropped down on the bed, Jaspal announced that he wasn't sleepy and stepped outside for a stroll. Kishan began to snooze. When he woke up the next day, Jaspal had already taken off for the fields. Packing lunch, Kishan drove to the farm. Balancing the account books, he smiled. His brother had been struck by the oldest, the most fatal disease — love. There was no one more miserable than a man in love — fluttering around like a happy butterfly one moment and twanging like a hopeless beetle in the next, feeling an awful ache and living a wild elation all at once. But as true as all of that was, love was beautiful, making a man marvel at the commonplace and ordinary as though he were seeing the world with new eyes. Kishan had seen Jaspal smiling at the bees hissing over the lupines. He'd also seen Jaspal grin at the blinking fireflies. Kishan knew too, that Jaspal had been the first to notice the blossoming of the succulents that week, the first to get up to relish the singing of the humming birds by the zinnias, the first also to drink in the fragrance of the inviting rosemary; and for once, Jaspal hadn't just walked on upon seeing the wild geraniums glittering along the fields, stopping instead to savour their ravishing purple. Kishan smiled again. Jaspal was spinning in the sea of pleasure and pain, wading at once through both rapture and torture.

Getting up, Kishan began to look around for Jaspal only to find him trotting around the farm on the horse. "Pali, aren't you hungry? You left so early this morning," Kishan asked.

"No, I am not," Jaspal replied nonchalantly. Then as if afraid that Kishan would read his mind and face, he rode off towards the cotton.

Watching Jaspal riding away, Kishan thought of how lucky the farmhand girl was to have someone as truthful as Jaspal fall for her. Just then a dreadful thought came to jab Kishan.

What if the girl and her mother rejected Jaspal? They were strange to begin with, always speaking in hushed tones, their mannerisms wary and doubtful. Kishan recalled how his own heartbreak had consumed, almost killed him. Instantly, he hoped Jaspal would never have to suffer that fate. He would do everything he could to help Jaspal. There was no way that he'd let his brother fall a victim to love.

SOPHIA

Isabel's fascination for the horse was turning into Sophia's nightmare. Isabel had started out by petting and feeding the horse every afternoon before lunch. Then, one day, the older of the two Sikh brothers stepped up to hand the horse's reins to her and Isabel took off on the horse, galloping around the fields in circles.

Sophia had let Isabel be, recalling her childhood passion for horseback riding in Guadalajara but things were quickly spinning out of control to where Isabel was now riding the horse around every afternoon before lunch. What was more, the older of the Sikh brothers had started to look at Isabel with lovesick eyes every time he walked over to hand the horse to Isabel.

Sophia had even noticed Isabel smiling a coy smile at the man and locking eyes with him. He now walked about the farm with stardust in his eyes, pining for a sight of Isabel as though he were living only for her. And worse yet, Isabel too, was edgy beyond belief. She rode faster and longer each afternoon as though to beat an uneasiness that had had the better of her.

From what the years had taught Sophia, it was clearly the unfolding of a romance. Infatuation was a fever, a foolish, fleeting emotion that burned bright only to fade fast. It didn't know right from wrong or good from bad. It could also turn dangerous, driving people crazy, pushing them over the edge of reason into an ocean of madness. She must act fast, put the drama to an end, blow out the spark before it began to blaze. She decided to flee to the safety of her family in Los Angeles immediately — get Isabel married as soon as possible. The last thing she wanted was for her daughter to get entrapped with a Sikh farmer.

"We will try our best to have the house ready before the hot summer sets in," one of the builders told Kishan as he was overseeing the plumbing at the upcoming farmhouse.

All at once Kishan began thinking of how wonderful it would be to have a lady in the farmhouse. That would make it a home. Jaspal and the girl had been drawn to each other from first sight. How perfect it would be if the girl and Jaspal got married soon. Then Kishan prayed like he never had before for that girl to fall in love with Jaspal.

At the rented rooms that evening, Jaspal did not pour himself any food even though Kishan had cooked a delicious chicken curry, watching on instead as Kishan ate dinner.

"Kishan, the labour that Allah Baksh sent us, has to be paid tomorrow," Jaspal blurted suddenly.

"Yes," Kishan replied, "I will get the money from the bank early morning tomorrow. Allah Baksh saved us in time. I've already hired another crew. It will start work the day after."

"We can't let her go!" Jaspal said.

Kishan kept a straight face. "Who? Who can't we let go?" he asked.

"Kishan, you will have to go talk to her," Jaspal said agitated.

Kishan took another bite. "Talk to whom?" he asked indifferently.

Jaspal frowned. "You know, that lady among the farmhands — Sophia, they call her. You must talk to her."

Kishan put his fork down. "Sophia?" he asked, faking surprise. "Why would you hold her? With her aching knees, she gets very little done! There's no way I will hire her again. Like I said, I've already hired a crew."

"It is not about the lady," Jaspal replied. "It is about her daughter."

Kishan rolled his eyes. "What about the girl? She is not up to any work either. All she likes is riding the horse, behaving as though she is not of this world. A dreamer is what they call her. I know mother and daughter can speak English but what do we care? Pali, I see no use for either of them. It's best that they get going." He dug into the curry again.

"Kishan, I never knew you to be such a fool! Can't you see that girl has taken hold of my mind? Dreamer or not, we can't let Isabel go!" Jaspal snapped.

Kishan let out a peal of laughter.

By morning, Kishan had it all planned — how he would approach Sophia and how he would present Jaspal as a desirable husband for Isabel. Confident that he would pull the deal through, he grabbed a bunch of wild geraniums and sped off to the farm with Jaspal. They were walking around impatiently, waiting for mother and daughter to show up when Miguel and the crew began tottering in, their strides brisk. The farmhands always walked about quickly on payday, Kishan recalled. He and Jaspal were all eyes for Sophia and Isabel, but strangely, even after the crew started work, mother and daughter were nowhere in sight.

They rushed to Miguel. "Where would Sophia be?" Jaspal asked. "And that daughter of hers?"

"Since today is our crew's last day on your farm, Sophia and Isabel packed up early. Sophia asked me to collect their wages. They are leaving for Los Angeles," Miguel said, smiling broadly, showing all his big black teeth.

"Leaving for Los Angeles? When?" Kishan asked.

"They will be taking the motor bus from Brawley later this morning. Sophia has family in Los Angeles," Miguel replied. "I'll have the money sent to her. Just hand their money to me."

Kishan knew they had little time at hand. He ran to Cesar, asking him to get the money from the bank and pay the labour at the end of the day. Clutching the wild geraniums, he and Jaspal drove off to Brawley.

A large crowd stood waiting for the motor bus. Kishan spotted Isabel right away. She was standing erect as she always did by her mother who was sitting on a large bag. Isabel saw them too. She was rattled but when Jaspal smiled at her, she pushed her brown hair away from her face and smiled right back.

Kishan walked to where Sophia sat.

Sophia got up immediately. "Hola. You are here?" she said. "Miguel would have sent the money to us in Los Angeles. Sir, you needn't have come."

Kishan looked around. It wasn't going to be easy. He couldn't for the life of him remember what he had planned on saying. Stepping up, he offered Sophia the geraniums. Accepting them uneasily, she looked around, her expression a cross between anger and anguish.

"Sophia, this is not about your wages," Kishan started. Pointing towards Jaspal, he fumbled before saying, "You see my brother Jaspal, over there. He is a good man, as good as a man can be. He wants to marry your daughter and make her happy."

Dropping her smile, Sophia gasped as if hit by a rock. She flung the flowers at Kishan and grabbed Isabel's hand. Isabel's mouth hung open. As Kishan stood there, trying to read their responses, letting go of Isabel's hand, suddenly Sophia began charging towards him, her eyes burning with rage as though she would strike anyone who tread close to her daughter. Kishan stepped back. He had no mind to fight Sophia.

"Sir, you are mistaking us," Sophia started. "Many a Sikh farmer from Arizona to here has shown an interest in my Isabel. But let me tell you, my Isabel is not just another girl that goes around picking oranges or pulling carrots in fields. What do you Sikh farmers think anyway? You can use and abuse a Mexican girl who comes to work your fields? How dare you chase after us? Stay away!"

Neither Jaspal nor Kishan budged. Fiercely, Sophia started again, "Good luck has smiled again on my Isabel. My cousin has a wealthy groom for her in Los Angeles. She will live a life of ease with one of our own. Now, what have we got to do with you Sikhs? Sir, I ask that you leave."

Kishan sighed. "Sophia, your daughter is no ordinary girl, but my brother is not an everyday farmer either. We own over three hundred acres and soon if God wills, we will buy more. You have seen our beautiful farmhouse coming up. Your daughter would be very comfortable there. And where is the question of using and abusing? My brother will take her in holy matrimony in the presence of your Virgin Mary. And Isabel will not be the first to marry a Sikh. Why, many Mexican girls in the valley have married Sikh farmers," Kishan said softly.

"Sir, I know that some Mexican girls have married your men, but I will only marry my girl within my community," Sophia said, frowning. "Now, if you and your brother are as good as you claim to be, leave."

"Sophia, can't you see Isabel will be happy on our farm? Did you see her riding the horse? She will never like it in the city with that wealthy man," Kishan said, his desperation mounting.

Sophia shook her head and looked the other way.

Kishan was at his wit's end not knowing what to do or say next when Isabel stepped up. "Mama, I like that horse," she whispered to her mother. Then looking towards Kishan, she said, "He is right. His brother is a good man. Kneeling on the dirt, his brother works harder than the farmhands that he hires. And Mama, even his eyes are truthful."

"Girl, who asked you?" a stunned Sophia shouted, losing it completely. "And what do you know about good or truthful? Why did I ever let you ride that horse? Jesus, if only I had seen this coming."

The motor bus zoomed in. Sophia picked up her bag and looked at Kishan. "Sir, we had better be going. Don't you try to stop us. I'll marry my girl to one of our own," she said. Clasping Isabel's wrist, she headed for the motor bus.

Following behind them, Kishan whispered ifs and buts. A stoic Jaspal said nothing.

Sophia climbed onto the motor bus. Instead of following her mother, Isabel freed her wrist from her mother's grip. Unhooking the necklace that she was wearing, she flung it towards Jaspal. Mounting the bus, she waved at him.

Jaspal rushed to pick up the necklace. Peering out of the motor bus window, Sophia shouted, "Go away! Go away!"

The motor bus took off, wafting mountains of dust.

"Let's drive to Los Angeles!" Jaspal exclaimed.

"Ah! Now you proclaim, 'Let's drive to Los Angeles!' Pali, when I was pleading with the old lady, you didn't utter a word," Kishan said. "Even the girl spoke up and did the unimaginable! Threw her necklace your way! But you stood there with that look on your face as if a drama was playing and it didn't pertain to you. How could you? We can't follow the motor bus to Los Angeles, not without the police coming for us!"

They dashed back to the farm.

Miguel was no longer the respectful crew leader who had come to work at The Rainbow Acres a few days ago. When Kishan enquired about Sophia's relatives in Los Angeles, Miguel shrugged and winked. Only after Kishan stuffed money in his pocket, did he open his mouth. "Sophia lost everything to the turmoil in Mexico. So, she snuck into America to give Isabel a better life," he said. "Isabel will soon marry a wealthy store owner in Los Angeles. She is in luck!"

"What we want is Isabel and Sophia's address in Los Angeles and we want it now," Jaspal said.

Miguel winked again. When Kishan stuffed more money into his pocket, Miguel pulled out a folded-in-four piece of paper from his embroidered wallet and handed it to Kishan.

"Pali, we must leave immediately," Kishan said, unfolding the paper and reading the address.

"Is everything all right?" Cesar asked.

"Yes, watch the farm closely. We will be gone a while," Kishan said rushing out with Jaspal.

Several minutes into the drive, Jaspal said, "Kishan, I didn't implore Sophia from fear of looking like a tramp. You were already pressing so hard. If I had joined in, the old lady would've thought us beggars!"

Kishan nodded. "You are right," he said. "Nothing can be gained by pushing. Since the girl is all that the old lady has left, we must convince her that her daughter will be happy with you."

Jaspal stretched out his arm and opened his clenched fist. Kishan pulled the Model T to the side and braked. All the while, Jaspal had held Sophia's necklace in his fist. The locket had a picture of the Virgin Mary and opened in the back. Inside lay a lock of Isabel's dark hair. Smiling, Jaspal snapped the locket shut. They looked up at the road. It was the start of another adventure.

SOPHIA

Mother and daughter bounded and bounced on the motor bus
headed towards Los Angeles. Sophia's head was whirling. She
knew well of the Sikh man's fixation with Isabel. Never had
she imagined, however, that he and his brother would come
following after them. But what had shocked her most was
Isabel's audacity. It was unbelievable how the girl had taken
such a bold stand. Looking towards the Sikh, she had called him
a good man and had even thrown her necklace his way. Sophia
sighed. Whatever would she have done if the motor bus hadn't
come in on time. She stared at Isabel who was wiping her eyes.

"Don't you go wasting your tears over strangers. Who are
these men to us anyway? You know how we have suffered.
I want the best for you as does our family in Los Angeles. The
right groom is waiting for you there. You will marry a man from
our community and live a happy life surrounded by family,"
Sophia said, placing her hand over Isabel's.

Isabel pulled her hand back and looked out of the window.

Clutching her bag, Sophia thought of the two Sikh brothers.
The way the younger one pleaded on behalf of the older, the
way his face puckered, and his eyes flickered when he spoke of
his brother's love for Isabel was applause-worthy to say the least,
a truly brotherly thing to be doing. A good brother never lets his
brother sink in anguish alone. In asking her for Isabel's hand, the
brothers had proved themselves to be decent and well meaning,
courteous and respectful. For a fleeting moment it struck Sophia
that her twin boys would have done the same for each other if they
had lived long enough to taste the absurdity of love. She shook
her head. It wasn't the time to look back or visit old traumas.
There were good people in the world all right, but she and
Isabel needed the security of family and community. Thinking
of family, tears sprung up in her eyes. First, her brother-in-law

Milano had rescued her from dissolution and now by welcoming her to California and helping her marry off her daughter, her cousin Santiago was reaffirming her faith in blood relations. Kinship lasted through life and beyond death. Having made it to the cherished land, California, she would always honour her family, keep them close and they in turn would watch over her and Isabel, sustain them through every high and low. No one else could do that. She blinked the tears out of her eyes and smiled. Happiness was having a caring family who came to hold you together when everything else fell apart.

"As a child, never had I thought that I would leave sunny Acapulco but here I am today sitting across the border in fantastic Los Angeles. Who could have known my story would sail me so far up along the coast, thousands of miles away from my hometown," Sophia said, sipping coffee with Santiago and his family in their large backyard under a blooming magnolia.

"Stories are no one's slaves. They follow their own course, not anyone's wishes or dictates," Santiago's wife Carla said biting into a cookie and laughing.

When the doorbell rang, Santiago's grandson Alberto ran to the door only to run back again soon. "Some people are here to see you Auntie Sophia,' he said. "They are waiting in the foyer."

"For me?" Sophia asked. Wiping her face, she got up and went inside.

When she saw the two Sikh brothers in the foyer, her eyes popped out. They had come after her and Isabel from Imperial Valley all the way to Los Angeles. Whatever would her family think of her and Isabel. Here they had barely landed in Los Angeles and two goons had come following after them. She must shush them out without ruffle or noise. "I told you not to follow us. I do not want trouble. Leave right away," she said sternly.

The younger of the brothers smiled and walking up, handed her yellow roses. She looked at his forthright face and then at his brother's lovelorn one and sighed. It was marvellous what love did to people — turned them into magnificent, compassionate, vulnerable beings. She could sense her anger and agitation slipping away but pulling herself up, she put on a ruthless face again.

"Sophia, a long time ago, in another land, I loved a girl," the younger one started, his brother standing quietly behind him. "I loved her more than any words can say, but I let her go because I saw a better life for her than what I could have given her at that point. But today, I ask you to give your daughter in marriage to my brother. He is good and honest and resourceful too. What's most important, he loves Isabel."

Sophia was suddenly benumbed. She wanted to touch the young man but stepped back and shook her head, wondering what to do. She was still groping for words when the younger one pleaded again, "Sophia, I would've never asked you to relent if I didn't think my brother a befitting match for Isabel or if we didn't have happiness to offer her at our farm."

Sophia's eyes were suddenly moist. "I know my Isabel would like it on your farm but, I am helpless. Having lost everything, the community is all I've left. If Isabel marries an outsider, our people will abandon us. My cousin has a nice groom for Isabel. I can't let my cousin down. Why, the wedding is scheduled for Sunday at the church down the road." Then blotting her eyes, she said, "If you wish Isabel well, go away!"

Setting the flowers down on a chair, she opened the door and hurried the brothers out.

Turning towards Sophia, the older brother said, "Tell Isabel, I will come for her."

Sophia's mouth fell open. She grabbed the arm of the younger brother who was still standing in the doorway. "Leave us alone! Do you hear?" she shouted. "Just so you know, I have a big family and the next time I see you or that brother of yours lurking around here, I'll have my cousin call the police!"

KISHAN SINGH

Slouching in the car, Kishan lamented how the matter had wriggled out of reach. Planning the next leg, they drove north to Jagat Singh's farm in Valencia.

On hearing the story, Jagat laughed. "It is not unusual at all. So many Punjabis — Hindus, Sikhs and Muslims — are now marrying Mexican girls," Jagat said. "Jaspal can marry the girl at a Mission in California."

So, there they were on Sunday morning, five of them — Jaspal and Kishan, Jagat and two other Valencia farmers — Bilawal Khan and Imran Aslam, in their best clothes, waiting across the street as Isabel's clan stepped out of the house and started for church. Seeing them, Sophia shrieked. Isabel lifted her veil and smiled.

Kishan had seen Isabel ride the horse with wild abandon at The Rainbow Acres. He had seen how she had flung her necklace towards Jaspal at Brawley despite her mother's grumbling. He knew the girl had some spunk and she proved him right yet again. Walking away from her people, she crossed the street and stood by Jaspal.

"Jesus, the girl has lost her mind!" Sophia yelled from across the road, stomping her foot.

A lean old man who Kishan imagined was Sophia's cousin, began charging towards Isabel, fuming and fussing. Walking up, Jagat Singh stopped him in his tracks and said, "The girl is an adult and she likes Jaspal. That's the end of the story. If I hear a sound, any sound, I will be forced to make some noise myself. Now step back."

Sophia's cousin froze. So did the rest of the clan. Jaspal began to lead Isabel to the car. Stopping midway and turning around, Isabel said, "Someone get my mother. I can't leave her behind."

Kishan rushed across the street to a shell-shocked Sophia. "Sophia, if you had any sense, you'd jump into the car with us!" Kishan said.

Sophia looked at him, completely stunned. Grabbing her by the arm, Kishan walked her to the car. Still startled, she climbed into the back with Isabel as Kishan snuck in the front next to Jaspal, speeding off for Santa Barbara, Jagat following behind in his car with Bilawal Khan and Imran Aslam.

After a hurried Catholic ceremony at the Mission in Santa Barbara, Jaspal and Sophia were pronounced man and wife. The white-haired, red-robed, Bible-holding priest hadn't any idea of course that at a church in Los Angeles on that breezy March morning in 1927, another groom had waited for Isabel only to be told that she had eloped with a Sikh.

SOPHIA

Everything was happening so fast that Sophia could barely get a handle on things. All she remembered was that she was daintily dressed up walking alongside her family to marry Isabel off at the church down the street when the two Sikh brothers showed up again, this time with three other men. All five stood in a bunch across the street from them, but even before they said or did anything, Isabel tossed back her veil and crossed over to join the men without even so much as looking back at her mother and family. It was then that a haze fell over Sophia. When she came to herself, the two brothers were driving her and Isabel to the Mission in Santa Barbara, where right before her eyes, her precious daughter began exchanging wedding vows with the older of the brothers as Sophia watched on dazed. What could she say when Isabel was gazing adoringly at her would-be husband and bouncing about like a bird in spring.

As the serene-faced priest performed the ceremony, Sophia wiped her eyes. Isabel had inherited her eyes, mouth and hair from Sophia's side of the family, but her spirit and will were her own — to do as she pleased, to live as she liked, to marry whoever that she wanted to marry. Sophia had loved everything about her daughter since the day that she was born. But the gutsy Isabel that she had seen that morning, left Sophia enthralled, making her admire her daughter to a newer, higher extent than she ever had before. Not only had Isabel shown that she would walk any length to follow her happiness, she had done it with glaring confidence. Sophia finally smiled. Her daughter was her own person no doubt but even in living her truth, she had echoed her mother. The steadfast stand that Isabel took for the man that she loved was no different from how Sophia had stood by Giovanni years ago by choosing to be with him over all else, leaving behind her family and Acapulco. Love found a way to triumph over everything.

Like a slowly rising storm, it shook up the forest, uprooting even the strongest of trees. All at once, Sophia was thankful that Isabel hadn't married the store owner in Los Angeles. He would never have made her happy. Secure, maybe, but not happy. Happiness was Isabel's blushing face during the exchange of vows, her soon-to-be husband admiring her as though she were a poem come to life, an artefact to be doted on till eternity.

After the ceremony, when Isabel came to kiss her, Sophia held her tightly. Her daughter was her spark, the miracle of her life, a promise unviolated, a gift to be prized not a lamb to be led around. By honouring her inner voice, Isabel had shaken her mother to rise and break free of real and imagined barriers and follow her heart even if it meant breaking away from family and community, momentarily. Sophia couldn't go back and change Isabel's tragic childhood, but that instance, she decided she would stand by her daughter every step of the way as she embarked upon a brave adulthood even if it meant obliterating the values that she had so tightly held on to for so long. There was no true adventure than embracing the unforeseen.

The younger of the brothers suggested that it was important to have a Sikh wedding ceremony too, and the older one agreed. So, thanking their friends and bidding them goodbye, the brothers drove Sophia and Isabel from Santa Barbara all the way up to their Sikh temple in Stockton.

The groom was most composed as he and Isabel covered their heads and circled around the holy book four times. Isabel went about the ceremony with a puzzled smile. The younger brother heaved with relief as though glad that they had pulled the endeavour off.

Later when Isabel and her groom rushed off to have their wedding photograph taken at a photo studio, the younger brother waited with Sophia inside the Sikh temple. Sitting in the courtyard, a befuddled Sophia was looking around when he came and sat by her. "Sophia, I know your name for a long time now, but I don't think you do mine," he said smiling. "I am Kishan Singh."

Sophia nodded and smiled back. "I may not have known your name thus far, but I know all else besides," she said.

"Like what?" he asked.

"That you can talk your way through anything, that you don't give up and that on any given day, you would go to hell and back for that brother of yours," she said.

He cringed his nose and laughed, stars shining in his eyes. She was convinced that they were the eyes of a man in love. He had shared with her the story of his failed romance from a long time ago but hadn't mentioned his present love. She wanted so much to ask him about the girl that he was so madly in love with but didn't. It wasn't her place, she figured. Not just yet. "Will you get married in this temple too?" she asked instead.

"It's called a gurudwara. And yes, I will get married here too, whenever I do that is," he said, smiling again. "Not only is the Stockton gurudwara our place of worship, it's also a focal point for all Sikh immigrants. By providing them with food and shelter, the gurudwara bolsters them forward on their American journey."

"Really?" Sophia asked.

"Yes," he replied, "thanks to the Stockton gurudwara, no Sikh has ever had to suffer hunger or homelessness or become a public ward in California. The gurudwara never shuts its doors to the destitute. It shelters impoverished Anglos too."

"Kishan Singh, what amazing heritage you bear," Sophia said, enthusiastically. Then softly, she whispered, "And the offering that is served here is so delicious that I had two helpings!"

"It's called 'karha'. For you, Sophia, and you alone, I will cook the sweetest karha every day of the year," he said, letting out a laugh so contagious that Sophia couldn't help bursting into laughter herself before hitting him hard on the arm.

KISHAN SINGH

Everything changed for the better when Isabel and Sophia stepped into Kishan and Jaspal's lives. The rented rooms bristled with new energy. Jaspal was humming all day, eager to return home every evening to be greeted by a chirpy Isabel. Sophia made the kitchen her haunt, cooking, embroidering and even sleeping there on a makeshift couch. Since Isabel had moved into the bedroom, Kishan had taken the sofa by the kitchen, where Sophia intrigued him with her endless talking. She had many stories, and Kishan had an ear for all her stories. The mother and daughter had begun to call Jaspal, "Jorge," but always referred to Kishan as Kishan Singh.

One evening after dinner when Jaspal and Isabel had sneaked into their room, one quietly after the other, Sophia pulled out a tray of sopas. As Kishan picked one up and bit into it, Sophia started off, this time about chocolate. "Kishan Singh, I would have glazed the sopas with chocolate, but we didn't have any cocoa beans about the house. I have a thing for chocolate, a love that's been passed down from my grandfather," she said with a dreamy look in her eyes.

Kishan nodded. The truth was that he didn't care for chocolate, finding it dark and bitter. Was it even a sweet, he had always wondered? A sweet had to be sweet all the way without a hint of bitter, like the Punjabi gur. Sweet to the core, gur came wrapped in fantasy. Made from ripe cane juice, the deep brown glob of wonder trickled with happiness, sparking the tongue, waking up the mind, dunking a person in elation. There was no point in even telling Sophia. She wouldn't even be able to imagine what gur tasted like. He would just remember to bring her some when he went to the Stockton gurudwara. They always had gur there. He smiled at Sophia who was still blabbing on about chocolate. "One day, I am going to launch my brand of milk chocolate. Smooth, creamy milk chocolate is an obsession across the world. I have made a few kinds of chocolate, but milk chocolate remains a dream," she said. "I guess, I will keep trying till my mind hatches the most perfect recipe."

"Good luck and good night," Kishan said. Finishing the sopa, he wiped his mouth and opened a book.

"Good night," she replied. Picking up another sopa, she bit into it, her eyes brimming with memories.

Sophia's memories of chocolate were happy ones. In time, Kishan discovered that she had others too which were far from happy — memories of a world lost to violence. Recalling them in passing, Sophia would shake her head as if to brush them off. There was one recollection, however, that clung the tightest to Sophia — of her two little boys, who despite having left the world long ago, always loitered around her, tugging her apron strings, eating her quesadillas, kissing her cheeks from the time she woke up to the moment she sank back into the kitchen couch at night. She would be happy to lunge into the past and relive her moments with her sons, going on and on about how clever they were, how one liked flan but the other loved pork chops and how one was great at chess and the other was an artist who drew long-legged frogs and ferocious fish. Returning to the present and not finding her boys there, she would become sad, wanting to sleep right away. The boys didn't leave her alone in her sleep either. Sometimes when Kishan read late into the night, he heard her conversing with them, instructing them to tie their shoe laces, finish their dinner and pick up their toys.

The next evening after dinner, Sophia would start prating again about her two boys. Again, Kishan would listen knowing as he did that telling the story of the two little boys was Sophia's effort to find peace because no matter to whom and however many times a sad story was told, it stayed sad.

With every narration, however, the narrator took another step closer to acceptance.

Sophia was an intermittent, hesitant narrator who couldn't face up to her past, always avoiding it, wishing it away as if fearful that it would pounce from a nook and stab her again, but gradually, Kishan was able to put her entire story together. It was an astounding tale of swimming against a tumultuous tide. He celebrated how moving beyond a gruesome past, Sophia had taken to sprinting, joking and laughing again. Her selfless smiles were even sweeter than her sopas. When she greeted him with her big embrace after long days on the farm, he dropped all his worries about pests and labour, harvests and loans. How strange was it, he wondered, that Sophia effortlessly calmed all his storms despite having sung a song sadder than that of any mourning dove in the vast desolate desert?

If a smile had a taste, he was convinced that Sophia's would be the taste of chocolate. He hoped that she would one day find her rainbow — live the beauty of her delicious dream of launching her own brand of milk chocolate. That would give her a reason to keep leaping forward and forging towards the future. Driving back home in the late evenings on many a day, he imagined Sophia flying high across a chocolate-streaked purple California sky.

SOPHIA

Sophia was proud of herself for mustering up the courage to share her story with Kishan. She couldn't, however, have imagined how deeply Kishan had internalised her odyssey across Mexico to California. In the ensuing days, when Kishan blurted out something from her past like how amiable a woman her grandmother Paula was, or what a marvellous beauty her mother was, or how at Acapulco, Sophia had whipped up exotic chocolate with chilli flakes, or how her husband Giovanni sang unforgettable serenades to her, for a while, Sophia would be left staring at Kishan, her eyes wide in amazement. Then shaking herself, she would wink at him, happy that her story had found a home in his mind. She realised that she couldn't have been more wrong in thinking of Jaspal and Kishan as outsiders. There were no strangers in the world, only friends waiting to cross paths with each other. By opening up her heart and smiles to them, she had freed herself from prejudice, discovered humility and in so doing, she was finally on her way to becoming the finest version of herself.

"Kishan Singh, thank you for listening to my story. I hadn't shared any of this with a soul, not even with my family in Los Angeles. But I felt comfortable letting it all out before you," Sophia told Kishan one evening.

"I should thank you instead," Kishan said, "for trusting me with your extraordinary story, for waking me to new realities, for reinstating my belief in people and dreams."

"Do you still think of the girl who you loved and lost?" she asked abruptly.

Kishan smiled. "Roop is a pressed flower in my memory, forever sparkling in the sunshine of my young love. Her destiny is to live in a cove of my mind that I visit on days when I am tremendously happy or awfully sad. On happy days, the questions always are, "What would Roop have said or done? Would she be happy too? Would she giggle uncontrollably?" On sad days, her absence bothers me as though by some queer twist of fate, her presence would have averted the sadness," he said.

"Stories of loss are also stories of beauty. Was it hard falling in love again?" Sophia asked.

"What?" he asked.

"Yes, you are in love. There is someone who is always playing in your mind like a favourite song. It is clear to see," Sophia said.

"Is it? How?" he asked.

"Oh, I have been around a while and know a few things. Only an infatuated man can radiate with love like you do. What's her name?"

"Amy," he said. "She is a librarian up in Elk Grove. I never intended to fall for her, love just got me in a flash. And I am glad it did. It's as though the universe has opened up before me, lighting my path with stars."

"Those who want to whistle will always find a tune. I bet that she is lovely," Sophia said.

"She is brown-eyed. Her hair is the colour of the setting sun. But what I like best about her is her spirit and that she has a mind of her own."

"And that she is enamoured of you and your stories." Sophia laughed.

"I would so like to think that she is, but honestly, I am not sure of that as yet," he said.

"Oh, how could she not be? You can weave galaxies with words, sending people spinning like planets, making them see rainbows and butterflies all at once. Truth be told, if it wasn't for your smooth talking, that reticent brother of yours would never have made a case with me."

Kishan laughed. "Sophia, what could we possibly have done without your approval?" he said.

Sophia slapped him on the back. Then turning serious, she said, "Everything happens as and when it is meant to happen. Like an inevitable pull, love drives the cosmos. Without it, the world would be desolate, and desolation is a wretched place to be in."

Kishan Singh is one of his kind, Sophia thought. He could rejoice fully in another's happiness, empathise completely with the sorrows of others. Most of all, it was the way he listened with his heart as though he would do all he possibly could to make a situation better, even urging her time and again to live out her dream of making milk chocolate. It was hard not to like a person like that. Through him, the cosmos had risen to offer her consolation for all the losses it had thrown her way.

When he drove her in the truck to the Catholic church on many a Sunday as Jaspal and Isabel took off driving around the valley in the Model T, it was as though one of her little boys had grown up and come back to hold her hand, making her feel wanted and loved, meaningful and important all over again. She looked forward to talking to him every evening. He filled her in with news of the outside world, sprinkling the talk with reminiscences about people in his life — his beloved Baldev Mama who lived with his two sons back in Punjab; his very sincere friend and advisor Harbans Singh, who was a restaurateur in Yuba City; his revolutionary friend Jeet Singh, who was fighting for India's independence from the British; a Chinese friend named Han-Gan who having bravely combated tuberculosis now owned a garment store in San Francisco and an acquaintance from his days in Angel Island, Nishan Singh who was now a successful peach farmer in Santa Clara Valley. Sophia listened closely, genuinely curious as she was about everything involving him and his life, starting with his name.

"What does your name imply?" she asked him one evening after dinner.

"Sophia, I've been named after the great Indian God, Krishna," he said.

"Is there a representation of Krishna in the Bible?" she asked.

"No," replied Kishan. "But just so you know, Krishna made a very fascinating God. He was both the humble flute-playing cowherd with peacock feathers in his hair, and also the majestic prince who guided a war with his intellect."

"Kishan Singh, do you and your brother play the flute too?" Sophia asked.

"No," Kishan replied, "I wish we could. Jaspal and I never came by a chance to learn."

"Is Singh also a God's name?" Sophia asked.

Kishan pointed to Guru Gobind Singh's picture on the wall. "Back in Punjab, Singh was the name bestowed by the great Guru Gobind Singh upon his fearless warriors who fought for righteousness," he said.

"I am sure there is a representation of Guru Gobind Singh in the Bible," Sophia said. "How could there not be one?" she asked.

Kishan shook his head. "Sophia, since representations in the Bible are so important to you, let me tell you that Guru Gobind Singh's father, the brave Guru Teg Bahadar, attained martyrdom for freedom of conscience. Like Jesus Christ."

Sophia let out a smile. Finally, she could make a connection. "What did you say the Guru's name was?" she asked.

"Guru Teg Bahadar," Kishan replied.

Sophia nodded. "Kishan Singh, next time you go to your gurudwara in Stockton, just be sure to bring back a picture of

Guru Teg Bahadar. We will put it up in the living room on the other side of the Holy Cross," she said.

Life from distant ends of the world was coming together at The Rainbow Acres. It was far from the reaches of Sophia's imagination. The Sikh Gurus and Jesus Christ were looking upon them from the walls. Kishan and Jaspal's chicken curry became marvellous when served with Isabel's wheat tortillas. Sophia's tray of sopas acquired an otherworldly sweetness when topped with the karha that Kishan made, everyone gobbling down the dish as though it were a magical delicacy. On winter afternoons, when Sophia and Kishan finished cooking the greens and corn tamales, they would call out to Jaspal and Isabel to eat, only to have Jaspal respond with a quick "Si" and Isabel with an eager "Haan."

KISHAN SINGH

Summer had seeped in when Kishan, Jaspal, Sophia and Isabel moved into the farmhouse on The Rainbow Acres. Furnishing the house and hanging the curtains, Kishan was over the moon. It was as though someone had plucked the scenes from his imagination and planted them there. On a wall in the living room, he hung a picture of Guru Gobind Singh, next to which Isabel and Sophia nailed the cross. On the mantle, they placed two pictures: the studio portrait of Jaspal and Kishan, and Jaspal and Isabel's wedding photograph.

Jaspal couldn't have his fill of the indoor plumbing. Having grown up drawing water from wells and sipping it straight from rivers, he revelled at water flowing out of shiny faucets. And Kishan was glad to finally have a bedroom of his own. Excitedly, he walked about his room, basking in its spaciousness. Crooning along as country songs played on the radio, he decided that now that he had a room of his own, he would buy books. Immediately, he wrote to Amy, asking for her recommendations and she mailed him back an extensive list of novels that he could buy. Kishan went over the list a few times. It included Erich Maria Remarque's *All Quiet on the Western Front*, Virginia Woolf's *Mrs. Dalloway*, E.M. Forster's *A Passage to India*, James Joyce's *Ulysses* and Franz Kafka's *The Trial*. He could scarcely wait to drive to the large bookstore in San Diego and buy all the books that Amy had recommended.

The following month, when Fourth of July came around, despite their pestering him to join them, Kishan stayed back as Jaspal, Isabel and Sophia left on a vacation with Allah Baksh and his family at the Grand Canyon. Kishan reflected on Fourth of July. The day marked the celebration of liberty, of justice being meted out. Liberty and justice were big and beautiful words that formed the cornerstone of Americanism. The irony, however, was that they were hard to put to practice. As much as Kishan delighted in rooting himself to America's phenomenal history that more than anything else claimed vehemently to uphold the ideas of justice and liberty, and as thankful as he was for waking up and working on the golden fields of wonder, he couldn't help muse about that mesmerising notion called, "Justice," wondering how America had delivered justice to him, to Jaspal and to Asian farmers across California. Many questions began seething inside him.

"Were the California Alien Land Laws America's idea of justice?"

"Was it fair to hold down Asian men who loved America and worked its land with their sweat?"

"Was it right to refer to them as 'Alien'?"

"Did not the mighty American Constitution in its Fourteenth Amendment, promise justice and liberty to all?"

Then thinking of the stalwart American document, *The Declaration of Independence*, which said, "We hold this truth to be self-evident that all men are created equal," Kishan sighed. The California Alien Land Laws were a blatant violation of that celebrated statement. Fourth of July had let loose a volley of questions for which he couldn't come up with any answers. All he could do was wait for the day when those limiting land laws would be repealed, when the brave Asian farmers would win their due and come to stand on an equal footing with the Anglos, their race and the colour of their skin notwithstanding. The repealing of the laws would mark the victory of the Japanese, who cleared and farmed areas of California that no one else had tread before. That day would also be the triumph of the Chinese farmers, who after being discriminated against for so long, would finally be able to call the fields they had been working on, their own. Much as that day would be momentous for the Japanese and the Chinese, it would also be the finest hour of the proud

Punjabi farmers, the courageous men who without a care of the hateful laws had not just cherished the California land but were ready to kill and get killed for it. That day when justice would be meted out to the Asians farmers, would come, sooner than later. Packing away that train of thought, Kishan took off for San Diego to buy books.

The birthplace of California, San Diego was a dream snuggled along the Pacific, its sunny beaches beyond all realms of fantasy, its weather defying a desert farmer's imagination. The sun in San Diego was bright and bountiful all year long without smothering or bothering, sweltering or charring. The mornings were soaked in sunshine, the afternoons warm, the evenings cool and the sunsets unforgettable. Locked in the San Diego harbour sat numerous, unfathomable secrets — secrets of the Kumeyaay, the original inhabitants of the land, secrets of the Spaniards who drove them away, and the newer secrets of the Portuguese fishermen who hunted the ocean for tuna. Driving through the city, Kishan admired the sprawling suburbs that were springing up, the broad, twining streets lined with gorgeous magnolias and splendid Spanish villas. He stopped by Mission Beach to join in the Fourth of July celebrations. Standing on the pavement with a striped banner that said USA in bold blue letters, he watched the Fourth of July Parade go by, smiling and waving at the children holding American flags. Following the children in the parade were a horde of men and women who held red and blue pinwheels that spun fanatically in the brisk breeze, reminding him spontaneously of the dust storms that swung through Imperial Valley. He noticed that closing the parade was a large horse-pulled carriage with over a dozen women in Betsy Ross outfits and a man dressed as Uncle Sam held the reins. Seeing the star-spangled saddles of the horses, he laughed.

The parade having passed, he began walking barefoot on the beach to take in the cool of the water, the sprightly ocean breeze blowing in his face. Pausing under a King Palm, he looked far out at the serene San Diego harbour, the desolate Coronado Island and then at the dazzling village, La Jolla, as it sat twinkling by the water. Turning around, he began gazing at Old Town, the very busy Pacific Beach and farther away at the Point Loma Lighthouse. There was something about that dainty old lighthouse. Untouched by the turbulent ocean, it was enticing, deep, timeless. Surviving many a tempest, it stood sublime, watching new stories unroll. A lone strong structure, it promised safe landings, offering a picture of mystique.

So enraptured was Kishan by the remarkable Point Loma Lighthouse that for a brief while, he forgot that the bookstore by Mission Beach closed before evening. Remembering in time, he rushed to the bookstore and sifted through books, finding many from the list that Amy had recommended. Purchasing them, he sat on the pavement watching the amber sun lapsing into the Pacific. Later partaking of the Fourth of July fireworks in Balboa Park, struck by the beauty of the Roman arcades flanked by pines and cypresses, he drank in the grandeur of the park's Spanish Renaissance-inspired buildings.

Balancing the account books under the old oaks one sun-drenched summer morning, Kishan thought about how hard Master Imitiaz Ali had worked with him on his Math facts back in Noor Mahal. If only his old teacher were around, he'd have been proud of how quickly and correctly Kishan now did the accounts, his accuracy even baffling the accountant in Holtville who filed the tax statements for The Rainbow Acres. Recalling his one-room schoolhouse in Noor Mahal, Kishan guffawed. Who could have thought that small noisy classroom would prepare him for a life across the oceans in as vast a country as America, which was well on its way to becoming one of the world's greatest civilisations. On some days, the past didn't seem so far away. On those days, Kishan could remember every detail of his boyhood with the same precision with which he did the account books. On other days, however, he thought that the past had slid to a far distance, separating itself from him by thousands of miles, incalculable time and immeasurable water. But the best days were the ones when the past flew effortlessly into the present. He always strove for days like those. On those days, he knew to revere the past but dwell in the present. The best part in the medley of past and present was that every man, no matter what his past, could work towards the future of his choosing. And no one knew about the wonders of work better than a farmer. Work and hope spurred a farmer on. With those two under his belt, a farmer could go far.

He looked out at the flowering cotton fields. The petals had gone from being pale white to a mild yellow and were now a pretty pink. Soon the flowers would turn red, wither and fall and give way to green pods, which upon ripening in the sun would expand and turn brown, bursting into fluffy cotton balls. Kishan's wandering gaze caught Jaspal, who was overseeing the labour that was tending the cotton. He knew Jaspal had put his soul in the cotton, rising with the sun to supervise the watering of the fields every morning. Kishan wondered about the cotton harvest. He hoped it would meet their expectations. Then he saw Jaspal walking towards him. Meeting him halfway, Kishan could see that Jaspal had been up even earlier than usual that morning.

"Pali, need you jump out of bed so early? Look at you — all washed up and wiped out. Why do you worry? The cotton is coming up well," Kishan said, looking at Jaspal's rundown face.

"Kishan, I have to start early. If I sleep too late, dreams come to grip me," Jaspal replied.

"I can bet that you even dream of crops!" Kishan laughed.

"I do. In my dreams, I see The Rainbows Acres. Sometimes, I see the fields back in Noor Mahal too," Jaspal said.

"Do you really?" Kishan asked.

"Yes, many times I dream that I am back in Noor Mahal, walking the trails along the wheat fields on a cold winter afternoon." Jaspal's eyes turned misty. "Then jumping ahead my mind takes me to the Vaisakhi festival, and I see myself reaping the golden wheat with my bapu, singing and dancing to the drums."

"That is a good dream to be dreaming," Kishan whispered.

"Nah," Jaspal replied. "I'd rather not dream that dream. It takes me back to that lost world, shakes up the present with questions."

Kishan stepped back, surprised that he was not the only one that morning, thinking about the past and the present. "What questions?" he asked.

"The mind wants both to let go of the past and hold on to it," Jaspal replied. "Most days, I look away from the past. On others, I want to share my Noor Mahal memories with Isabel. She is a good listener, but there are things that she will never know."

"Like what?" Kishan asked.

"She will never know the lost wheat fields back in Noor Mahal or the smell of simmering saag that filled up my house on winter evenings. She will never know how influenza came in through the dark of the summer nights and tore my world apart. She will never know the reckless farmer boy that I was before boarding the ship to California in search of new moors."

Kishan nodded. He knew from having lived it himself how hard it was for a boy to be forced into manhood. He knew something else besides. "Isabel may never know the fields and family you loved and lost, but what she knows is enormous," he said touching Jaspal's shoulder. "She knows hope. Clasping to it, she continued seeking flowers through riots and massacres, sadness and despair to find love, to discover that there was no beauty greater than truth and no truth braver than goodness. Seeing goodness in your eyes, stirred by your song of loss and longing, she walked out of your dream into your life, lighting the The Rainbow Acres with her persistent hope to where you have now regained both family and land in the new world."

Jaspal smiled. Together they began walking to the farmhouse, the morning sun sliding down their backs.

SOPHIA

Late one night, Sophia lay in her bed thinking about The Rainbow Acres and how that farm and the farmhouse upon it had become her world — every twig, branch, tree, and field on the acreage swirling within her like the River Colorado meandering through the canals. Much like the rainbow that the farm had been named for, her life was the outcome of rain and shine, of passions and strife. She was glad for The Rainbows Acres. It was her home, blazing her light, inspiring her to seek out butterflies on every flowering shrub, to love and to dream. She smiled at the expanding universe around her, her heart burning with gratitude. She knew that nothing could say, "Thank you" better than milk chocolate. Her life was a story laced in strength and endurance. Now was the time for her to share her saga through her creation. She must match her pursuit to the beat of the universe, make her milk chocolate and swash the cosmos with joy. She rose from the bed and walked to the kitchen in small measured steps. It was a dark moonless night. The summer air was heavy with unfulfilled promises, the lingering quiet of it broken by the hooting of a faraway elf owl. Slowly, she gathered the ingredients — sugar, milk powder, cocoa and butter, scenes of Acapulco and Guadalajara playing in her mind. She saw an eager-eyed little girl running along the beach, dashing on to become an engaging woman in a flowery white dress pulsating with a throbbing bliss until she hit a large opaque cloud and fell. Despite trying to pick herself up time and again, the woman fell down again and yet again.

Sophia mixed the sugar and cocoa and set the blend aside. Melting butter in a saucepan, she added the milk powder and then the sugar and cocoa blend, whisking till the mix was smooth and glossy. Like the beach by her house in Acapulco, the ocean breeze far more zealous than the ocean. She turned off the stove and stirred a little longer. Her chocolate was her song that had carried her from Acapulco through Guadalajara and Bahía de Kino to the shiny California earth. It must convey her odyssey, the depth and decadence of her travails. She must colour it with the fragrance of her journey. Not with hints of vanilla or with plum or peach water, but with the myth of her lore. She reached for the bottle of gardenia essence and dropped a little into the mix before pouring the dark flowy paste into the moulds. Just as she put the mix on the kitchen counter to set, an old folk song came to play in her mind.

Farewell my love,
I'm sorry to cause you pain;
I promise to send a letter, my love
To say when we'll meet again.
Don't follow across the prairie, my love,
Don't follow me where I gain.
But wait till I send a message, my love,
Till then I will miss you so.

Sophia became still. "Giovanni," she whispered. A gush of desert breeze blew in through the window, breaking the summer calm, caressing her face, sending her hair flying. "Love outdoes death. You live in my song. It took me a long time, but tonight, I have finished the trek, made my dream chocolate. And God knows that it is worthy of my struggle, deserving of being the food of Gods."

A weight lifted off her heart, rose up and dissipated in the air. Sophia let out a sob. Even as she cried as though she would never stop, she knew she had finally pierced right through the centre of the opaque cloud to reach over to the other side where large, fragrant gardenias bloomed, vivacious butterflies fluttering around them in circles. It was her space to roam about, to waltz in and to sing new songs in. No longer a captive to the past, she was free like a butterfly in love with the rising sun.

"Mama, what will you call your milk chocolate?" Isabel asked Sophia as they prepared batch after batch, packing them in baskets to be sold at Farmers' markets across Imperial Valley, starting with Holtville.

"California Delight," Sophia whispered.

"Hmm, great name," Isabel said. "The gardenia essence lends the chocolate an unmatched taste and texture. It's smooth, sleek and alive all at once."

"I hope it will make people smile. God knows when life turns topsy turvy, milk chocolate can pull out a sunken smile," Sophia said. "I'll donate a part of the proceeds from the chocolate sales to a charity that is working to rebuild revolution-torn Mexico."

When Kishan drove mother and daughter to Holtville, scores of people — Chinese farmers and Japanese workers, Swiss cotton sowers and talkative Mexican farmhands, smiling Anglo policemen and nodding Catholic missionaries — stopped by to try Sophia's chocolate, twirling their eyes and tongues with delight, smiling at faraway gardenias, buying chocolate baskets for wives and lovers, mothers and daughters, children and cousins. Sophia applauded the diversity around her. Like butterflies, people had flown far out from their homelands in search of brave new starts and rapturous pastures, forming a rainbow of immigrants that wove California together. She thought everyone had a look about them that was exultant, springing from ploughing, digging, sowing and striving, the California sun blazing in their faces.

She stretched out her hands, priding in their power to create, to spread elation. In making her milk chocolate, she had earned her place and dignity, stepped into the larger community and announced her status of being Californian. She smiled a big smile. And wasn't in the least surprised to see that a lot of faces were smiling back at her. Every day was a journey. The odyssey never ended, going on and on instead in a perpetual quest of open roads and yet newer beginnings. And wild ambiguous milestones made it worth taking.

KISHAN SINGH

Waving the hot summer goodbye, Kishan eagerly welcomed autumn as 1927 streamed along. The sun rose early each morning and a cool breeze blew all day. One couldn't spot even an accidental cloud in the sky. Fluffy cotton balls, however, formed tiny clouds atop the cotton fields. The much-awaited instant had arrived. The cotton was ready for harvest. As Mexican crews spread across the fields picking cotton, Kishan could see that the harvest was nothing like what they had hoped. It had been destroyed by tenacious pests. It jolted them hard. They barely broke even with cotton. Recalling the endless toil, the exhaustive watering and fertilising of the cotton, the pesticide dispensing from time to time, Jaspal shook his head in dismay. "Kishan, perhaps it would be best to focus on melons and vegetables. The queen of crops is mysterious," he said. "She doesn't grace just any farm. From Noor Mahal to here, she continues to elude us."

Kishan stared at Jaspal. The poor harvest had flustered him to the core, but it couldn't diminish his fixation with the shining white balls. Touching Jaspal's shoulder, he said, "Pali, we mustn't give up on cotton. Not now, not ever. Cotton alone can put The Rainbow Acres in the league of prosperous farms in the valley. Having experienced cotton-growing first hand, we're now better prepared to surge past the odds next time."

He began researching at length, gradually managing with help from the Farmer Bureau to get an appointment with a scientist at the Agriculture College up in Davis. The scientist expounded on how long-strand cotton was resilient enough for the desert and the best fit for canal irrigation, underlining the best ways to go about farming it. He even shared with Kishan the two keystrokes for growing cotton successfully. The first was to burn the cotton shaft to scratch right after the harvest.

With the shaft gone, there being nothing left to gorge on, most of the pests perished instantly. The second stroke involved exterminating any remaining pests with three sustained dispersions of pesticide right before the next harvest. Imbibing the rules, Kishan pressed Jaspal to not give up. "A farmer has to be brave and take risks," he told Jaspal. "Cotton is the crop for the daring. We mustn't lose heart. In time, we will hit it off with cotton."

Though sceptical about the heavy expenditure involved and risk at the heart of the venture, Jaspal agreed to take a chance on cotton again.

On a trip to Holtville to purchase farm supplies, Kishan heard about the new swift tractors and cotton strippers that were being launched across the country, denoting a marked shift from labour intensive to mechanical farming. Of late machines were more reliable than Mexican labour, which was no longer easy to hire. Forming unions, the farmhands now talked of rights and contracts with the same passion with which they spoke of Jesus Christ. Even the docile Mexican women among the workers now conversed in an elevated tone. Where many of them would have twisted an arm to marry a Punjabi farmer and become a landowner's wife in the past, mouthing labour unions slogans, they were now treading new roads, pursuing liberty.

Uncanny as it was, one day shortly after his visit to Holtville as he sat eating lunch by the old oaks, he saw a young Mexican woman walking towards him. He had seen her around the valley and knew that she was married to a Sikh farmer, Mal Singh. Kishan got up. Her flushed face told him that she had been walking a while.

"My name is Rosa," she said hurriedly.

"Hola," Kishan said. "I am Kishan Singh. Hope all is well at your acreage. How is your husband?" he asked.

"He is fine. He is always fine with a bottle of whiskey tucked under his sleeve. The farm is fine too, ensuring that his whiskey never runs dry. But I am not," she replied.

"Are you not well?" Kishan asked hesitatingly.

"My husband is always drunk, yelling at me on the slightest pretext," she replied unhesitatingly. "He eyes my every move with suspicion. There is money enough for his drinking and blowing off but not any for me to buy even a dress."

Kishan looked at her face. She was no older than twenty-five and Mal Singh was approaching fifty. Clearly, she had married him hoping for a life of ease but had met with stifling control instead. What Kishan couldn't figure for the life of him was why she was sharing all that information with him. He barely knew her or her husband.

Rosa read the confusion on Kishan's face. "I heard of how kind you have been to the labour on your farm, encouraging everyone to send their children to school. So, I stopped by to enquire about factories up north. I want to work in one, it pays better than working the fields," she said.

Kishan was fazed. "Have you thought things through?" he asked. "If you stay on in the valley, you would be a farmer's wife and not have to worry about earning wages. Would you rather be a factory worker over that?"

"It is best to make work my amigo, earn money and live how I want to than be at the mercy of a drunk who watches me like a hawk," she said coldly. "Today, workers have rights but many Punjabi farmers' wives in the valley have none."

Kishan nodded. If he were in her place, he would have done the same. "There are bottling factories, packaging factories and food processing factories in San Diego where you can find work. There are a lot of working-girl boarding houses too, where you can live," he told her.

Rosa smiled. "I'll jump onto the next bus going west," she said, her dark eyes blazing.

Kishan could tell that her grit would sail her across. Then it struck him that a woman could use more than just grit on the path out west. Reaching for his wallet, he pulled out some money. When he handed it to her, she shook her head. "Thank you, but I have money to get by for a bit before I find work."

"It's not a loan," Kishan said. "Only a little something to help you on your journey."

She thanked him. "I'll head straight to the bus stop," she said, clutching the money.

Watching her walk away, Kishan wondered about her long cotton skirt. It was wide. It would keep her from sprinting, he thought. Just then he saw her stopping by the vegetable fields to pull her skirt down, revealing loose black pants that she was wearing underneath. She grabbed one end of the skirt, twirled it in the air before swinging it far into the fields and hurrying away.

Kishan felt the surging gush of freedom. It was invigorating and uninhibited, just like her flight.

A few days later, he heard that an angry and very drunk Mal Singh was cursing his runaway wife, calling her bad luck, an ill-bred, shameless woman who had sped off with her Mexican lover at night. As Mal Singh went about pouring himself glass after glass of whiskey, his Punjabi friends offered to find him another wife — this time, a Mexican girl no older than eighteen, who would keep her gaze low, know her place in the house and behave like a wife. One Punjabi farmer from Brawley even suggested that the new girl's waist had better be small. Because the ones with smaller waists, he said, always bore sons.

Shortly after, on a visit to San Diego, Kishan saw a Mexican labour union leader addressing a rally. Eager Mexican workers were chanting his name. There were several women workers, too. Kishan thought their eyes were like Rosa's, raring with zeal. He smiled. He was proud of Rosa, the girl who had got away, thanks to the labour activists, thanks to the winds of change, thanks most of all to the invincible human spirit, which, when it chose, could break all and any barriers.

Time was zipping, spreading out a canopy of stirring hopes. Kishan was working long days, tending tirelessly to cotton, managing accounts and waving at the new speeding cars that occasionally ran down the valley's old dusty roads when early in 1928, Amy wrote to say that she would be attending a Librarians' Conference in Los Angeles on a weekend the following month. "Kishan, if you are able to take some time off from the farm, perhaps you could come by and see me," she wrote.

Kishan's heartbeat picked up. "I'll be sure to drive out to Los Angeles that weekend to see you," he wrote back to her immediately. Finally, they would be seeing each other again after so long and what could be a better place to meet than in fantastic Los Angeles. The city was now booming with people from all over the world, its population likely to double in the coming decade. He smiled at the most amazing part of all. The University of California in Los Angeles was growing by the day — black, white and brown students flocking together in shopping areas, at the movies, in restaurants and on beaches. He and Amy could catch up in Los Angeles without worrying about spurring a racial riot. Besides, he had something to tell her, something important. If only he could speed through time and bolt to that weekend right away. After days of marking the calendar without fail, when at last the weekend came around, Kishan took off for Los Angeles very early on a Saturday even though he and Amy had decided to meet over dinner later that day.

Reaching there late morning, Kishan walked around Hollywood, immersing himself in the many sounds and smells of a city on the run. Buicks and Jaguars were speeding down highways as pedestrians snacked on buttered popcorn and decadent ice-cream. Strolling by the large Mediterranean-style villas, Kishan rejoiced at how the city was evolving into a hub of American modernism, doggedly embracing technology and diversity. Stopping by Charles' Book Store, he spotted William Faulkner's *Soldiers' Pay*. "It's a debut novel," the young girl at the bookstore said.

"I'll buy it," Kishan said. "One must take a chance with a debut novelist. Besides, I like that it's slim."

At a café, Kishan flipped through the pages, trying to get a feel of the book. A line popped up at him. He read it again and then again. "Women know more about words than men ever will. And they know how little they can ever possibly mean."

Kishan smiled. Faulkner was perhaps right. Women had so many words for every moment and occasion and the reason women were generous with words was because many of them didn't think them valuable enough. He thought about how, on the contrary, he treasured words, always wanting to know more of them. One could even say that he loved words. He had a word for every person in his life. That was his way of understanding people. Jaspal for instance was purposeful, Sophia resilient, Isabel optimistic, Allah Baksh wise and Amy happy. Snapping the book shut, he smiled. The book had done its job, hooked him, got him thinking. He would read it as soon as he returned to The Rainbow Acres.

Stepping out of the bookstore, he noticed that the bright afternoon had stepped up to greet a bustling evening. Brushing his hair, he slipped into his newly purchased shirt, dabbed cologne and drove out to have dinner with Amy.

The restaurant was the oldest on Santa Monica Beach. The sepia pictures on the walls told sunny California stories of surfers and swimmers. On an old piano, the pianist played Western classical, splashing the evening with a rhythmic jubilance. The waiter, a young college student, told Kishan that the pianist was playing Bach. Kishan thought the music was strangely reminiscent of fast-blowing winds, of violet blooms on alfalfa, of reading Rumi on a rainy day.

He had his eyes on the door when Amy came in. Just as he had imagined, she was wearing green and smiling too. She looked knockout beautiful, as entrancing as the last time that he'd seen her over three years ago. "Kishan, I can't believe it has been so long since we met last," she said, embracing him.

"Yes, it has been long," he sighed, pulling out a chair for her. "And what a spin it has been for me from the lush Central Valley to the dazzling desert."

She let out a fitful laugh. "Tell me about the desert," she asked, sitting down.

Reclining in his chair, he was about to start off about the colours and sounds of the desert, about cotton and carrots, melons and lettuce, when he noticed her laugh had stirred up a cough, sending her eyes watering, turning her face red.

He held up a glass of water for her. Waving her hand, she continued coughing and wheezing. He put the glass down and watched on as she pulled an inhaler close to her nose and took a deep puff. The gasping ceased. "Asthma has been bothering me a lot of late," she said smiling. "No matter what I do, I can't put it to rest."

Kishan nodded. "Amy, before I go on about my life on The Rainbow Acres, there is something important that I must tell you," he said.

"About what?"

"About asthma."

"Asthma?" Amy was surprised.

"I met a flaxseed farmer down in Imperial Valley. He lived in Fresno before, where he grew grapes. When I asked him what impelled him to move to the desert, he said it was his wife's asthma. The woman suffered severe bouts up north, but ever since moving down to the desert valley a few years ago, she hasn't had a single attack."

"Really?" Amy asked.

"Yes," Kishan replied. "And she is not the only one. The man said he knew other people besides who having moved to Imperial Valley have finally rid themselves of asthma. Some doctors recommend it too."

Amy took to thinking. "The warm weather must help," she said.

"If I were you, I'd talk to the doctors right away. And you know there is a library in Imperial Valley?"

"Wow, someone has my move all planned!" Amy exclaimed.

They ordered white wine and seafood, she lobster and he trout. Between mouthfuls, she filled him in about her days, speaking very softly, smiling where she would have liked to laugh, cautious not to kick up a bout of coughing again.

"Amy, the desert is mesmeric, the mornings are bright and sunny, the evenings cool, the sunsets heart-warming, and the nights breezy," Kishan said, trying to enchant Amy to the desert. "What's more, winter rains though sparse make the desert gleam with astonishing colours, leaving the meadows replete with wildflowers. And the best part — rains also leave behind haunting rainbows. You'd have to come down and see for yourself."

"For rainbows, I will." Amy said, "Rainbows are so much like books, telling stories of survival, adding colour to our lives, holding out hope."

"And new possibilities," Kishan said. "Promise me you will think seriously about moving to the desert."

She nodded.

After dinner, slurping pistachio gelatos on sugar cones, they walked past tourists and street artists to reach the top of the Santa Monica Pier. Kishan shared with Amy that he and Jaspal had finalised talks with a Swiss farmer about purchasing his five-hundred-acre property. They would soon be farming eight hundred acres in Imperial Valley, he told her.

"Kishan, how wonderful it is to see your dream taking you from height to height," Amy said, rippling with joy.

Kishan looked into her smiling eyes. The contradiction hit him again. Neither could he fall madly in love with her nor could he forget her. He saw that her bright eyes were looking right back into his. It was an infinite moment, making him oblivious to beginnings and ends. In that instant, Anti-Miscegenation Laws, race and culture submerged into nothingness. It felt as if he and Amy had never been away from each other, as though they would be together forever. Her words from a long time ago rang in his mind: "Kishan, there are no laws that forbid friendship. And the Anti-Miscegenation Laws will be revoked too. It is only a matter of time."

He felt strong and hopeful, glad to be alive. Suddenly, the unreachable seemed attainable.

Sitting down on the pier, they watched dolphins dancing on rolling waves. In the skyline, turned peach by the sunset, a lone star blazed, putting the street lamps to shame. Applauding its unabashed glitter, they laughed.

SOPHIA

Jaspal and Isabel's first born arrived on a windy day in March of 1928, swirling The Rainbow Acres with delight. Jaspal and Isabel asked a euphoric Kishan to give the little boy his name.

Holding the unusually restless little boy, Kishan thought long before saying, "Jaymal. His name will be Jaymal after the legendary sixteenth-century Indian chieftain, Jaymal Singh, who dauntlessly fought for his land."

Jaspal smiled. "The ballad of Jaymal Singh is a celebrated one and was sung often in our village, Noor Mahal," he told Sophia and Isabel. "I even heard the bards sing it outside of the Golden Temple in Amritsar the one time that I'd gone there to offer thanks after harvest."

Soon Sophia and Isabel were showering the little boy with kisses, calling him Jay.

From that point on, everything about the acreage was about little Jay. Jaspal and Kishan bought him toy cars and tractors, planes and ships, and sang Punjabi lullabies for him. In time, they would build him a tree house on the old oaks, they told Sophia and Isabel. They prided in how Jay had stout arms and legs and how he picked himself up right after a fall. Brave Sikh boy, they called him. Sophia rejoiced in how Jay's hair was thick and straight but curled towards the ends, how it was dark with hints of gold, how his Spanish heritage shone brightly in his deep brown eyes, his arched hairline and his high brow.

Jaspal and Isabel, Sophia and Kishan had barely had their fill of holding, nurturing and loving Jay when his brother followed just as they rang in 1930. Kishan thought Jaspal and Isabel's second son had the brightest forehead so when called upon to name him, Kishan called him Jasjit, meaning a person of honour and acclaim.

"Because Jasjit sounds so musical," Sophia said eagerly, "it is best that he should go by Jason after my grandfather, Jacin, who played the banjo with passion."

Jay and Jason were great names, Sophia thought for the brothers to gallop out into the world with. The Rainbow Acres was aglow with the spatter of tiny feet and ringing laughter. Jaspal and Isabel, Sophia and Kishan took turns to meet the boys' numerous needs. Soon, however, the boys became the driving force of the adults, bringing smiles to their days, adding a spring to their steps, making them dance to faster tunes.

KISHAN SINGH

Kishan talked to Jay and Jason all the time as the babies crawled and played on the living room floor. He even told them stories about tall mountains and bubbling rivers; about deep-blue oceans and multi-coloured fish; about the burning sun and the placid moon; about the endless skies and an amazing aviator called Charles Lindberg; about thirsty deserts and pouring rain; about cunning coyotes and greedy rattlesnakes; about ripe crops and happy harvests; about bothersome pests and helpful sprays; about efficient tractors and diligent combine harvesters.

The babies would babble and smile at him, wrapping their pudgy hands around his fingers, their shiny eyes laughing. Kishan took it that the boys liked his stories. Every evening, he told them new, more fantastic ones. There was one story that was his favourite to tell, the story of land.

"Land is a wonder," he would tell the boys. "Along with the sky and the oceans, it makes up the world. A man can't own a chunk of the sky or cut and claim a wedge of an ocean, but a lucky man can own a piece of land. He can live, laugh, love and farm on it. Land makes an everlasting friend. It can outlive fire, floods and storms, even time."

Listening to that story, Kishan thought the babies gabbled louder, smiled bigger, clasped his fingers tighter and kissed him much more, smudging his face with drool.

"Pali, we had chased the queen of crops from Noor Mahal to here. And today, she has finally graced us! It is the start of a new beginning!" Kishan told Jaspal doubling with laughter.

It was the fall of 1930 — luscious, unforgettable and steeped with jubilance. They had reaped a bountiful cotton harvest even exceeding by a little, the valley's average yield per acre to where the local newspaper had reached out to them for tips so that other cotton farmers could increase their subsequent production. "There is no secret mantra to cotton," Kishan told the newspaper men. "All the most glorious of cash crops asks of a farmer is time and effort. From weeding to fertilising, watering to pesticide dispensing, a farmer must consistently give cotton his all, topping it all with the will and passion to succeed."

Jaspal was gratified but unusually quiet, an all-encompassing peace spreading across his face as he smiled at Kishan. How they had hoped, waited, longed for that day. Overcoming tremendous odds, they had finally managed to kiss elation. The brimful cotton harvest at The Rainbow Acres had finally washed away the pain of the monsoon-wrecked cotton so many years ago in Noor Mahal. Kishan laughed. Nothing beat the taste of success. Uplifting and heady, it was already making him dream new dreams, impelling him to take yet newer roads.

Riding high on the cotton wave, he and Jaspal were over the moon, rapidly paying off their loans and pursuing new stretches of land across the valley. Adamantly following an ambitious lead, they purchased a thousand-acre foreclosed strip in the spring of 1931, continuing with their cotton adventure on it. Since Jay and Jason were born in America and were hence natural-born American citizens who were eligible to own land, Kishan and Jaspal had registered all their land in the boys' names. The Alien Land Laws were backsliding from Kishan's mind each day. Every now and then, a newspaper would carry an article about how those laws would be repealed soon but Kishan knew better now than to chew over those laws, focusing instead on buying yet more land.

Now that they were farming nearly two-thousand acres in the valley, Kishan began to rely on book-keeping machines and the accountants in Holtville to do all the accounting for The Rainbow Acres. Glad to not have his nose in the account books all the time, he started finding ways to implement sustainable agricultural methods to maximise yields. After the Stock Market crash in New York, the dwindling economy and the Dust Bowl had rendered the farmers in the Midwest penniless. California, however, was holding its own, opening its doors to the Dust Bowl refugees. California farms must produce more to keep the country going, to feed themselves as well as the nation in crisis, Kishan told Jaspal.

He wrote to Amy regularly, vividly sharing his adventures under the desert skies. After their meeting in Los Angeles, he had driven up to Sacramento once to see her. He would have liked to drive her in his new Buick to the air-show and later to the Seattle vs. Sacramento baseball game being played at Buffalo Park that day but realising that Sacramento was nowhere as diverse as Los Angeles and hence not the best place to roam around together, they had decided to catch up inside the Elk Grove Library itself. He cherished every moment of that meeting, watching her thoughtfully as she went about talking and smiling in her life-infusing dark green lace dress. Returning to The Rainbow Acres, Kishan wished ardently that Amy would come down for a visit soon because some evenings on watching the auburn sunsets, he found himself aching for her and uttering her name, hoping that hundreds of miles away, she would hear him and run outdoors in time to catch that dazzling amber of the dipping sun before it sank into oblivion.

Kishan was writing to big-name corporations discovering ways to supply melons, vegetables and cotton to them; exploring avenues to market Sophia's milk chocolate through the length of California and chasing leads to buy more land in the valley when 1932 came bursting in like a desert flash flood breaking barriers, spreading out possibilities as endless as the Pacific. Kishan applauded President Hoover's initiative of building the All-American Canal to systematically channel the Colorado waters into Imperial Valley. The idea of a large, planned canal was astounding, with the potential of changing forever the lives of Imperial Valley farmers, giving them a chance at an up-until-then inconceivable success.

"We are in luck," he told Jaspal one sun-soaked July morning. "Running eighty miles along the Mexican border and branching into hundreds of concrete canals, the Colorado will feed Imperial Valley's half a million acres before jumping into the Salton Sea. Nothing stands between us and smashing success anymore. Soon our produce will be flooding the nation's markets!"

"That's incredible," Jaspal said.

"Yes," Kishan replied. "The All-American Canal would make a flabbergasting wonder, entwining the vision of an artist with the precision of a scientist."

As he raved on about the canal, Sophia came in. "Isabel has gone into labour!" she said. "There is no time to wait. As I see it, the baby could come any moment. Third babies don't wait long!"

Jaspal and Sophia took off immediately with Isabel for the hospital and Kishan stayed behind to watch Jay and Jason. Taking the boys out into the fields, he showed them around. It was an inviting day, brittlebush blooms lighting up the acres. The labour was packing away the last of the sweet onions and the peppers. Soon the boys were rolling in dirt under the oaks and laughing. Large honeydew melons lay waiting to be harvested. Farther away, Kishan spied the gleaming cotton. Basking in the summer sun, the cotton would be ready for harvest before frost came along. Come autumn, they would reap another heaping harvest. He smiled. Then thinking of the soon-to-be-born baby, he walked up to the boys. "Let's go inside and wash up. Then we will go and see the baby," he said, gathering the boys in his arms.

As he was walking towards the house, Cesar rushed in with news. Jaspal and Isabel were now parents of a baby girl.

Kishan let out a laugh. There couldn't have been a better year than 1932 for a little girl to come along. The year had pluck. For the first time ever, there was a woman Senator, Hattie W. Caraway in the American Senate. And a daring girl called Amelia Earhart had taken over the world, flying a plane by herself all the way from the Newfoundland to Ireland in less than fifteen hours. 1932 was a caravan of wonders, unleashing adventure, extending an invitation to the fearless to live their dreams. Jaspal and Isabel's little girl had responded to that brave call. She was spunky right at birth. Unlike her brothers who were born at home, she had arrived in style at the newly opened hospital in the valley.

Driving to the hospital with the boys, Kishan thought the medical facility a wonder. Equipped with remarkable new medical gadgets, the hospital was a manifestation of modernity, of fast-changing times. The maternity wards were cosy with zippy yellow curtains in the windows and delicate ceiling fans. Isabel and the baby lay relaxed, nurses fussing over their every need.

Sophia, too, was hugely impressed with the hospital. "The hospital makes things so easy," she told Kishan. "Isabel is hardly as tired as she was after she had delivered the boys. I must say anaesthesia is the honey of paradise. Savouring it, Isabel slept like a very pleased child herself and when she woke up, her little girl came along as easy as a breeze."

"That is true," Isabel said smiling. "Having a baby in the hospital is a mere whiff, more restful than gruelling."

Kishan held the little girl. Twitching her chin, wrinkling her forehead, the baby looked at Kishan. Her dark eyes were like the ocean, deep and mystifying and her nose though button-sized showed promise of sharpening up. "She is lovely like her mother!" he exclaimed.

Turning towards Isabel, he asked, "What will you call her?"

"Juliana," Isabel replied smiling. "It sparks my mind. I have always admired the fifth-century BC Roman General, Senator and poet Julius Caesar. Like our little girl, he too, was born in July."

"Juliana," Kishan whispered. It was a melodic name, flowing like a song. Jay, Jason, Juliana were perfect names indeed for the children to march and merge into America with. Taking a deep breath, he smiled. The air was imbued with the fragrant happiness that a girl brings to a family.

Kishan drove Sophia, Jay and Jason back to The Rainbow Acres as Jaspal stayed behind with Isabel and Juliana at the hospital. Arriving home, Kishan saw a pale green envelope in the mailbox. Quickly, he reached for it. Walking into the living room, he ripped the envelope and opened the letter. Reading along, he let out a chuckle. It was the day of sensational surprises. Finally, Amy would be coming down to visit The Rainbow Acres.

Looking out of the window, he smiled. The most outstanding of all the colours on the rainbow was without a doubt the colour of love. He closed his eyes. A string of vignettes ran through his mind. He saw the Satluj swinging in the canals by Noor Mahal, Roop smiling by the old serai. Then he saw the Colorado jumping along The Rainbow Acres, Jay and Jason playing by the old oaks, Juliana prattling in her cot, Roop's silver anklets twinkling inside his closet. Those anklets were a timeless refrain about falling in love and about the lengths to which he would go, the selfless sacrifices that he would still make for love. He clutched the letter tighter. Suddenly Amy's soft laughter filled up the room, flowing and fusing with Roop's smile. The mynahs in Noor Mahal and the cuckoos at The Rainbow Acres were singing in unison. The past and present were blending, the quaintness of Noor Mahal meshing with the promise of Imperial Valley. A tale from an old village had uncoiled to meet the story that was unfurling in the heart of the desert. He could hear Jaspal laughing in the far distance. "Pali, the day is as perfect as it could get. Bright and beaming. Like California," Kishan whispered.

"Kishan, ready for another adventure, are you?" he heard Jaspal whisper back.

"With you, over and again. With a brother, life is one big adventure under the indigo skies," Kishan murmured.

He was still smiling with his eyes shut snug when a pudgy hand came to pull one of his fingers. He knew it was Jay. Shutting his eyes tighter, he continued grinning. Two little hands came from the other side and pulled his arm. He knew it was Jason. Smiling some more, he still didn't open his eyes. Not ones to give up, soon the boys were tugging his shirt, pulling at his trousers. Buckling up with laughter, Kishan opened his eyes.

"Now, you are a naughty set of brothers, aren't you?" he asked, grabbing and tickling them.

It was the boys' turn to double up and giggle.

"Uncle Kishan, do you have a story today?" Jay asked, still in splits.

Kneeling on the rug, Kishan drew them close. "I have a story, one that I've never told you boys before. It's about the joy of having a brother."

"Brother?" Jay asked.

"Yes," Kishan said, "having a brother is a stroke of luck. When you have a brother, you can roller-coast to fantastic dreams. When you have a brother, you walk tall, knowing that your back is covered."

"I have a brother," Jay said, pulling at a button on Jason's shirt.

"Baather," Jason echoed in baby language.

Kishan held the boys tight. "Yes! Aren't you both lucky? Because when you have a brother, you can paddle past loss and denial. When you have a brother, you can overcome the most dreadful of storms. And catching a remarkable rainbow, you can make a new beginning. Together."

SOPHIA

August 20, 1932

Dear Santiago,

Even though the many letters that I have written you over the last few years have been returned unopened, I am instinctively impelled to write you another. You may choose never to respond, but I hope you will read this one all the way to the end.

You gave me a new life. By extending the vision of brighter days, you helped me grow wings, so I could take the flight across borders. You held up a light in the darkness and I lifted myself and embarked on the journey. For this, I am forever indebted to you. The journey was difficult, but led by the promise, I carried on. Unknown to me, within that journey lay another journey — my Isabel's quest for love. In supporting my daughter in her pursuit, I have hurt you. God knows that the last thing that I ever wanted was to repay your kindness with ingratitude, but my story willed it otherwise. The human journey is not the travel of the sun or the moon. It cannot be predicted. One cannot fight one's story, it always wins.

The two Sikh men who abruptly showed up on Isabel's proposed wedding day, are now my family. One is my son-in-law and the other a long lost son who has returned to walk by me. Stars from a different galaxy, both light up my life, reminding me that in every stranger lies a kindred spirit waiting to be discovered. Through them, the universe has offered me comfort and refuge, compassion and empathy but most of all the courage to keep dreaming. I am also a proud grandmother now to three delightful little children. A cross between proud Sikhs and conscientious Mexicans, they form my world, their eager eyes and rippling laughter imploring me to live my potential and fulfil my purpose.

I rejoice in the various turns and twists of my journey, but the destination is my treasure. *El Dorado* is a state of mind — a quest of one's truest self, an endless adventure under the golden sun. It is the manifest realisation of the dream that came to sit like dew in my eyes in Bahía de Kino, and for that I have only you to thank.

Enclosed with this letter is a box of my own brand of milk chocolate which is for sale in Imperial Valley and if God so wills, it may soon be selling across California. My chocolate is both a veneration of what was and a celebration of what is. I hope it will endear me to you again and you will find it in your heart to forgive me. In so doing, you will oblige me yet again.

Yours lovingly,
Sophia

ACKNOWLEDGEMENTS

I would like to thank farmers across the world. They work the land, live by the seasons, nurture life, conserve the planet and spread hope. They are some of the most virtuous people and we owe them our very existence.

In particular, I thank the pioneer Punjabi farmers of California, whose stories of strife, struggle and fantastic success have motivated me to write *The Rainbow Acres.* Much like Kishan Singh and Jaspal Singh Dhillon in the novel, those pioneers enriched the California landscape with their hard work and the courage of their beliefs. Today, following the lead of the pioneers, Punjabi farmers of California, notably Didar Singh Bains, Karm Bains, Charanjit Singh Batth, Sarbjit Johl, Baldev Munger, Kable Munger, Jaswant Singh Bains, Gurdev Thiara, Baveljit Samara, Kuldip Atwal, Harry Brar, Jasbir Kullar, and Tut brothers — Surjit, Ranjit, Pritam and Amarjit — along with numerous other visionaries, are farming hundreds of thousands of acres of California's prime agricultural land. Their success is a manifestation of the great California Dream and I thank them all for their inspiration.

California's remarkable Punjabi-Mexican community of the early 1900s was a beautiful coming together of two cultures, a vibrant, truly secular bi-ethnic set-up. Through Kishan Singh and Sophia's brave odyssey across borders in *The Rainbow Acres,* I celebrate that melding of cultures and salute all immigrants everywhere, who in fleeing oppression, persecution and hopelessness, undertake perilous journeys in search of new beginnings, sometimes starting with nothing more than the clothes on their backs and the fire of their dreams. Toiling in the new land, they not only survive but also succeed and thrive. Their perseverance is a triumph of the human spirit and the world is a better place because of their enterprise.

Many thanks to Professor Karen Leonard and Professor Bruce La Brack for informing my perspective of the Punjabi-Mexican community through their articles.

My thanks to the lovely Chandan Bhullar for propelling me forward on my publishing journey. Heartfelt thanks to Ashok Chopra for his generosity of spirit and valuable help.

I am grateful to my publisher, Ajay Mago for believing in my story. Special thanks to my exceptionally talented editor Dipa Chaudhuri for her guidance and insights.

My loving thanks to my son Nik for being the first reader. It is his love, curiosity and wonder that shine through this story. A very special thank you to my father, Dr. Ranbir Singh Sarao, for reading the manuscript and offering me feedback. Many thanks to my beautiful mother, Sukhdarshan for her immense love and encouragement. Thanks also to my brother Ajaiveer Singh Sarao for adding to my perspective about old Punjab, its landscape, flora, fauna and traditions. Thank you to Mrs. Satya Dhir and Dr. Sunita Dhir for their many kindnesses. Thanks also to my uncles Viren Joshi and Amarjit Singh Kaleka for their support.

Many thanks to Raveen Khehar, Rupa Subramanium and Nirmaljit Singh for their well thought out comments on the manuscript.

I also thank my readers for taking a chance on my story. Please know that in so doing, you are also helping a cause. As diligent as farmers are, they are also the hardest hit in the face of calamities like floods, droughts and crop failures. A part of the proceeds from this book will go to the disaster-struck farmers of District Sangrur in Punjab, India, who are battling an enormous financial and emotional crisis in the face of landlessness and destitution.

Finally, and most importantly, thank you Lalit Dhir, for inspiring me with your extraordinary work ethic, for spurring me on and for loving me. You are the reason. This book would not have happened without you.